The

CHARMED
CHILDREN *of*
ROOKSKILL
CASTLE

The
CHARMED
CHILDREN *of*
ROOKSKILL
CASTLE

Janet Fox

Viking

VIKING
An imprint of Penguin Random House LLC
375 Hudson Street
New York, New York 10014

First published in the United States of America by Viking,
an imprint of Penguin Random House LLC, 2016

LIBRARY OF CONGRESS CATALOGING IN PUBLICATION DATA IS AVAILABLE

ISBN: 978-0-451-47633-3

Printed in the USA

10   9   8   7   6   5   4   3   2   1

Designed by Jim Hoover

To Kathi, mentor and friend,
and to Jeff and Kevin, with love

chatelaine, *n.* *(shat-l-eyn)*

2. An ornamental appendage worn
by ladies at the waist, supposed to
represent the bunch of keys, etc.,
of a mediæval châtelaine; it consists
of a number of short chains . . .
bearing articles of household
use and ornament. . . .

—*Oxford English Dictionary*

It is your bane,
This chatelaine.

By flesh and bone,
By rock and stone,
I'll charm a child
To call my own.

Fish and hunchback,
Boot and chest,
Cat comes crying.
For the rest:

The devil's sign,
The dog and bell,
A nesting pearl
Within its shell,

Eel and anchor,
Last, the heart.
All complete,
All now a part

Of chatelaine.

Its magic dark,
A prison cold,
A witch's mark,

A cruel fate,
A childling's bane:
The thirteenth charm
Of chatelaine.

Your soul will sleep
Within its keep,
Your life will linger
Dark and deep;

By rock and bone,
By blood and stone,
Not life, nor death,
But lost, alone.

I'll charm, I'll claim
With chatelaine.

1

The Fifth Charm: The Cat

IT IS 1863.

The winter winds shriek and moan around the castle turrets as the nightmare finds him, poor cat-boy John.

He runs from room to room until he finds a place to hide,
and then he hears but two things: the clattering and the ragged
hish, hish of his own breath.

Quit breathing so loud, you fool, or you'll never breathe again.

His heart pounds in his ears and his chest aches as he holds
himself still and silent.

The clattering—irregular, metal on stone—stops, and the
dread silence that follows almost stops his heart, too.

Now where is the blasted thing?

The only sound cat-boy John hears beyond the pounding

of his heart is a soft jingle—as of light rain on a bucket, or a bracelet on a moving wrist, or the whisper a falling star would make as it scatters, broken, across the sky. *Oh, the heavens help me.*

Then, a *click, rasp, click,* like a clock being wound, and there it is again, not ten feet from where he stands pressed against the wall behind the tapestry, the cold stone seeping through his thin shirt and up through the soles of his bare feet, the smell of wormy wool full in his nose, suffocating him, the horrifying thing only feet away now and closing in on him, *metal on stone, metal on stone,* his heart a *thump, thump,* his eyes pressed tight as the tears leak out beneath his lashes, his breath held in his tight-drawn chest.

As one tear descends his right cheek and cleaves a line down to his chin he thinks again, *The heavens help me.* Except that heaven is far, far from this place of unearthly creatures.

How he wishes he could have saved the others before him—the fishmonger's daughter, the hunchback boy, the singing girls—but he is only a boy, brave but not brave enough, more mouse than cat, and at the mercy of a monster too dreadful to behold.

No, he is not the first to be taken. Nor will he be the last.

One of John's own cats, fresh from the night's kill, betrays him, cat-boy John. Poor lovey kitten drops a mouse on John's bare right toe before she speeds away to escape the monster.

The last John hears is a string of accursed words in a voice that comes from the depths, perhaps from the devil himself: . . . *by flesh and bone* . . .

Outside—beyond the thick walls, the frozen moat, the barren yard, the ringing stockade—the moon slips from behind a skidding cloud as the screams whisk away into the forest. Even the sneaking stoat hunkers in terror as the boy cries with the ripping pain of losing his very soul.

2

London, Fall 1940: The Blitz

THE PIECES THAT made up Katherine Bateson's world were scattered across the landscape and over the ocean, far and wide, blown about by the winds of war. Kat herself felt like one of the clocks in Father's workshop, all wheels and plates and springs and pins strewn across the table, waiting.

But she squared her shoulders and told herself to hold her wits together. That's what her father would want, and what her brother and sister needed. Especially given the urgency in Father's letter to Mum, the letter sending the children away.

"Are you sure?" Robbie pressed against Kat's left arm. She tilted the photograph so he could see. "Wow, it is," he said, sounding awed. "A castle."

More like a not-so-majestic ruin, a shadowy box with

peaky turrets rising out of the ivy, but maybe the photo didn't do justice to the name: Rookskill Castle.

"I bet it's got battlements," Rob went on. "And ramparts. I'll bet there are dungeons. Secret passageways and hidden rooms. And ghosts."

"Ghosts?" Amelie popped up from the floor like a bobbin, round eyes in her round face, curls bouncing.

"All castles have ghosts," Rob said. "They moan. And carry clanking chains"—he raised his arms straight forward and stiffened his body—"that they rattle at night when they're coming for you!"

"Robbie," Kat said, a low warning.

"I can't wait to learn more sword fighting," he said. "I'm already a whiz." He took a stance.

"I doubt we'll be fiddling with swords," Kat answered. "They'll have us at regular lessons."

"Lessons! You're being stodgy again. It's a castle," Rob answered. "Who in a castle gives regular lessons during wartime?"

"Read Father's letter, Rob. Rookskill Castle Children's Academy, that's what he says." She unfolded the letter.

> Aunt Margaret's cousin Gregor is the
> eleventh Earl of Craig, and a good man, recently
> married. They need the income, as Lord Craig

has taken ill. I met with Lady Craig at the castle not long ago, and she seems devoted to children, having none of her own. As I was thinking of sending the children here, I helped her secure instructors of my acquaintance. And I have reason to be back in Scotland from time to time. A sound choice for the children, under the circumstances.

Kat paused. "So there you have it. Father secured instructors. We'll be learning."

"You are dull, Miss Stodginess. Of course we'll be learning. But it won't be sums and history and Latin. We'll be learning how to parry and form up and shoot arrows. Practical things we can use against the Jerries." Rob thrust his imaginary sword, made an imaginary block. "I've heard that the Jerries are planning a landing on the beaches in Scotland. We'd best be ready."

Kat folded Father's letter around the photo, tucking both back into her pocket. Amelie's eyes slipped from Kat to Robbie and back. "I like ghosts," Amelie said. She still held her drawing pencil clutched tight in her fist. "Maybe there'll be a ghost like Mr. Pudge."

Kat smiled. "Ame, it's an old place that looks like a castle, and we'll be in school. And it's Great-Aunt Margaret's cousin.

And Father may visit. I'm quite sure there won't be any ghosts."

Kat had plenty of real things to worry about. For one, Robbie might be right: the Germans could land on their shores at any time. Kat worried about Father and his reasons for being in Scotland, and about Mum and Great-Aunt Margaret being left in London while the Germans continued their incessant bombing. And at twelve, Kat had started in a new school and was trying to sort out where she belonged and who her friends might be, and now she had to leave. She twisted the watch that wrapped her left wrist.

Ghosts ranked low on Kat's list of worries.

"You must look after Rob and Ame," Father had said. "I'm counting on you." It was what seemed ages ago, in midsummer, and he was readying to leave. His tools lay on the bench before he fitted them one by one into the sleeves in the felted fabric. The clock he was done fixing tick-tocked on the table behind them.

She wondered how he could do two such different things— the one, mend clocks, and the other, so dangerous. He didn't even look the sort for the other, and she said so straight out.

He smiled, pushing his glasses on top of his head and resting his hand on her shoulder. "Don't judge a book by its cover, Kitty. There's often much going on inside. I do what I'm good at. And I do it for you, and your mum and Rob and Ame, and everyone who loves 'this precious stone set in the silver sea.'"

His voice lifted a little with the quote. "Your mum has many cares. So you must promise to do your bit."

Kat had promised, yes, but she wished her father wasn't so noble. She wasn't sure she could bear it if he should be caught.

Now she was sure about only one thing. That castle in Scotland to which he wanted them sent would be cold. Warm clothes essential. And she would be head of the three young Batesons.

Father's parting words to her were, "Remember, my dear. Keep calm."

And biting down the swell of tears, she'd whispered back, "And carry on."

As Kat was packing, Great-Aunt Margaret called her to the library.

"Your father is wise to send you to Gregor's," Aunt Margaret said. "Well away from this dreadful noise and strife." She paused. "Although I must say Scotland is a bit dodgy. An umbrella is of no avail against a Scotch mist." She, like Father, liked aphorisms. Mum had once said it was the way Great-Aunt Margaret kept her mind sharp; Father had whispered that if Kat's great-aunt's mind was any sharper, she'd impale her pillow.

Yes, she used to be so sharp, so logical and precise. But, to Kat's dismay, Great-Aunt Margaret had lately gone a little dotty, perhaps more now with the bombing and the stress of war.

Mum stood at the tall window, her hands clasped behind her, her fingers weaving patterns, in and out, in and out, like she was kneading dough.

Great-Aunt Margaret rose from her thronelike chair. "Now, come over here, dear. 'Time and tide wait for no man.' I have something for you. To keep you safe." She took Kat's chin in the fingers of her right hand and laid the finger of her left alongside her nose while she widened her eyes. Kat knew the gesture: it meant, *This is our secret.*

How it could be with Mum there, Kat couldn't imagine. She glanced at Mum, who raised her eyebrows as if to say, *Be kind.* So Kat played along, forcing down a smile. "Yes, ma'am."

Great-Aunt Margaret dropped Kat's chin and took a step back, and her hands went to her waist, to her belt of soft leather. Pinned to it, dangling from it as it had every day in all the years of Kat's memory, was her great-aunt's chatelaine.

The chatelaine had been a gift to Margaret from her mother upon Margaret's marriage, and Kat knew it to be a precious family heirloom. Wrought of silver and marked with the smith's stamp, the chatelaine contained three useful items that hung from slender silver chains joined on a silver hoop. "Yes," said her great-aunt. "This will keep you safe." She was removing the chatelaine from her belt.

To give to Kat.

"Oh, Auntie, no. I couldn't." Kat raised both hands in protest and looked to her mother, who pursed her lips. *What if it should be lost?*

"Nonsense." Her great-aunt's response was firm even as her stiff fingers fumbled. "I'm having a bit of trouble. . . ." She lifted watery eyes to Kat. "Help me, my dear," she said. "Come, now. I insist."

Kat stepped forward, hesitant. She unclasped the chatelaine and held it up. The three items—pen, scissors, thimble—swayed as they dangled from her fingers.

Aunt Margaret leaned toward Kat, her lips close to Kat's ear, and dropped her voice to a whisper. "It's quite magical, you know."

"I'm sorry?" Kat whispered back. "Did you say magical?" *Oh, goodness.* Kat saw worry in the set of Mum's face.

Aunt Margaret straightened. "Yes, my dear. I shall explain. But do remember this: be careful with magic." She fixed her eyes on Kat's. "Do you hear me, Katherine? Magic is tricky. There is always a price to pay for its use."

Mum went with them to King's Cross Station to catch the train. Kat turned in the seat of the hackney as they pulled away from the curb, catching a glimpse of Great-Aunt Margaret standing at one of the tall windows with her hand in solemn salute.

The cab splashed through deep puddles and rain pelted the roof. They passed mounds of rubble, men in their clinging wet work clothes clearing flattened homes with picks and shovels and barrows. They passed St. Paul's, rising stately and seemingly untouched from the ruins around it. Pride surged in Kat. The bustle of London—motors and buses and black umbrellas—continued as if there was no war. Londoners described the bombings as "blitzy," as if they were some kind of nasty weather.

Most of the kids she knew were staying put, working after school hours to help clear roads of broken bricks and glass, and here she was, fleeing. She shut her eyes. No, she didn't like the bombings one bit, the sirens wailing, the dark root cellar, the shuddering blasts, the plaster raining down, Ame crying out. She didn't like shaking so hard her teeth chattered. Still, Kat would rather stay. Stay with Mum, stay in London, stay and be strong.

She felt anything but strong as the station grew close and home slipped farther away.

Mum, squeezed between Kat and Amelie, cleared her throat over the *splish-splosh-rumble* of the cab. "Kitty, I must tell you. In the Service office with me there's a couple with a son about your age. They want him out of London, too, so I thought to recommend this place. He'll be on your train."

Kat twisted sideways. "Oh, Mum, you didn't."

Kat's mum was always trying to fix her up with friends. She didn't think it was good for her eldest daughter to spend more time with facts and figures and puzzles and Father's clocks than with people.

"I'm not happy sending you off. It's because your father wants it." Mum fiddled with the buttons of her coat. "Please don't fuss. It's only for a little while. Just until the war is over."

Nothing that Kat had heard or read convinced her that the war would be over in a little while. "Why can't we all stay together? Why can't you and Aunt Margaret come away?" Kat bit her lip. Her words sounded small and selfish.

Mum frowned. "Kat. I'm needed here. And your great-aunt insists upon staying. You understand."

Yes, Kat understood. But she needed her mum, too, and with Father on a mission so delicate he couldn't reveal his whereabouts even to Mum, what if . . . Kat swallowed her protests past the lump in her throat.

Mum reached for Kat's hand, holding it tight. She said softly, "You have your great-aunt's gift? I'd hate for you to lose it."

Kat nodded. The chatelaine was pinned to her waistband and stuck inside her pocket.

Mum's face relaxed into a smile, and she sighed. "I'll miss you all, my little sweets."

Robbie, sitting across, looked up from his reading. "When

we get back, we won't be little or sweets. We'll be knights." He was putting on a brave front.

"I'll still be sweet," said Ame, her voice plaintive, "and I wish we didn't have to leave."

In the station they jostled among the troops and travelers, lugging their trunks behind. Thick steam twined hissing around them, shuddering engines roared to life, brakes squealed, whistles sounded, and the ground shook with the thunder of trains coming and going. Kat clutched her sister's small hand tight.

"Ah, there they are!" Mum said, and walked forward, waving.

"Ow! Kat, you're squeezing," said Amelie.

The boy stood with his parents. He wore a tweedy jacket, his hands jammed in his pockets. His hair, browner than Kat's, was straight and brushed to one side, where it rebelled from its slicked-back situation. He had a narrow face and brown eyes, and was taller than Kat, which was a comfort, as she was usually the tallest in her grade.

"All here, then," Mum said with forced cheer. "Kat, Rob, Amelie, meet Mr. and Mrs. Williams. And you must be Peter."

"Hello, there." Mr. Williams stuck his hand straight out at Kat. "Pleased to meet you all."

"Ruddy Americans!" said Robbie, catching the accent at once. "Wow!"

Mr. Williams let out a deep laugh. "I am, anyway, and Pete's spent most of his life stateside."

Kat tried not to stare at Peter. She shook hands with his father and nodded to Mrs. Williams.

Mrs. Williams sniffled, and her eyes were rimmed with red. "Here we are in London because I insisted, although who could have known the war would come to this? And now to have to send him away. . . . Oh, I know it's for the best, but I do so wish . . ."

"Mom. It'll be okay. Don't worry."

Kat didn't know what she'd expected, especially of an American boy, but Peter's voice, despite its flat twang, was gentle and soothing. She straightened and lifted her arm to place it over Amelie's shoulder.

"Besides, my dear," said Mr. Williams. "This whole war business will be over in no time, and we'll all be back together again. Think of this as a little holiday for the children. Don't you agree, Mrs. Bateson?"

"Why, yes, of course," Mum murmured.

The conductor approached. "Need help with the trunks?"

Mr. Williams stowed the trunks, and the conductor helped them into their car, latching the door behind. They all leaned out the windows, hands reaching down. Kat held Amelie by the waist so that she could grasp Mum's uplifted hands. Ame stifled a sob, and Kat's throat swelled. Rob's eyes glistened as he pressed against the glass.

"Bye, my loves, bye!" Mum called as the train lurched away. "Stay safe!"

Mrs. Williams burst into tears and buried her face in her husband's shoulder. The train tunnel closed in and curved away from the platform, and their parents slipped out of sight.

Long after the others had settled into their seats, Kat pressed her face to the rain-streaked window as the warehouses and rugged outskirts of London melted into a gray haze. The multiple tracks skinned down to one and the city thinned away. Kat clutched the watch on her wrist, pressing the snapshots of home into her memory.

The three Batesons sat on one bench in the rocking train car; Peter sat across from them, jacket off now and shirtsleeves rolled up, his hair trying to fall from stiff confinement.

"So!" Robbie rubbed his eyes hard, then bounced up and crossed to perch next to Peter. "You're a ruddy American! Do you know any cowboys?"

Peter grinned.

The boys talked (well, Robbie jabbered on and Peter responded in friendly fashion), and the train pulled north into the creeping shadows of a countryside blacked out in the face of war.

Kat shoved her hand into her pocket and clutched her great-aunt's chatelaine. Her fingers kneaded and worked at it, the three items rubbing against one another like the bones of a bird, and she squeezed so they made imprints in her palm.

In times like these, according to Great-Aunt Margaret, magic bubbled up, rising out of the confusion and strife of war. Troubled times stirred up magic like dumplings in a stew. "And one must be prepared," she'd said, folding Kat's fingers over the chatelaine, "with appropriate countermeasures."

In times like these, thought Kat, magic—if such a thing were real—wouldn't help. War was a dark fog covering everything. Kat could wish for the war to end all she wanted, and it wouldn't do any good. Really, even Robbie's attempt at swordplay was more useful than this chatelaine. Kat sighed. Poor Aunt Margaret, spouting nonsense. Her sharp mind was withering away.

This chatelaine was just one more thing for Kat to worry over.

She stood, swaying with the train's motion, clutched the edge of the brass luggage rack above, and pulled down her valise. With her back turned, Rob and Peter and Amelie couldn't see Kat as she unfastened the chatelaine from her waistband and dropped it into the dark well of the open valise, watching as it disappeared underneath the more practical things, the sweaters and hats and mittens, that Kat believed were truly important to their well-being.

For an instant, she caught a dim light emanating from the

chatelaine, a soft blue glow, but then decided it was only a reflection off the silver.

Cold. At that moment Katherine Bateson was certain that the chill and drafts of a Scottish castle would be their greatest threat.

3

Claw

DEEP IN THE dark well Kat sees something shiny. Glowing. Faintly blue, like hard-packed ice.

It moves, creeping, and she backs away until her spine is up against the cold stone wall of the well, backs away as it creeps closer, and then she sees. It's a hand, but not a normal hand. It's a claw hand, sharp, curving, wicked, crawling on knife-edge fingers straight toward her, one scraping shiver at a time, and she wants to scream but she can't, oh, she can't . . .

4

The Number Thirteen

THE TRAIN LURCHED and the lights flickered and Kat woke up with a jolt, her back pressed against the cold hard corner of the bench. The muffled scream died in her throat as she remembered that she was on a train, Ame's head across her lap, Rob and Peter talking, London far behind, and the northland still far ahead in the dark night.

Kat clutched her book of math games, searching for the page she'd been working on before she'd drifted into the nightmare.

"Never mind Los Angeles," Peter said. "New York, that's the place." His elbows rested on his knees, Robbie fixed on every word. "The city that never sleeps. Skyscrapers and shows. And lights. It sparkles. New York is lit up day and night."

Kat slapped her book shut. Amelie stirred and whimpered.

Peter caught Kat's sour expression and looked stricken. "Oh, gee. I'm sorry."

The blackouts had spoiled her for lights, and the only kind of sparkle she knew now was the kind that preceded a blast. Even the windows of the train had blackout curtains, the conductor coming through at dusk to make sure they were all drawn good and tight.

It wasn't Peter's fault.

Ame whimpered again. "Bad dream," Kat said. Peter bit his lip and nodded.

"At least it's a castle," Robbie murmured. "If we have to leave home, I mean."

"Yeah," said Peter. He looked away, fidgeting. "What time is it?"

Kat wrapped her fingers around the watch on her wrist. "I forgot to wind it," she lied.

"Ah," he said, rubbing his eyes. "Must be late. I'm going to try to catch some shut-eye."

"Me too," Robbie said, yawning wide and leaning back.

Peter reached up and dimmed the lamp, and the green velvet and mahogany and brass sank into dusky darkness. Kat didn't fall back asleep for a long time, not wanting to return to the well and the claw-fingered hand.

They changed trains in Edinburgh in the wee hours. Peter

carried the sleeping Amelie through the station, and Kat silently thanked him for it.

Their second train was only two coaches long and threadbare. There was no brass or velvet, just muslin curtains tacked over the windows. The four sleepy children were nearly the last left aboard when the engine crawled to their stop at Craig Station.

It was a gray dawn, thick with mist, and there was no one on the platform. They hauled their trunks from the luggage car to the middle of the waiting room and heard the train as it roared to life again and made away, leaving them alone on the raw eastern lands of Scotland, the smell of the sea heavy in the air.

Regret and worry filled Kat as the train's clacking faded into the distance.

The waiting room, no bigger than a small parlor, was silent and empty and dimly lit. Kat and Peter exchanged a look. He raised his eyebrows, and she lifted her shoulders. "We're supposed to be fetched from the station, that's what Mum told me," she said, uncertain.

At that instant the outer door opened, the overhead bell jingling, and the smallest man Kat had ever seen blustered in, slamming the door behind him. The thin windows rattled in their frames. He paid the children no notice as he marched across the waiting room to another door that led into the darkened ticket office.

Open, slam, rattle-rattle.

Amelie tugged at Kat's sleeve; Kat leaned down. "He's such a wee man," Ame whispered.

"A dwarf, I think," Kat whispered back, and Ame's eyes went round.

"Ah," Ame said, nodding. "There's always a dwarf in the best magical stories."

Kat was about to correct her—this wasn't a story, and there was nothing magical about to happen—when the wooden ticket window shutter, which had been drawn down behind the bars, slammed upward and Kat jumped. Lights buzzed and blinked and brightened.

"Can I help ye?" The dwarf's voice, belying his size, boomed through the waiting room, his accent a strong brogue.

His head was now of a height with theirs. He'd changed into a proper cap with a badge on the brim: STATIONMASTER.

Peter and Kat stood side by side at the counter. Kat put on her most grown-up expression. "We're to be met," she said.

"We're on our way to Rookskill Castle," Peter added.

"Refugees," Kat said. "From the Blitz."

The stationmaster looked from one to the other. Then he shook his head. "I shouldn't, if I was ye."

Kat wrapped her fingers around the edge of the ticket counter. "Shouldn't what?" A chill crept up her spine.

"It's a peculiar place," the stationmaster said, rolling his *R*s.

"Been so forever. Hainted, that's what they say. By ghostlings. You bairns, you childlings, oughtn't be going there. Don't like it, and now all you childlings coming up from London regular . . ." His words trailed off as he pursed his lips. "Odd noises, specially at night, like grindings, and screeches, and whatnot, is what I'm told, though I try to steer clear, I do, specially at night. When I have to go up there on business I make it quick-like. Not a one wants to go near the place. And poor Lord Craig, bless him, not seen these many months, not since just after . . . well. Peculiar, that's what."

"Odd noises?" Peter asked.

"Grindings?" Amelie asked from below. "And screeches?"

"Haunted?" Rob piped in from behind, sounding not so brave.

"We were told he's taken ill. Lord Craig, that is," Kat said. "So maybe that's why—"

"Hainted, it is, with grindings and screeches," the station-master put in darkly. "I count three bairns from down south before you lot." He shook his head. "Came in last week. Haven't seen 'em since, neither." He shuffled a stack of papers. "Next train back to Edinburgh leaves at noon. You want tickets?"

Before they could answer, from behind them Kat heard the outer door open again.

"Are you here for Rookskill Castle?" This man was as large as the stationmaster was small, almost a giant, filling the door frame only because he was bent at the waist. "Let's go then."

Amelie tugged at Kat. "See? A giant. Just like—"

"Yes, I know, Ame," Kat interrupted. "The old magical stories."

"I shouldn't, if I was ye," came the low voice of the station-master.

Kat glanced back at him; he was frowning behind his bars. The giant took her trunk in one paw and Robbie's in the other, and said to Peter, "You take that 'un, now."

Off they went. *Keep calm.*

What waited outside was not a motorcar but an open-seat wagon drawn by four black draft horses. "Yer too many for her Ladyship's horseless," the giant mumbled. He threw their trunks into the back and lifted Amelie up by her waist to sit at the front; the rest of them scrambled up to find seating on the bench behind him.

Kat's heart thumped something dreadful.

There wasn't a proper dawn; it was too foggy. The cold fog beaded on Kat's beret and wrapped the wagon and the road ahead in gloom, and she couldn't get the lay of the land. Kat tucked her gloved hands into her armpits. The wagon jostled and shuddered. Kat was sitting between Peter and Rob so that her shoulder bumped against Peter's. It couldn't be helped, and though she wouldn't admit it, it gave her some comfort.

As did her sensible packing. She wore warm woolen trousers; yet, even so, her knees were knocking.

She saw something of the village, wreathed in mist, as they passed through—small and silent, no souls strolling among the thatched-roof cottages or in and out of the shuttered pub with the sign of a spread-winged blackbird: THE ROOK. The road wound upward from there, back and forth, like a hawk hunting, turn and turn again, the wheels making a hawklike squeal as they rotated in the muddy ruts. The drays puffed steamy breaths as they hauled their load up the hill. The smell of damp decay filled the air.

All of a sudden they were at a gate. The giant, who hadn't said a word since the station, got down and opened the gate on its grating hinges, then pointed at Peter. "You," he said, "close it behind."

When Peter climbed down Kat missed his shoulder at once, and then dismissed that thought right away and clutched at the watch on her wrist.

The gate was an iron monster with crossbars, and at the very top of the arch she could make out an odd symbol. It was the number thirteen inside an ornate circle, with the letters *RC* flanking it.

Kat guessed that the *RC* stood for Rookskill Castle, but the thirteen? Maybe it was the house number. Did castles have numbers? And if so, who would choose the unhappy number thirteen?

Silly, she scolded herself. Numbers weren't happy or unhappy. Numbers were solid things, things you could depend on.

But as the wagon passed under the gate, she couldn't suppress a shudder and wouldn't look up at the thirteen that stared down at them like a winking eye.

From somewhere in the misty wood came the echoing *off-off* of a rook.

5

Rooks

THE CIRCLING BIRDS of Rookskill Castle could tell a tale. Back and back—time weaves a tapestry. It is 1746, and a terrible conflict lays waste to the land and people.

A girl, Leonore, contemplates her misfortune. She has not been able to fulfill her marriage vow. She holds her chatelaine, a wedding gift of mysterious origin, dangling it from her fingers. It dances in the firelight of her room, the most beautiful thing she has ever owned. Even in the utter dark it casts a faint blue light. Touching it sends a shiver, a cold spike right through her heart.

She cannot deliver a child to her lord. He plucked her from nothing for this alone, having disposed of the three unfortunate wives who came before her—he picked her for her peach-cream skin and thick black hair and her youth. Picked her from the village, after the other lairds refused him any more of their daughters. At least she has escaped her father's fist, the bruises and the fearful hiding.

The chatelaine. Finely wrought of silver, jewelry to hang from her waist. Wrapped in velvet inside an inlaid coffer and placed upon the marriage bed, resting on the white linen beside an inky feather that drifted in with the breeze. No one, not her lord nor the servants, could tell Leonore who placed the coffer there. The only precious thing her new husband gave her was an engraved thimble, a thimble that now lies within her embroidery box.

She plays with it, the chatelaine, its thirteen charms twisting and clinking, and she wishes she could trade it for the one thing that would save her. Even a healthy girl-child would buy her time. She fears the fate of her lord's former wives. And she wishes he would view her with sincere affection.

Leonore is lonely and frightened, her only friends the birds she feeds from the sill of her high window overlooking the wild waste that stretches toward the sea, the birds that cackle and caw.

The rooks.

6

The Lady

The castle loomed out of the fog at the end of the winding lane, after what seemed an age. Kat sat up straight, and Peter let out a low whistle.

It was much bigger than the picture had made it seem, a real castle with many turrets rising up through the gloom bit by bit, and it did look the sort of place that would house ghosts.

And knights. To their left stood a half-ruined square keep topped by battlements; to their right, a high wall with turrets. The keep's narrow windows slotted the wall like blank eyes, and Kat imagined someone aiming an arrow from one straight at her heart. The moat bed was a rocky trough of thorny weeds.

As they crossed the bridge Kat shut her eyes at the bony rattles made by the wood straining beneath their weight, then opened them as they passed beneath the gate arch, its rotting gate hovering overhead. They entered a broad court.

A parapet led away from the keep to join a giant stone bulwark of a building. A portion of the roof of the parapet walk had fallen in, and the wall that circled the court to their right was a mass of fallen stones, but this part of the castle before them seemed newer and grand. The windows were like stretched-thin black eyes, and the castle was three stories tall with tight brickwork. A dead vine wound around the door frame like a thick rope and the whole was topped by a peaked slate roof poked through with narrow chimneys.

A freshly hand-painted wooden sign was mounted on posts beside the entry: ROOKSKILL CASTLE CHILDREN'S ACADEMY.

Gooseflesh crept up Kat's arms. She'd tumbled headlong into a fairy tale, like Alice down the rabbit hole. The wagon pulled alongside the massive stone front and crawled to a stop. The horses chuffed as the wagon creaked and groaned, and it smelled damp and cold and faintly moldy.

The giant lifted Amelie down and waited as Peter, Rob, and Kat scrambled to the ground. Kat found it hard to breathe. Even Robbie held his tongue. Peter leaned back as he looked up at the front of the castle, and Amelie tucked her hand into Kat's.

The giant said, "I'll take your trunks round. They'll be in your rooms." And he clapped the horses with the reins and rattled off.

"He's quite nice," said Amelie. Kat looked down. Ame was gazing after the wagon. "That giant man."

Amelie was usually right, but Kat wondered if this time she didn't have it wrong.

"It's not what I expected," murmured Peter.

They stood in a cluster before the door—it was more than twice Peter's height. Peter cleared his throat and was raising his hand to knock when the door opened.

Kat had steeled herself for cobwebs and dust and an aging butler with a toothless leer, so the sight of a crackling fire in the hall and electric lights and Turkish carpets and cozy fur-nishings behind the plump, vacant-eyed maid in uniform was a huge relief.

The maid was young and pretty. Kat glanced at Robbie, who was of an age to develop instant crushes, and his cheeks already glowed like the bed of a hot fire. The maid seemed to take no notice; she said, "I'm Marie. Her Ladyship asked me to show you in. I'll take your coats."

The mist had been so thick that their coats were soaking. Marie bustled off with the dripping load in her arms.

Robbie went straight to the fire, rubbing his hands. "Just as I thought. Scary on the outside, but that's only to put off the enemy. All castles are like that," he said. "Hello, what's this?" He moved to a tea table set beside the fire. "Look! A pot of chocolate!" Rob set to pouring himself a cup at once. The rich fragrance filled the hall.

"I'm not sure . . . " Kat murmured.

"It's quite all right," came a soothing voice with a boarding-school British accent. "I made it for you myself."

They turned. A woman moved from the shadows of a doorway on the far side of the hall. As she stepped into the yellow light of the lamps the children grew still. Kat became aware of the slow *tock, tock* of the great clock on the mantle and the snap of the fire in the grate.

Kat dropped into a curtsey—the woman had that kind of presence. Shiny, that was how she seemed, like silver polished until it gleamed. Her smooth, porcelain skin stretched over her bones, all angles and points, her eyes were sharp as a badger's, and her hair was swept up and silky and so fair it was almost white.

As impressed as Kat was, she thought Peter would do well to close his mouth, and she had to ignore Robbie entirely.

The woman walked toward them, her arms open in greeting. She shook hands with each of them in turn. "I'm Eleanor, Lady Craig. You may address me as Lady Eleanor. Welcome to the Academy at Rookskill Castle. You must be the Bateson children and the Williams boy. Peter, yes? My, you are tall." Peter straightened to full height. "And Katherine, and Robert— young man, it's hard to believe you are only eleven. And you, dear little thing, you must be Amelie." Amelie's hand sought Kat's again the instant the Lady let go. "We're so happy to have you in our humble refuge. Katherine, Robert, and Amelie, you're practically family, too, at least to my dear Gregor. Is London dreadful? I understand there are frequent bombings?"

Robbie launched right in about the bombs and fires and rubble and broken windows, and how he was heroic and not at all scared, and the Lady listened, nodding and making sympathetic noises. Kat tried to distance herself from Rob's all-too-detailed descriptions by focusing on the Lady. She was beautiful. And yet, there was something *off* about her that Kat couldn't put her finger on.

When Kat had taken the Lady's hand, it was so cold. Almost icy, and hard. If Kat hadn't been looking she might have thought she was shaking hands with one of Father's calipers. The Lady had stared intently at Kat as she gripped Kat's hand.

Robbie nattered on and on, and the Lady wasn't really listening to him. She murmured as if she was, but she glanced at Amelie, and then at Peter—she took a good long look at Peter. She didn't look at Kat again.

The Lady was fashionably dressed in a tailored tweed Norfolk jacket with a slim skirt, a tartan scarf crossing diagonally over one shoulder and tied at her waist. As she folded her arms, the jacket lifted just a little, and Kat saw. Dangling from the Lady's skirt waistband was what looked like a chatelaine.

Goodness, Kat thought. *Another chatelaine?*

Kat's great-aunt's chatelaine held practical items—the pen,

the scissors, the thimble. But on the Lady's chatelaine were charms, though Kat couldn't see much except a shell and a silvery heart.

"Oh! You have—" Kat began, and then as the Lady turned her eyes Kat's way, Kat stopped. The Lady dropped her arms to her sides and her chatelaine disappeared again beneath the hem of her jacket. The Lady's sharp glance was like a spider crawling over Kat. Kat's little inner voice said, *Don't mention the chatelaine.* She scrambled to find words. "You have a lovely home."

The fire popped and hissed, and Kat's mouth went dry.

"Thank you, my dear," the Lady said at last.

Kat, still scrambling, pointed past the Lady's head. "And that's quite a nice portrait of you."

The Lady turned. "You are mistaken," the Lady said. "That is Leonore, mistress of this castle in the mid-eighteenth century and married to an earlier Lord Craig." The huge portrait that dominated the front hall was of a woman who could have been the Lady's twin but for the difference in the color of their hair and the antique fashion of her clothing. The black-haired beauty in the portrait wore the same plaid as the Lady Eleanor, and her piercing blue eyes were watchful. "The villagers maintain she haunts the castle yet. Of course, ghosts of highlanders are often about the moors, and sometimes invade the keep."

The lady who ran their new school talked about ghosts as

if they were ordinary. Real. A shiver ran up Kat's spine and she gripped Ame's hand. Silence fell over the hall, broken only by the snapping of the fire and the slow *tock* of the clock, until the Lady spoke again.

"We have all the modern conveniences in Rookskill Castle. And we are far from the bombs and strife of war, thank goodness. Our small farm and garden provides fresh goods, despite the shortages. Even eggs enough for every day, and with the academy I've been able to secure some extras, like sugar and cocoa. You're fortunate to be here. Your formal lessons will begin as soon as the remaining instructors arrive."

The clock on the mantle gonged nine times, low and loud, nine o'clock in the morning.

"I do apologize," the Lady continued, "if things seem out of sorts from time to time. My dear husband has been gravely ill. But we all do our best. We shall carry on." She looked directly at Kat as she said this and gave her a slim smile, and Kat was forced to smile back.

Carry on.

"You'll find school uniforms in your rooms," the Lady said, "which you shall wear at all times except weekends. We did our best in getting the sizes right. Marie will advise you of the other rules. Marie?"

Marie appeared from the end of the hallway.

"Show the children to their rooms," the Lady said.

Marie started up the wide staircase, and the children followed. The Lady remained below. Kat could feel the Lady's eyes on her back.

As they reached the landing Robbie said, "Darn! I forgot to drink the chocolate."

7

The Fishing Girl

AMELIE AND KAT shared one room on the third story, and the boys shared another. From the outside the castle was blocky and regular, but inside the stairs curved in a spiral, and the hallways were narrow with unexpected bends and dead ends. Columns rose up like great trees. Dim light filtered down through the stairwell.

Kat was lost almost at once.

"The Lady insists we lock you in at night," Marie informed them, wielding a ring of keys. "She says I must see to it that there are no night wanderers. My room is just down there." She pointed.

Lock us in? thought Kat, with a shiver. *What's that about?*

"Where are the others?" Rob asked. "The other students?"

"About," Marie answered, with a vague wave of her hand.

"When do we start lessons?" Robbie pressed. "I hope we practice other stuff, too, you know, what we'll need to fend off the Jerries. Like swords. We'll have fencing, won't we? And archery? This is a castle, after all."

Marie looked befuddled. "Don't know about any of that. Proper lessons begin tomorrow, that's what her Ladyship said. Because you missed breakfast, you're to have lunch early. You'll meet the others at supper. The Lady insists on early supper, before sunset." She turned, paused, and then said, as if reciting, "If you hear any odd noises, it's nothing. Castles as old as this are filled with odd noises." Marie disappeared around a turn, keys clanking as they hung from her hand.

Odd noises, odd rules, and an even odder building. Kat rubbed her arms, then looked down at Amelie. Her sister's eyes were round as saucers.

"I miss home," Ame said.

"Me too," said Kat.

Robbie cleared his throat. "Right, then. Want to go exploring?"

Kat wanted to find the other students. She wanted to know why Marie mentioned odd noises, like the stationmaster. She wanted to know why they had to be locked in at night. She wanted to know why they had to eat supper before the sun set. But she said only, "I think we should unpack our trunks." And added, "And I don't think the Lady will take kindly to exploring."

"She didn't forbid it now, did she?" Robbie challenged. "Besides, it'll take me all of five minutes to empty my trunk."

Boys.

"I'll go with you," said Peter. "At least we can wander up and down this floor."

Amelie and Kat unpacked in their spacious room. They had their own bath and a large fireplace, and they shared a monstrous bed plumped with a fat quilt. Their uniforms were folded in two neat piles on the bed and consisted of a heavy wool plaid skirt in the same tartan the Lady wore, white shirts, a couple of sweaters, a dark gray boiled wool jacket, and heavy wool stockings, all very warm, which was some comfort. Kat stowed her things in the giant dresser that hugged the wall between two tall windows.

Amelie picked at the comforter. "What do you think of the Lady?"

"She seems nice enough," Kat said.

Ame nodded. "I don't like her, either."

"Now, Ame, we don't know her yet," said Kat. "Father said she seemed all right."

"She's not like the giant," Ame said. "He's special." She shifted off the bed and went to the window, pulling aside the curtain and looking out.

Kat shook her head. That was Amelie. Their great-aunt didn't have to tell Ame to be imaginative.

"I miss Mum," Ame murmured. "And London. And Aunt Margaret."

"I know," Kat said. "Me too. At least Father said he'd visit from time to time."

"And I miss Mr. Pudge," Ame added, "although you don't believe in him."

Kat tried not to smile.

As Kat moved about now, folding and sorting, she paused before the clock on the mantle, a beehive clock with a thin band of inlay around the face. She wound it and set the pendulum going, but it wouldn't stay running for more than a few beats. She turned it around and opened the back, examining the works.

In Father's shop there were anywhere from one to a half dozen clocks at any time, all waiting for repair. When he was home, he went there straight after breakfast, laying out his tools, lining them up in order before beginning work. For years, Kat had watched him, her chin on her hands, her eyes on the gears, pins, and cogs that he removed one by one and laid out to repair or replace. He'd name parts for her as he worked: the arbor or axle, the barrel with its mainspring, the tiny jack man that struck the bell. It wasn't until last summer that he'd turned one clock—a small beehive much like the one before her now—its back open, toward her.

Her hands had trembled a little as she started, but after she'd disassembled the first layer of the works she grew bolder, and her father watched her, interjecting only a little. She'd cleaned and oiled the parts, and reassembled them, tightened the screws and adjusted the balance, and then set the clock to running. It gave a satisfying *tick-tick*.

Father had placed his hand on her shoulder. "Well done. You've got a knack for this, Kitty. Like with puzzles, eh? You've a mind for patterns and a careful, patient hand."

Kat's heart swelled with pride.

After that, for the next few weeks, he'd allowed her to assist him, until one day when she grew restless and began to chatter. In a moment of inattention she swept her arm across the workbench, knocking tools and clock parts and Father's wristwatch, which he'd taken off and placed on the bench, onto the floor with a clatter.

Her eyes stung as Father picked things up one by one. She stood, her back to the wall and her hands behind her. He said, so quietly she hardly heard him, "Cut to the chase, Katherine, or all is waste." And with his index finger he tapped the face of the wristwatch, its glass cracked, as he placed it on the bench before her. "I like to think you're more grown-up than that."

Later, crying herself to sleep, she'd thought, *I'm not like Ame, all flighty and full of stories. Nothing like Robbie, either, with his wild ideas. Nothing like.*

Father had left days later, and she hadn't helped him again.

Now, the clock on the mantle in front of her was clogged with sticky oil, and some of the screws had come loose, so she decided she'd work on it when she could. She turned it back to face the room, its hands frozen at 12:05, and went to finish emptying her valise.

As she stowed the last few things in the dresser, she fingered her great-aunt's chatelaine. If it hadn't been for that magic business and the other odd things her great-aunt had said, Kat would have found the chatelaine at least useful. Not like the useless charms she'd seen on the Lady's chatelaine. If Kat had to do some mending, for instance . . .

And there it was again, playing on her fingers. A winking blue glow that seemed to come from the chatelaine itself. She shook her head. Not possible. Some trick of the light.

And yet.

Magic, that's what Great-Aunt Margaret had said.

"So," Aunt Margaret had begun. "Three items of particular significance. First we have"—and she extended one long, gnarled finger—"the pen. You understand?"

Kat had heard this one before. She nodded.

"And?" her great-aunt prompted.

Kat knew an aphorism was demanded. "The pen is mightier than the sword."

"Brilliant. Your excellent memory is a gift." She smiled. "Of course, this pen has been replaced. The original was not dreadfully useful, requiring ink pots and the like and always clogging. But this pen"—Aunt Margaret removed the pen by unscrewing it from the holder from which it dangled—"this pen was made to fit and given to me most recently upon my birthday. By your very own father, the dear boy."

Kat looked quickly between her aunt and Mum. Aunt Margaret's eyes sparkled. Mum lowered her eyes as if to say, *Patience.*

Aunt Margaret continued. "This pen has a special ink that writes even under the direst circumstances. Something new, invented by . . . well, I have no idea. But it will write of its own accord, no need for an inkwell, no blots or clogs. It's quite the thing, a pen that writes of its own accord."

Writes of its own accord? Right. That would be a neat trick. Father would have winked.

Aunt Margaret recapped the pen. "Now," she said, "here we have a pair of scissors. These are original to the chatelaine." She lifted the second item, a tiny silver triangle into which fit a pair of scissors. There was an elegant small clasp over the top so that the scissors would stay put; Kat unhooked the clasp, and Aunt Margaret slid the scissors out of their case.

"These, my dear, are indeed magical scissors." She leaned toward Kat as she spoke and lowered her voice.

As Kat watched her great-aunt's bright eyes, she knew better than to laugh. If she said they were magic, then, by golly,

Kat had better pretend they were. She had to suck on the inside of her cheek to keep the smile down.

"They will cut anything," Great-Aunt Margaret said. "That's the important thing, Katherine. These scissors will cut . . . *anything*." Her face went still and grave. "'We are the two halves of a pair of scissors, when apart, Pecksniff; but together we are something.' Mr. Dickens, my dear, as you well know," she added, eyebrows raised. "Although you may find something more suitable to say when the need arises," she added cryptically. "Something of your own to say. You understand?"

Kat nodded. But by then she was thoroughly befuddled.

Great-Aunt Margaret replaced the scissors and lifted the third item, also hooked to its slender chain. "Ah." She sighed. "The thimble. You know what that means."

Finally, Kat allowed herself a smile. "A kiss," she answered. Aunt Margaret had read *Peter Pan* to them so often that the cover was coming apart from the binding; Robbie played at being one of the Lost Boys, especially since taking up fencing. Kat teased him about losing his marbles.

"Well, yes," Great-Aunt Margaret said, seeming disconcerted. "That, of course. Thimbles also have often been given as wedding gifts and love tokens. But this thimble has a magical aspect. This thimble can catch souls."

Kat had to bite her cheek hard. *Honestly.* "Aunt Margaret," she began. "How can anything catch a soul?"

Her aunt reared back, her eyebrows arching. "Katherine, you really must become less pragmatic. In times like these we require other equally important qualities. Like imagination. And faith. And hope. Remember, dear, hope springs eternal in the human breast."

Magic. Imagination. Hope. Great-Aunt Margaret was quite out of her mind.

Now, the only thing Kat hoped was for this war to end so they could all go home. She dropped the chatelaine among her sweaters and shut the drawer.

"Look," Amelie said. "Come and look."

Ame stood at the window, staring out into the garden. Kat moved to her side.

The view was toward the back of the castle. The fog had lifted into a gray autumn sky. The garden was barren and cold, the annuals gone and the shrubbery bare twigs. Some patches of early snow showed in the hollows, but the ground was otherwise bare and brown. An allée of trees stretched in a narrow band toward a woodland; beyond the farthest edge of woods Kat thought she saw a thin sliver of silvery water. That way was southeast, toward the North Sea and the continent.

Toward the war.

Toward Father, who was there, somewhere across the water, in danger but doing what he must.

The woods, the rough coast, the moors beyond were

treacherous and would be an easy place in which to be lost, especially in fog. There was no need of a castle moat, no need for shuttered gates. They were all here until the bitter end, and Kat swallowed the lump in her throat. She touched the cold glass with her fingers before she turned away.

But Amelie tugged at her sleeve. "No. Look." Ame pointed down into the near garden. Kat leaned against the glass to see.

Straight below them a small girl with blonde hair sat on the stone edging of an empty round fishpond. How Kat hadn't seen her right off was a mystery. A hound dog circled the girl and nosed the grass at her feet. As Kat watched, the girl reached into the rocks and lifted something out, and for an instant there was a flash of silver in the child's hand. Kat blinked and rubbed her eyes.

The girl held nothing.

"She's wearing a summer frock," Kat murmured.

"She's catching fishes," said Amelie.

"Ame, that pond is dry, silly." But the girl dipped her hand into the dry rocks again and again, and each time, something fishlike shimmered in her hand and then winked away. Kat shuddered.

"I feel so sad for her," said Amelie, leaning against the window, fingers splayed on the glass. "She's lost something. Can you see it, Kat? She's looking for something in the pond."

Kat took her sister's hand. It felt so cold, Kat had to rub

Ame's fingers between her palms. "You have a kind heart, Ame." But a vague uneasiness stirred inside Kat.

The door burst open behind them. "Kat!" Robbie fell into the room, Peter on his heels, Robbie's eyes like saucers. "Kat! You won't believe it. We found a secret hiding place. A hidden room. With something—or someone—locked inside that makes terrible shrieky noises."

Kat looked at Peter, who nodded, then back at Rob.

He was white as the cliffs of Dover. "Sure as sure," Rob said in a low voice, "sure as sure, it's a ghost."

8

The First Charm: The Fish

IT IS 1746.

Leonore leans against the door frame, listening. Her maids gossip about someone who lives at the edge of the village and who can use magic.

A conjurer, a magician, newly arrived . . . or maybe not. Who appeared from the mists of the moors, or the hollows of the hills . . . no one knows.

When questioned, her maids tell Leonore that he can help her, yes, surely, for he is the magister. She finds her own way to the ramshackle hut.

The magister listens while he stirs his fire. When Leonore falls silent, this is what he tells her. He can make her wishes come true. The chatelaine that hangs from her belt holds, he says, an ancient magic, and he can release it. Then she can use this magic for a child, not her own, exactly, but a child nonetheless.

"There is a price," he says, and stirs his fire. There is always a price.

"I'll pay," she says, and pay she does.

The magister takes in trade a part from her. No: he takes a part *of* her.

By flesh and bone, by rock and stone; I'll charm a child to call my own.

"The child must see the charm he will wear," the magister says. "He cannot be asleep or with senses dulled." When he whispers the incantation she's to recite, the fire dims.

Leonore shivers. She hears the cruel words. But she wants a child so badly . . .

The magister watches as Leonore retreats into the mist. He has begun to work his own magic, and she does not know how he will use her, how he will twist her dream into a nightmare. She does not know that the chatelaine was his gift to her. She does not know the terrible things the magister will do.

Leonore of Rookskill Castle will make magic to please her lord. But when she returns to tell him, her changed left hand hidden by a glove, she finds that he has been thrown by his stallion and lies in a deathlike stupor. She must find a willing child quickly now, quickly.

"I bring you good news," she says to her unconscious lord as she stands by his bed surrounded by weeping servants. "Of a child to come."

For which she has sacrificed to the magister a finger. Payment made of flesh and bone.

Leonore makes a gift of the fish charm to the child Rose in the very presence of the child's mother.

The fishmonger's wife, making deliveries, has been complaining, say Leonore's maids. "All these children! All girls, worse luck. I can't bear it! To keep them fed and clothed . . ." Leonore sees the opportunity she needs, and pays a visit to the hut by the shore.

Rose, the youngest girl, is beautiful and sweet and— Leonore hopes—an easy mark. She prays that a child so much desired, even if only a girl, will spur her lord's recovery and secure her future, as he wakes to see she is able to give him an heir. With the magister's enchantment Leonore can confound her lord, make him believe the child is theirs by blood and bone.

"Aye, then, go and live in the castle, Rose," Rose's mother says. "You'll have a fit life, you will. You have my blessing." And she mumbles, "And I've one less mouth to feed, thank the heavens."

Leonore holds a silk handkerchief to her nose with her gloved hand.

The fishmonger's wife is glad to see such emotion in her Rose's new protector. She herself wipes away a tear or two before chasing down Rose's older sisters.

Leonore feels emotion, for certain: she can scarce stand the fishy rotting stench in the dark and crowded cottage. She's grateful when Rose moves outside to examine the charm by the light of day.

A moment later, as Rose hangs the charm around her neck and Leonore repeats the whispered words from the magister, the child cries out, then slips into a vacant-eyed silence. Leonore bites her lip. Was that a cry of pain? Has she done something wrong?

But no—Leonore assures herself that Rose's mother is right. Rose will have a fit life in Rookskill Castle as the daughter of a lord, even if the enchantment has changed the child in some way Leonore does not yet understand.

It is only as she makes her way back to the castle that Leonore feels something else. The charmed child Rose walks behind her, silent as a shadow, frail as a wisp. But Leonore is stronger than she was before she cast the spell, less the young bride and more the rightful lady. She smiles for the first time in years. Instead of feeling lighter for the loss of the little fish charm, Leonore's chatelaine feels a wee bit heavier.

She brings the charmed Rose to her lordship's bedside. "See what I have made for us?"

But he does not stir. His staring eyes are fixed upon a point in the space above his head.

The chatelaine tugs on Leonore's belt. A newfound strength snakes through her blood. A thin strand of white weaves through her black hair. The rooks, her only friends, wait at Leonore's window.

9

The Secret Room

"SIT DOWN AND catch your breath," Kat said to Robbie. But it was to Peter she looked. His eyes were almost as round as Rob's.

"He's right about the secret room," Peter said. "We found it because of the noises."

"Grindings," said Rob. "And screeches."

Peter lifted his hands in a shrug, nodding, and goose bumps rose on Kat's arms.

"It's got to be a ghost," Rob whispered. His eyes widened. "Say. Maybe it's that Lady Leonore."

"Like the fishing girl," said Ame. "Except she didn't screech."

"Amelie," Kat said, trying to keep the tremor out of her voice, "that girl couldn't be a ghost. Likely she's one of the other students."

"No, she's a ghost, because she's disappeared," said Ame.

Kat turned to the window. Sure enough, there was no sign of the girl, who'd been there only moments earlier; the dog wandered the lawn alone. A rook perched on the pond coping, its head cocked, looking down at the stony bottom.

Kat twisted the watch on her wrist. *Carry on.* She faced the boys. "I'd like to see for myself."

Peter squared his shoulders. "Okay."

"Robbie, you stay here with Ame, okay?"

"No problem," he said with a shudder. "I wouldn't go back there for anything."

Kat plastered on a brave smile before closing the door on Robbie's white face and Amelie's round eyes.

She and Peter crept down the hallway past closed doors, turning corners and finding their way in the gray light.

"This place is so confusing," Kat whispered. "It's nothing inside like it appears on the outside."

"It's like a puzzle box," Peter whispered back.

"Right." Kat glanced at him. He was clever and friendly. An unexpected shyness grew in her. "Did you see anyone else?"

"No," Peter replied. "Rob rattled a couple of doorknobs before I stopped him, but nobody came out."

The castle did creak and groan in the way of old places, but nothing shrieked or clanked yet. A dank, musty odor permeated everything, and the carpet was worn and tattered. Kat tried not to think that the grim portraits of long-nosed ancestors with dark eyes watched them as they tiptoed down the hall. She didn't want Peter to know she was frightened, but she was glad to have him there, even if she couldn't tell him so.

After twists and turns they reached the stairwell. They crept down the stairs, the window on their right.

At the next landing Peter stopped. He pointed to the wall at the turn of the stair.

Kat stepped forward, and a sound, a low murmur, seeped from the very wall itself. She leaned in, cocking her head, when a short high screech made her jump, and then she heard a staticky hiss, and she backed up the stairs and right into Peter, so that she jumped again.

He shook his head and pointed past her, at the wall, and she moved back down the stairs, and there it was, the thin outline of a door fitted so tightly in the wall that it was well hidden from all but the most discerning eye.

Now she leaned her right ear flat up against the thin crack. And heard a sharp *screech*, and a *click-click*, and worst of all, silence.

Until a *thud* and something moved, unmistakably coming right toward her.

She turned around fast and caught Peter's wide eyes, and they both ran up the stairs, top speed, taking the steps two at a time until they reached their floor, and they made it around the corner into the hallway the same instant they heard the door open on the landing below. Kat pressed her back against the wall, her chest tight, knees trembling, eyes closed, and ears wide open. She heard the door below them close, and then a dreadful pause, as if someone on the landing was checking the air, *sniffing us out,* she thought, until whoever it was headed down the stairs, away from them.

She and Peter waited until all sounds faded.

And waited and waited. The castle grew still and silent, but for the wind, which moaned now at the windows.

Peter stood with his back against one wall, Kat facing him with her back pressed against the other. She thought her lungs would burst, until she had to let the air out, gasping.

He whispered, "Well, unless ghosts walk down stairs, it's not a ghost."

Kat shook her head, both relieved and worried. "No. But it might be worse."

Peter tapped on the wall and Kat listened, poised to run, but finally they were satisfied that the secret room was empty. They examined the door, up, down, and around, but couldn't see the way to open it. They tapped, and pushed, and tried to pry—Kat broke a fingernail on that attempt—but it wouldn't budge.

"How do you know?" Peter asked when they'd given up and

were making their way back to their rooms, Kat chewing on her damaged index finger. "How did you know what it was?"

Kat said, "Because I've heard a short-wave radio before." In fact, she'd seen one up close.

When Father brought a short-wave wireless home a couple of weeks before leaving, he'd shown it only to Kat. "Here, Kitty, have a look. I knew you'd be interested. Just keep it under your hat."

It was about the size of her valise and was rigged up to be carried like a backpack. He'd dialed up a colleague and let her listen in on the test. It had screeched so she had to stop her ears with her fingers. Father had said, "Noisy all right. But it might save someone's life." She'd touched the case with gentle fingers.

It might save *his* life, that wireless.

"Why's it worse to have a short-wave radio here than a ghost?" Peter asked. "A ghost would be far more trouble. Moving through walls. Moaning and howling and keeping us up at night, and maybe up to evil tricks. At the very least, scaring the devil out of me."

A ghost would scare the devil out of Kat, too, but she wasn't going to admit that to Peter. Really, he was so honest. Blunt. She wasn't sure what to think, since the boys she knew at school were all aloof. Peter's straight brown hair now fell across his forehead. In the time since they'd left London—which already felt like a million years ago but was only yesterday—his bangs had come unglued. Kat rather liked them that way, but she wasn't about to admit that, either.

She stirred herself to be logical. "Think about it. A short-wave here would serve what purpose?" Kat asked. "We're supposed to be on the lookout for spies in our midst. Mr. Churchill said so."

Peter's expression moved from amusement to surprise, and he stopped in his tracks so they were facing each other at a turn in the passage. "You think there's a spy here?"

Kat set her lips. She knew something about spying. "It's possible."

"Well, it couldn't be the Lady," he said.

She lifted her eyebrows. "And why ever not?"

"Maybe she has a wireless out of sheer practicality." He paused. "She's living up here nearly alone, and with her husband ill and all."

Kat wasn't keen on the Lady, what with the small girl left out in the cold garden, the Lady's chilly personality, and now Peter obviously thinking the Lady very fine indeed. Kat folded her arms across her chest. "I'm not at all sure about her."

"I like her well enough," Peter said in a tone that suggested he liked her quite a lot.

"Why would she have a wireless behind a hidden door if it's just practical?"

Peter shrugged. "You're too suspicious."

Kat chewed her lip. "Maybe she's in league with someone else."

"Maybe. Or maybe she doesn't know the wireless is in there. Maybe someone discovered this hidden room and is using it for his or her purpose."

"I guess that's possible," Kat said grudgingly.

"At least it's not a ghost."

"Right," Kat said. No such thing—was there? As if in answer, a grumbling groan drifted up from below. Kat glanced down the dusky hallway, suppressing the urge to run. *The furnace, or maybe the wind around the outer walls. Right?*

Peter's voice startled Kat. "What do you want to tell Rob and Ame?"

"I guess we should—"

"Here!" Marie's voice, sharp, came from behind her. Kat almost leapt out of her skin. "Just what do you think you're playing at?"

Peter said, "We were trying to find the, um, you know, where—"

"If the Lady discovered you wandering about the hallways, you'd regret it," scolded Marie. "Back to your rooms at once. And stay there until I fetch you."

Peter and Kat hurried down the hall.

"Where did she come from?" Peter whispered.

"I don't know." They'd reached Kat's room. "I thought the hall was empty."

"This place is definitely spooky," Peter said.

Kat couldn't agree more. Her heart was thumping. She opened her door. "Rob? Ame?"

But Kat's room was stone cold, silent and empty.

10

Flesh and Bone

IT IS 1746. The magister makes Leonore a gift.

He says, "Here is a finger to replace your own, the one you have given up for the charmed child Rose."

Flesh and bone.

Leonore asks, "How could you make a finger that can replace the one heaven gave me?"

"Ah," says the magister as he turns to stoke his fire. "This is so finely wrought that none shall see it for what it is in the broad daylight. Only in the dark shall sight and sound betray; only the light of the full moon shall reveal." He does not add that heaven could never be party to this making. He does not add that his skill of invention is bought with old magic. He does not tell her what he does with her payment of flesh and bone.

"To keep this gift," he says, "you cannot leave the castle or the town or the fells that surround them."

Payment made.

When the charmed fish-girl Rose does not bring Leonore's lord back from the brink of death, Leonore wants to try again.

She should have taken a boy first, and now she will. Her lord would want a boy to be his heir. She will go back to the magister and ask for a boy, before the heather purples the fells. A boy that Leonore can save from a life of misery, a boy she will raise from poverty and shame, much as she has saved Rose.

And there is that other thing, that feeling that came from her chatelaine with the charming of Rose, a feeling almost as good as love. With her cold new-minted finger she pushes the charmed Rose aside.

Her sacrifice is blood and bone. But the children sacrifice something far more valuable.

By rock and bone, by blood and stone, not life, nor death, but lost, alone . . .

11

Ghosts

THE EMPTY ROOM made Kat's heart pound like a drum. A pack of playing cards lay scattered across the floor.

Then Rob's hand thrust out from under the bed and waved close by her feet.

"What in the world?" Kat fell to her hands and knees, and Peter dropped down next to her. Rob's and Ame's white faces shone in the gloom.

"A ghost! Right here!" Robbie whispered.

"I tried to tell Rob it was all right," said Ame. "It's a nice ghost, like Mr. Pudge. But Rob made me get under the bed."

"That's because I wanted you to be safe," Rob said crossly.

"There are no ghosts," Kat said, her voice trembling. "Come on out."

But Robbie shook his head. "It's still here."

Kat looked around the empty room, warding off a shiver. "Where, then?"

Robbie pointed. "There."

"Ah," Kat said, as his finger waved toward the window. She took a breath, letting her insides settle. "Another someone out in the garden."

"No!" came Rob's coarse whisper. "Not outside! Look in the lavatory."

"The lavatory?" Kat was sure Robbie must be wrong. She opened the bathroom door and looked inside, and . . . she couldn't help herself.

Kat cried out and stumbled backward.

"Here!" shouted Peter from behind her, yelling at the figure by the sink. "What do you think you're doing?"

Kat didn't want to chase the boy. She'd already given him the fright of his life, she could see that much in his face. And she was sorry for his twisted, painful-looking shoulder, and he ran dragging one leg, pinwheeling his arms. Peter followed him out the door halfheartedly and stood and watched until the boy disappeared.

Kat pulled herself together. *Keep calm,* for pity's sake. Even if she was shaking all over.

When she bent to look under the bed again she found the two pairs of round eyes. "It's all right," Kat managed. "He's gone. Only a boy. A poor crippled boy." Then she leaned back on her heels and said, "But how'd he get in here, anyway?"

"I don't know," Robbie said as he and Ame crawled out from under the bed. "We were playing Go Fish, and all of a sudden he was here in the room, watching us."

Amelie nodded. "He was here out of nowhere. Like a ghost would do."

"Are you sure he was real?" Rob asked.

"He looked as real as you," Kat said, but she didn't feel at all certain. "What do you think, Peter?"

Peter pushed his hair off his forehead. "He ran like he was real," he said. "I think."

"Did you touch him?" Rob asked. "Was he solid?"

"Sure he was. I couldn't see through him," Kat said. "Ghosts—if they exist, and I'm not saying they do, because I'm quite certain they don't—but if they do they'd be transparent." *Wouldn't they?* Kat turned the watch on her wrist. She didn't want to admit that she'd been scared to touch him, as if he might feel . . . cold. Or that her hand might slip right through him. She shuddered.

"He made noises, too," Peter said. "I heard his footsteps."

"Ghosts can make noises," said Amelie. "Moaning and groaning noises."

"Speaking of noises," Rob said, "what about the noises behind the hidden door in the stairwell?"

Kat and Peter exchanged a glance. She hoped Peter wouldn't tell them about the possible spy. One spooky thing was enough for their first day. "A tree branch rubbing against the window in the hall above," Peter said.

Rob narrowed his eyes, suspicious.

"How do you think that boy got in here?" Kat asked. "If he was real, he had to get in."

Ame said, "He walked right through the wall."

Kat tapped her watch. "That's it," she said, brightening. "That's it, Ame. Brilliant! There must be a hidden door, like the one in the stairwell. We just have to find it."

A sharp rap on the door made them all jump, and then Marie poked her head in. "Lunch," she said. "Follow me."

Kat hoped they'd see the other students of the academy as they went down, but Marie said no, they were already in the middle of a lesson. "You'll start tomorrow. That's what her Ladyship said."

They followed Marie down the stairs to the grand front hallway and then through the castle, back and back. Kat found it hard to make a mental map with so many twists and turns, though she did her best. She passed at least one parlor and several small libraries and something that looked like a museum full of dead animals and antlers, and everywhere were shields or hauberks on the stone walls hung with the Craig tartan.

Marie stopped before a set of massive oak doors and tugged at one to let them inside.

The dining hall—for it was a great hall—was paneled in dark wood and watched over by rows on either side of metal-armored men, each holding a different weapon. Robbie ran down the line, from one suit of armor to the next.

"Just look at these!" he gushed, his voice echoing. "Look at that claymore! Look at that broadsword. A two-headed ax! Golly."

Amelie tugged at Kat's sleeve and Kat bent down.

"They're worried," Ame said.

"Who are?"

"The men," she said. She paused before one of the suits of armor and lifted her small finger to touch the glove with its rows of knuckle spikes.

"Ame, there are no men," Kat said. "These are empty suits of armor. How can they be worried?" A little shiver wove across her shoulders.

"But they are," Amelie said. Her voice was tinged with impatience, and she placed her fisted hands on her hips. "Something awful is happening here. Can't you feel it?"

Of course she couldn't. But Kat couldn't deny that something was very wrong. The suits of armor stood still and cold, rank on rank of gleaming metal men. Amelie walked down the row, touching each and whispering something.

The table at the far end of the hall was set with four places, and Marie pointed out the buffet and then left them to eat alone. It was eerie in this great hall with the cold fireplaces and the cold men and the high arching clerestory windows shedding a gloomy light.

But hunger got the best of Kat when she surveyed the buffet. It was quite a feast—lamb and potatoes, gravy and green beans, all steaming and fragrant in warming trays, and even a vanilla custard for dessert. Such a lot of food, what with rationing, even if the Lady said they had plenty. Despite feeling watched by those blank metal eyes, they dug in, and Robbie entertained them with battle notes and historical facts.

Kat ate well. But as soon as she was starting to feel stuffed and relaxed, the thought popped into her head that they were being fattened up, like in those dark fairy tales where children stumble into enchanted castles and bad things happen when they are least prepared and most satiated.

She pushed her plate away without getting dessert.

As they left the hall they took a wrong turn right off.

They passed small utilitarian rooms, some with washbasins, some with great pantries lined with dry goods. They saw a baking room and a canning room, but everything looked unused and dusty, and Kat got to wondering who was feeding them when Robbie piped up, sniffing, and said, "We can at least find the kitchen. Why don't we follow our noses?"

Kat sniffed and smelled it then, the rich buttery odor. They followed it back until they pushed open a swinging door, and there was the kitchen, and standing in the middle and talking to herself, the cook.

She was a large woman and introduced herself right off as Miss Brodbeem, but, aye, they could call her Cook.

"But what are you children doing wandering about, then, hey?" She turned away, pacing between the great center table and a sink, carrying things back and forth. "I never for the life of me saw such a place, and it's only because of you lot and for him that I stay. Why, I never believed all the talk, but here I am and . . . Here!" She stopped her pacing and whirled as they were creeping out of her domain. "Just where do you think you lot are off to, hey?"

They froze, Kat's hand clutching Ame's tight.

Peter cleared his throat and said, "We didn't mean to intrude."

"Intrude? Intrude! Have you lot eaten all you need? Did you get the luncheon? Yes? Well, then. What did you think? I try my best to prepare a feast for every meal, but does anyone appreciate it? Does anyone even eat it? I wouldn't know, now, would I, because no one ever tells me. I'm just told, do this, do that, but I'm left as ignorant as a newborn babe. Her Ladyship . . ." And here Cook dropped her voice and muttered things under her breath that Kat couldn't hear.

"We quite enjoyed it," Kat said.

"It was delicious," said Peter.

"We loved it!" piped up Amelie.

"It was smashing. Really, really excellent. Especially the vanilla custard. That was," said Robbie, searching for some extreme epithet, "that was brilliant."

"Oh," said Cook, and she drew her apron right up to her eyes, dabbing them aggressively, "oh, you lot are lovely. Would you like some apple tart? The apples are straight from the orchard. I only now finished the making of it, and wouldn't you know, here you are."

Kat smiled, and Cook pulled stools around so they could sit, and they all ate the tart happily and listened as Cook described her menus, and Kat decided that they had established their first solid friendship in this bleak, peculiar place.

Her lack of sleep the night before—sitting upright in a rocking train was no way to get a good sleep—caught up with Kat now that she had a full belly. Marie stormed into the kitchen and led them back to their rooms, scolding them the entire way for leaving the dining hall and "wandering." She reminded them not to be late for supper, which began at the hour of five, and to change into their uniforms, since she couldn't be always chasing after them what with her many duties, and she left, still scolding, her voice echoing down the hallway.

When Amelie stretched across the large four-poster, Kat only lay down to keep her company, but once her head settled into the pillow, she fell into a deep slumber.

12

Spikes

KAT IS BACK in the well. She's found a soft cushion of dried leaves, but it's not a comfort. Wind moans over the top of the well, and a rook screeches, *Off, off,* and something scrapes toward her. That hand, that curving claw hand, scrapes across the floor.

And then, more horrible, a disembodied face lifts out of the shadows above the hand, a face she knows, a sharp pale face framed by silvery hair, a ghostly face. Lips curve in a smile, and the teeth look like the spikes on a saw blade.

The teeth grind metal on metal as the face and the claw hand make straight for her.

13

The Second Charm: The Hunchback

I̲T̲ ̲I̲S̲ ̲1747.

The villagers shun him, the hunchback boy. Abandoned in the dark of night at the chapel door for his deformity, he does not know his parents. He will not be missed. Leonore will save him from a life of lonely submission, from a barren childhood of painful memories. She will do this—charm the child—as much for him as she will for herself.

For the hunchback boy the magister asks only for an ear, a small sacrifice. Something she can hide beneath her hair.

"And this ear I've made for you, no one seeing you in daylight will know it's not your own."

No, not in daylight. And only her vacant-eyed husband sees and hears Leonore by the light of the full moon.

The boy serves the chapel at which he'd been deposited, since the priest is too old to carry the heavy cross and too arthritic to polish the silver. For his labors the boy is given refuge: he sleeps in the transept, eats in the rectory, and rarely strays far from the chapel.

The chapel is sanctuary, the magister tells her. You cannot charm him in the chapel. You will have to catch him outside.

Gathering wood, she reasons. He has to be out gathering wood for the fireplace that warms the rectory. She sends her man to offer her forest to the boy. She finds him alone in her woods, the rooks hovering overhead, their guardian wings folded tight, and she offers him the charm. She holds it before his eyes, and he marvels at the silver thing she's taken from her chatelaine. It looks so much like him.

It floats in the air, reflecting the light. "Here's a pretty silver chain for you to wear it on. Won't you put it round your neck?"

The boy looks up. The beautiful lady standing before him is so sweet. Perhaps she's a saint, come down from heaven to save the poor boy who sweeps out the nave and passes out the offering box.

But then he trembles. If she's a saint, she'll know: he is imperfect. He backs away from her. "Can't," he says in a broken voice.

"Can't?" For an instant, she does not look sweet. But then she is again. "Of course you can. It's a gift."

Should he tell her? It had only been once, one time, when the fair had come through town. And oh, he'd wanted to see it, see the jugglers. And it was only a few coins from the offering box. The terrible punishment he'd suffered at the fair—being taken for one of the freaks—had been enough of a lesson. Hadn't it?

The beautiful lady takes his hand and folds his fingers around the chain. A braided circle of white hair crowns her black locks like a halo.

The silver charm dangles from the chain in his hand. The more he looks at it, the more he thinks it looks like him. As if it has been made for him. In the shape of this charm, his deformity is beautiful.

Yes, take it. He'd paid for his sin at the fair, as he'd been tossed about for a freak, laughed at and muddied and bruised. This charm is but a small gift, a balm for all the hurts laid on his crooked back. A saint would want that. And if she is a saint, maybe this bright charm will even cure his ills . . .

Tim smiles up at her, and when she smiles back, he fancies that she is made of shining silver.

14

Chatelaine

THEY WOKE TO a furious pounding on the door.

"Up! Up!" Marie ran into the room. "The Lady will not tolerate a late supper! Up at once! I can't be responsible for you at every turn. Oh, you should be in your uniforms. Now there's no time. Just come down at once." She *tsk*ed as she ran out again.

The back of Kat's neck was slick with sweat as she tried to shake off the nightmare. Amelie rubbed her eyes fiercely, a rumpled mess in her twisted wool jumper.

"Come on, then," Kat said. Her hands trembled.

"I don't need to eat," Ame said, grumpy. "Want to stay here."

"We've got no choice."

Kat tried combing out their hair—Amelie had terrible

knots and cried out more than once, and Kat finally gave up, saying, "That will have to do."

They rushed down the great stairs into the central hallway and turned left, and—"No! It's right. Sorry, Ame"—Marie calling them along, so Kat followed the sound of her voice until they finally reached the dining hall.

Now fires roared in both fireplaces. Light streamed in from the high windows; the sun had come out from behind the clouds while they napped. The table was spread again for a feast. Everyone stood at their places at the table, including Peter and Rob and three other children, two boys and a girl. It was clear that they'd all been waiting for Kat and Amelie, and they glared at them as they stumbled in. Rob and Peter wore their uniforms, and Kat tried brushing her messy hair back from her face, feeling the blush of embarrassment.

At the head of the high table, raised above the table where the children waited, stood the Lady Eleanor, and standing next to her was a man. Kat thought he had to be Lord Craig, though he didn't look ill in the least.

Kat dragged Amelie as fast as they could move until they stood before the Lady, and then Kat dropped into a curtsey; Amelie copied her, mumbling annoyance. "Sorry, my Lady," Kat panted.

The Lady Eleanor lifted her chin. Her white-blonde hair was swept into a side chignon, and she was dressed to the nines. She wore the kind of gown that wouldn't keep anyone warm unless they lived in the equatorial regions, where bare arms covered only by black above-elbow gloves would be a relief. Her dress was shimmery, full-length, body-hugging, although she wore an elaborate belt from which hung a Scottish sporran made of leather and a scarf in the Craig tartan. All the male eyes in the room were on the Lady. Kat would've liked to kick Peter in the shins. Robbie was almost drooling.

"You will dress in uniforms for every occasion," the Lady said, her voice cold even as she gave them a thin smile. "We eat before sunset here. You will not be late again."

"No, ma'am." She curtseyed again, this time to the man. "Good evening, my Lord."

At that, the man burst into mocking laughter.

Kat stiffened, first at the sound of that laugh, and then at the looks she—and the man—received from the Lady.

"'My Lord'!" the man said, sputtering with laughter. "She called me 'my Lord'!"

"Yes, well, she is an ignorant girl," the Lady said, loud enough for Kat to hear.

Kat's hand tightened on Amelie's.

"You can call me Sir," the man said with a narrow-eyed grin, "but I'm no proper lord."

The Lady turned cold eyes on Kat. "This is not my lord husband," she said. Her teeth gleamed in a smile that didn't reach her eyes. "This is Mr. Storm, one of your instructors. Now that you've all arrived, and the other teachers arrive tomorrow, lessons shall begin."

"About bloody time for something interesting to begin," murmured the boy standing a few feet behind Kat. "Been a bloody bore here so far. That bugger had us locked in study hall all day, he did, while he was off someplace."

That "bugger" Mr. Storm held the Lady's chair for her and swept his hand for her to sit, and the Lady gave him a look that would freeze a polar bear, though he either didn't see or didn't care. When he pulled his chair out to sit, Kat heard the scraping of the chairs behind her and she tugged Amelie to the two empty places at the table, while stealing another look at Mr. Storm.

Instructors come in all shapes and sizes, but Mr. Storm didn't fit Kat's idea of an instructor. To be honest, he hadn't fit her idea of a lord, either. He was built square, and wore an ill-fitting tweedy jacket that seemed too small for him, and he had a flat haircut that left his blond sprigs shooting skyward. He still shook with laughter like a heaving barrel, and Kat thought that, really, her comment wasn't all that funny. It was as if he was privy to some secret joke.

The Lady, bristling, motioned for them to eat.

Although it had been but a few hours since lunch, a feast was laid before them yet again. Mutton, potatoes, beets. Kat rubbed her forehead, still groggy from her nap and unnerved by her nightmare, trying to balance the coldness of the Lady with the comforts of the food and the castle.

The others at the table made introductions. The rude boy was Jorry Phillips, who was from Belgravia, the swankiest of London's neighborhoods. Jorry was as thin as a rail, with a long nose and a sour expression and a red smear of birthmark that emerged from the collar of his shirt.

"Don't much care for all this meat," Jorry said. "Mother's raised me as a vegetarian, and to be fit and healthy. But without a balanced meal I have to eat this. It's probably going to make me sick. Plus we're not allowed to be outside without permission, so there's nothing to do here but sit about, no calisthenics or other vigorous exercise. I've been doing push-ups in my room, but it's hardly enough, you know. We'll all be fat as hogs soon, eating like this. That Mr. Storm isn't much of an instructor, if you ask me. Claims his field is history."

Kat was glad to be a couple of places removed from Jorry.

She was seated on one side next to the younger of the two boys, Colin Drake. Colin was sweet and eager, chattering away about anything that crossed his mind. Kat thought he and Robbie, close in age, would make a fine pair of bookends, and indeed, they seemed to be striking up a friendship, talking about the armor and fencing and castle living.

She turned to the girl on her other side. "Isabelle LaRoche," the girl said, with the faintest accent. "You've come up from London, yes? My mother's English and Papa's French, and we were in Paris until last spring. Papa got us all out ahead of it." Kat knew Isabelle meant the German incursion into France. "*Heureusement,* I was able to bring my clothes from Paris. This uniform is so dull." Isabelle smoothed the collar of her white shirt—it looked as if she'd starched it—and raised one eyebrow as she surveyed Kat's outfit.

Kat plucked at her wrinkled jersey.

Amelie, on Isabelle's other side, said, "I think the uniform looks well on you."

Isabelle preened a bit. "*Merci.* You may be about my size, since I am small for my age. When we're not in uniform we can play dress-up. We'll try things from my closet. Yes?"

Kat brushed at her jersey again and picked at her food.

Isabelle leaned over to Kat, whispering. "The Lady, she is glamorous and has beautiful clothes."

Beautiful, but odd. Kat glanced at the Lady, whose chignon swept artfully over one ear. "She does."

"But I must tell you, something's peculiar in this academy."

"Why do you say that?"

"I saw something, when we first arrived. It was very strange." Isabelle dropped her voice further.

"What was it?"

"A boy. I watch from the window when no one is around."

Isabelle shrugged. "He is good-looking, you know? Anyway, he is feeding *les chats*. But I watch the boy, and I realize that his eyes, they do not really see. He is like a ghost. And as I watch, well, I glance away for just a moment and then . . . poof!" Isabelle snapped her fingers.

"Poof?" Kat echoed. A chill crept over her despite the fires raging in the fireplaces. "You mean he disappeared?"

"*Mais oui.* I only look away for an instant, and I could not see him after."

Like the girl by the pond. "His eyes—was he blind?"

But Isabelle shook her head. "*Non, non,* nothing like that. Something else." She leaned closer to Kat and dropped her voice. "He is standing, frozen, before he vanishes. His eyes are all wide and . . . nothing." Isabelle pointed to her own blue eyes, now round and staring. "Like this." She waved her fingers. "Marie says he is ill, but that is not how it looked to me. Unless he is ill in the head."

"Marie knew about him?"

"Of course," Isabelle said, pouting a little. "When I see him wandering about, looking *enchanté* . . . how do you say? Enchanted. I watch for him. And I see him again, once more. He feeds his cats, but he is again looking *enchanté*."

Kat shifted. "Did Marie say anything more? Does he live in the castle?"

Isabelle shrugged and ate a delicate bite of food. "Some-

where with his cats. I haven't seen him since the second time."
Then she leaned toward Kat, one long curl of her hair sweeping
forward over her shoulder. "He wears a long necklace. I see it as
he bends to his cats. I have very good eyes."

"A necklace."

"Yes, an odd thing. A necklace with a charm at the end. The
charm is shaped like a cat." Isabelle hesitated. "It reminds me, a
little, of the charms on the Lady's belt."

Kat sat straighter. "The ones she wears on her chatelaine?"

"Ah, you know some French? You know of *la châtelaine?*"
Isabelle seemed excited. *"Oui, les charmes sur sa châtelaine.* The
Lady hides this chatelaine she wears. Once when she does not
realize I can see it, I catch a glimpse of one charm." Isabelle
leaned even closer so that only Kat could hear. The boys were
devouring their dinner, all four now chattering loudly about
football. "That charm was"—Isabelle dropped her voice to the
lowest of whispers—"the sign of evil."

The room darkened with sunset just as Isabelle said the
word *evil.* The only light in the hall came from the fireplaces, a
dull red glow. A chill like tiny feet crawled up Kat's spine now,
bringing up goose bumps all over.

"Sign of evil?" she whispered back.

"Like this." Under the table Isabelle made the familiar hand
sign for the warding off of evil things, the horns—*les cornes*—
of the devil.

Kat shuddered. "Are you sure?"

Isabelle nodded, solemn. *"Mais oui."* She picked at her food. "I am thinking the Lady wears this charm to ward off bad things. But the handsome boy, he found bad things even so, of that I'm sure."

Isabelle's eyes dropped away. Her dark hair formed perfect ringlets. She didn't seem the practical sort; no one would call her stodgy. Maybe she even liked to tell scary stories. Maybe she shared Amelie's imaginative streak.

So the boy with the cats wore a necklace charm in the shape of a cat and seemed enchanted. Two other ghostly children wandered about the castle as if lost. And the Lady wore on her chatelaine the sign to ward off evil. Why would the Lady wear such a thing?

Unless there *was* something evil in this castle, and she wore it for her own protection. Perhaps the ghost of the Lady Leonore did wander the castle, with an evil purpose.

Kat shook herself. What was wrong with her? There must be a logical explanation for everything. Of course. It was just a matter of picking things apart, like opening the back of a clock and taking out the mechanism bit by bit to discover how all the pieces fit together.

"My Lady?" Kat said, standing up and lifting her voice to be heard above the chatter.

Everyone froze. The Lady, sitting straight up in her chair at the head table, appeared to have eaten nothing, her hands flat on the table before her. She stared down at Kat, one eyebrow lifted. "Yes?"

"Where are the others?" The blood rushed into Kat's cheeks, and she thrust her trembling hands behind her back.

"The other . . . ?"

"The other children. We saw them, earlier today. A girl wearing a gauzy frock out in the cold garden, and a crippled boy. And . . ." Isabelle nudged Kat hard in the thigh, so she stopped herself from saying something about the cat-boy. "Why aren't they at supper?"

The fire popped and snapped in the silence. Mr. Storm stopped chewing and stared. "Other children?" he mumbled.

The Lady braced her hands on the table and then stood. "I'm afraid I must leave you. It's time for me to tend to my husband. Please, finish your supper under the watchful eye of Mr. Storm." She gave Mr. Storm a swift glance, then glared at Kat. "In the future, you will refrain from addressing the upper table."

The Lady left the hall.

Every male eye in the place followed her sweeping form. Robbie, Kat understood. But she admitted to being disappointed in Peter. And disappointed in herself for caring what he thought.

After the great doors closed behind the Lady with a *thud*,

they ate in silence, the boys' chatter dropping away so it was quiet all around. Even Mr. Storm was silent, although he made loud unpleasant noises as he chewed his food and heaped his plate.

Marie came in with hot chocolate, and Kat wondered at such extravagance, having cocoa in the midst of war, and remembered that the Lady said she'd stockpiled sweets. But she must have had some foresight, since even Kat's own parents hadn't guessed the war would last so long. The children each drank two full cups, even Kat, while Mr. Storm helped himself to several glasses of claret.

The fires burned lower and lower and the room grew dim, and Kat found herself nodding in her chair, even as they drank their chocolate. The next she knew, Mr. Storm was gone, the fires had smoldered to ashes, the room was thick in shadow, and they all sat as if in a stupor. Kat couldn't tell how much time had passed.

Peter stood up. "Got to get to sleep," he mumbled. "Must be the long trip, but I'm beat."

They left the hall as a group, the half-eaten meal remaining on the table, with no sign now of Marie nor Cook, and somehow they found their way to the stairs, dragging themselves up to their rooms. Kat held Amelie's hand as much for herself as to keep Ame moving. As they passed the portrait in the hall Kat could have sworn the blue eyes of the Lady Leonore followed her.

Isabelle, Jorry, and Colin had rooms down the hall from Kat and Ame, but they were barely able to murmur good nights before falling into their chambers.

Kat must have washed and changed and helped Amelie wash and change, but she didn't remember a thing about it later. At some point she heard the lock on the door snap shut from outside.

Trapped, was her last waking thought.

15

Tricks of Magic

GREAT-AUNT MARGARET looms. *"Do you hear me, Katherine? Magic is tricky. There is always a price to pay for its use."*

"What price?" She doesn't really want to know. She doesn't believe in magic, after all.

Her great-aunt holds out her hand and it changes from flesh and bone to something terrible—a hand made of shining silver, with fingers like knife blades—and she drops her chatelaine onto Kat's open right palm. The chatelaine glows blue and grows colder and colder until it's so icy, Kat must let go. When it hits the floor, the three silver charms—the pen, the scissors, the thimble—shatter into a thousand pieces.

Great-Aunt Margaret screams like a high-pitched bird. *"You did not pay the price!"*

16

Moon

IT IS 1747.

With the second charming Leonore pulses with joy. Although she hears Tim's cry of pain and sees his face go blank like Rose's, she dismisses it. She has rescued the hunchback boy from a miserable childhood and terrible memories. She will give her lord the gift of a son and has saved herself in the bargain.

Her chatelaine weighs heavier on her belt, but it is a weight she can bear. This weight feels almost . . . glorious.

Leonore brings the boy before her lord.

But that very night her lord wakes from his accident at last, and by the light of the full moon, he sees her. He sees her shining silver ear, her mechanical finger. He sees her deformity, hears the whining of wheels within her mechanical finger, and calls her a witch—and he is revolted. He does not love her; he will not keep her; the children make no difference; and he casts her away, staggering from his bed, brandishing a blazing stick from his fire.

Weeping, Leonore gathers the children and goes no farther than the ancient keep, for it is a cold dark night and the woods are full of wolves. She huddles in the keep with Rose and Tim, who watch her with blank eyes.

The Lord of Rookskill Castle, hearing rumors, burns to the ground a ramshackle hut at the edge of Craig village that is said to be cursed by evil.

Leonore sees from her tower when her lord takes a new young wife who promptly gives him a son, and Leonore's heart breaks with the pain of rejection. But then she wonders, for her lord and his new wife grow old and die, and their heirs, and great-heirs, all grow old and die—and she does not. She and the children remain in the keep for many, many years, she and Rose and Tim, always young.

What kind of magic does she possess?

The rooks keep her company. They have unnatural skills and whisper their news. She hides with the children in the keep's dark shadows. Her hair will change from black to black and white to white and black, and finally to silver-white.

The cold color of the moon.

17

Storm

THE WORDS ECHOED in Kat's head as she heard the snap of the lock in the door. *You did not pay the price!* She lay in bed, shaking, clenching her fist as if it still felt cold.

Sunlight streamed through the open curtains, a rare sunny day in Scotland. She'd have taken a dreary London rain for anything, and Father and Mum and even Great-Aunt Margaret. Outside the glass Kat heard the harsh call of a rook: *Off, off, off,* it cried. And then, more distant, *War, war.*

War. Why had Father sent them to this awful place?

Father. She had to prove to him that she could survive. *Keep your chin up, my girl. Keep calm.*

Kat splashed cold water on her face and got herself dressed in her uniform before dragging Ame out of bed. As soon as

Ame was moving about, Kat opened the door and peered into the hall. Light spilled along the hallway from the far windows, and from somewhere below she could hear the clatter of dishes.

It all seemed perfectly normal. But she was sure now that it was not.

There was only one other person she could talk to about it, even if he was a boy. A bold American boy who made her feel shy, so that she had to remind herself again to keep calm.

She knocked at Robbie and Peter's door, and Peter opened it almost at once; they were both dressed, although Robbie looked like he'd wrestled with his bedclothes and lost the battle.

Kat tugged Peter's arm to pull him into the hallway, out of Robbie's hearing.

"I think we were drugged," she said in a low voice.

He ran his hands over his face. "I did sleep well, but I thought it was because I was exhausted."

"I didn't sleep well. And it felt wrong, that kind of sleep."

He pursed his lips. "Why would we be drugged?"

She placed her hands on her hips. Bad dreams and poor sleep made her shyness give way to irritability. "I don't know. Because we're in the house of a spy, maybe? Maybe someone is using us as a cover for spying, and when that someone wants us out of the way, we're drugged." *That, or we're in a house haunted by evil magic, and we're being enchanted,* she thought, but didn't want to say that out loud.

She wanted to pry the puzzle apart, piece by piece, attack it logically. But what if there was no logic to it? What if this castle *was* haunted and there *were* ghosts?

For once, Peter said nothing. She didn't want him to think she was being silly, with her imagination running wild.

"It's the only thing that makes sense," she said. "You just don't see how important it is because America isn't in the war."

"Okay," he said with a sigh. "I get it. If there is a spy about, we'll unearth something eventually. Then we can make your Mr. Churchill happy."

Marie appeared at the end of the hallway and began knocking on doors. "Breakfast. Come at once. Come along, now, all of you."

As a still-sleepy Isabelle, silent Colin, and staggering Jorry joined the other four to troop downstairs, Kat whispered to Peter, "I wouldn't drink any chocolate."

"I don't think . . ." he began, but when she cast a look his way, he shrugged and said, "Okay, fine."

At any rate, there was no chocolate at breakfast, and no Lady Eleanor, either. Mr. Storm was there, however, heaping food from the buffet onto his plate.

"History lessons straight after breakfast," he said in a blustery voice, sounding every inch the tutor. "The other instructors will be up later today, and then we'll fix our permanent schedule."

It was Robbie who spoke up. "You have the strangest accent." When Mr. Storm turned his head sharply toward Robbie, Robbie added more softly, "Sir."

Mr. Storm smiled with his teeth. "I'm Welsh. But I was raised in a far corner of the country, so my accent is unusual."

"Mr. Storm lost his small sailing vessel on the rocks off the point." They all turned as one as the Lady Eleanor entered the hall. "It was quite propitious. I was seeking instructors as I set about to open my little academy, and the sea brought us Mr. Storm. He was on a circumnavigation of the British Isles at the time. A naturalist's hobby. Quite extraordinary that he should wash up here, and that he should have this expertise in history and natural sciences," the Lady continued. "Later this afternoon, thanks to referrals from Mr. Bateson, a Miss Gumble and a Mr. MacLarren will be arriving to instruct you in grammar and maths."

Robbie raised his hand. "Will we be learning any fighting skills?"

The Lady looked puzzled. "Fighting skills?"

"You know, fencing and archery, that sort of thing. We need to be ready for the Jerries."

"I don't think—" she began.

"Just the thing!" spouted Mr. Storm. He grinned like a madman, and once again Kat had the feeling that he was in on some private joke.

"Well, perhaps," said the Lady with a dark sideways glance. "Maybe Mr. MacLarren—"

"Nonsense! I can assist. Fighting the Jerries, eh? I have all the necessary skills," said Mr. Storm.

Robbie grinned and shot a look at Kat.

The rest of the meal was conducted in silence. The Lady didn't appear to touch her food. The same could not be said of Mr. Storm, who ate like a trooper.

Straight after breakfast they were shown into the morning room off the entry hall. It was made up to serve as a classroom, with a handful of desks and a chalkboard up front. They chose seats and they found small notebooks and pencils ready, but no textbooks.

"Right, then," said Mr. Storm, rubbing his hands and marching back and forth at the front of the room. "Who can tell me something of the geography of Scotland?"

After geography Mr. Storm gave a rambling lecture on recent history of the British Isles, and then more ancient history, and then he launched into something more than a little unexpected.

"I should like to discuss historical artifacts," Storm said. "As part of our lessons touching on archaeology, yes?" Storm smiled with his large teeth. "My area of expertise is in the realm of artifacts that may have peculiar properties. Magical properties, as evidenced by the association of these artifacts with mysterious and unexplained events."

They all waited in utter silence; even Jorry was still.

Storm held up a small black-and-white photograph. "Who can tell me what this object is called?"

Kat almost fell out of her chair.

Isabelle raised her hand, and Storm said, "Yes?"

"It's a chatelaine," Isabelle said. She glanced sideways at Kat, who was trying to keep her face from showing her surprise. *Another chatelaine?*

The chatelaine in Storm's photo held a large number of dangling charms, and Kat strained to see them. Without thinking, she blurted, "But I have one that's nothing like that."

"Yes, Miss Bateson?" Storm said, watching her carefully. "You have such a thing? A chatelaine?" He tucked the photograph away.

Kat's face went hot. "Ah, well . . . my aunt, she, um, has one."

Storm stared at her for another minute before saying, "Miss LaRoche is correct. This is a chatelaine. But this one has a special place in history. This chatelaine is said to have the power of enchantment. It once fell into the hands of the cruel prince Vlad of Romania, who used it to overpower his enemies before he sent them to their gruesome ends, and perhaps it explains the rumors of his longevity. But Vlad lost it, alas for him." Storm smiled, toothy. "Some archaeologists in the service of the Reich should like to find it."

Kat was stunned. Her teacher, in his first lesson, claimed

that he knew of a chatelaine with the "power of enchantment." She looked again at Isabelle, who was now taking notes as if her life depended on it and avoiding Kat's glance.

"Yes, many people would like to get their hands on such an object." He paused, then went on. "After Vlad lost it, this chatelaine was next seen in Scotland some two hundred years ago. This report is one reason I was circling the coastline until the loss of my sailboat."

"But if this chatelaine thing is found by the Germans, sir," said Jorry in a buttery voice, "Germany might use it the way Vlad did, to overpower their enemies." Then Jorry muttered under his breath, "Not that I believe in such nonsense. Utter rot."

Kat wasn't sure she liked having anything in common with Jorry.

"Ah, yes," said Storm. "Having that kind of power in Germany is something England and her allies would not like. If it is indeed in Scotland, it is possible that the hunt is on. A scavenger hunt of sorts. We can all keep our eyes open, yes? At least in our own little corner of Scotland." He paused. "It's what Mr. Churchill would want, eh?" And he stared hard at Kat.

She squirmed.

They were dismissed, "until the other instructors arrive."

"Good grief," Kat said to Peter when they were well out of earshot. "What was that all about?"

Robbie, who had hung back in the classroom, ran up, gleeful. "Mr. Storm will teach me sword fighting! Starting this afternoon, right after lunch. He's going to take me out to the courtyard and give me a real sword and everything."

"Robbie, I don't think—" Kat began.

"Don't be stodgy," Rob interrupted, glowering. "You're not Mum." He stuck his tongue out and turned and ran on, whooping, to tell Colin.

Kat clenched her fist.

Jorry, catching up with them, said, "Storm is ridiculous. Why in the world would he mention magical artifacts?" Storm emerged from the room, and instantly Jorry's expression changed. "Interesting lesson, sir," he said.

Kat bit her cheek.

"Ah, thank you, Mr. Phillips," Storm said. He turned to Kat. "You have one, then? A chatelaine?"

"It's my aunt's," Kat said, which was true enough. "A family heirloom."

"It must be very old, yes?"

"I guess." Kat fidgeted.

"Perhaps you have a picture?"

"It's not like the one you showed us. It's much more simple."

"If you should find an image, I should like to see it. These antiquities collect magic just as they collect dust." Storm smiled his toothy grin.

Collect magic? Kat searched for words. "I'm sure my aunt's is only a piece of jewelry."

"Indeed," Storm murmured, narrowing his eyes at her. He turned back to Jorry. "Keep an eye out for anything unusual, eh, Mr. Phillips?"

"Oh, I will keep an eye out, sir." Storm retreated down the hall. As Storm disappeared around the corner, Jorry muttered, "Completely daft. Artifacts collecting magic? Bonkers."

Peter and Kat watched in silence as Jorry marched away.

Kat twisted the watch on her wrist. "I hate to admit it, but Jorry's right. Storm's crazy." As loony as her great-aunt.

Peter said, "I wouldn't mind having an object with magical power. But here's what I think: Storm is a treasure hunter."

"Treasure hunter?"

"Yeah. One of those people who hunts for valuable artifacts. He may be an archaeologist or historian or maybe not, and he may or may not be crazy. But I don't think he's done much teaching."

"That seems certain." Kat chewed her lip, then shook her head and sighed. "Well, at least Robbie's getting his wish."

"And it's a sunny day, and we're out of school for a few hours. We can go for a walk and explore the grounds if we get Storm's okay. Maybe we'll uncover some of that spying you suspect is going on."

"Spying? That *I* suspect? What about you? Don't you

suspect something peculiar's going on here?" she asked.

Kat blushed furiously as she swore Peter was trying not to laugh.

It was a brilliant, blustery day, and Kat's nightmares had begun to fade in the sunlight. Maybe the other children they'd seen were from the town, and the Lady was unaware of them wandering about the grounds. Maybe the Lady was unused to children and put off by Kat's blunt questions. Even Isabelle's mention of the hand sign charm had taken on an innocence in the light of day. After all, the Lady's charm was to ward off evil, wasn't it? Not to invite it in.

But it was odd that the chatelaine, such an unusual piece of antique jewelry, had begun showing up over and over. It was almost as if Great-Aunt Margaret had known.

Colin begged to join Kat and Peter on their walk. He reminded Kat of a puppy, dogging their heels and panting a little, nosing off from side to side as they made their way down the allée of trees behind the castle.

Rookskill Castle was a hodgepodge of buildings, as they could see now from the outside. The moat ended halfway around the older buildings, so that the imposing and ramshackle ruin out front, the one that seemed so frightening when they arrived, was the ancient—mostly abandoned—part of the castle, and the grand house the Lord and Lady lived in and where they were all staying was a much newer addition opening onto the formal garden behind.

As they wove through the garden now they passed the small pond where Kat had seen the girl. The pond was dry. A little tickle ran up Kat's arms as she thought of the girl's invisible fishes.

As they entered the allée, they turned back to look at the castle.

"That should be your room," Peter said, pointing, "and I think that's where the stairwell would be. Looks so normal from the outside."

"But it's so confusing on the inside. There's nothing that would show up as a hidden room," Kat said. "But then, this place is not what it seems. From the outside," she added.

"Hidden room?" Colin asked eagerly.

Peter coughed. "Just imagining there might be some in that old place," he said, and Kat knew what he meant. Best not to alarm susceptible Colin until they understood what was happening.

"Maybe we could explore inside the old castle, too," said Colin. "I love the idea of finding hidden rooms. Can we?"

"Maybe," Kat murmured.

The sun was fine, although a snapping breeze came up off the ocean, and it carried a sound. They stopped at once, straining to hear.

"What is that?" said Colin.

"It sounds like singing," Kat said. "Like it's coming from the sea."

They walked, quickly now, all the way down the allée to the cliff edge, where the land fell into the rocks and surf, but there was nothing, just the crashing of waves, and over them barely, a sound like voices, a wordless song in harmony.

"I'll bet it's some hollow in the rocks where the wind is whistling through," said Peter.

"Of course," Kat said, relieved. "That's what it is. Why, in my great-aunt's attic, when the wind blows hard, it sounds like a whining voice. Amelie thinks it's her ghost friend, Mr. Pudge."

"But what if it is ghosts?" asked Colin. "The villagers think the Lady Leonore haunts the castle."

Kat put her hand on Colin's thin shoulder. "There are no such things as ghosts," she said as firmly as she could. "So you needn't worry."

The space between his eyes was occupied by a deep furrow.

"Look, Colin. There's a logical explanation for everything," she said.

Yet, as they made their way back toward the castle, the singing followed them, mournful and filled with longing, making Kat sad.

18

The Third and Fourth Charms: The Boot and the Chest

IT IS 1820.

Ah, the cruel, cruel sea. As the years pass, the villagers think the caves along the coast house mermaids. They hear sweet, sad voices that lift and swell and ebb like waves. They leave the caves alone, not wishing to disturb the sorrowful selkies.

But the voices belong to girls charmed by Leonore.

After years of hiding in the keep, haunting Rookskill Castle and terrifying the human residents who come and go and live and die, Leonore craves again the feeling that comes with charming children. She has taken care of these first two, Rose and Tim. They have not suffered the loveless anguish of a childhood like her own.

When the fire—such a tragedy!—consumes the timbered

house on the village square, it leaves twin girls orphans. Leonore can rescue them from fear and sad memories. She can give them bliss. That she feels bliss as well . . . that's an added sweetness.

Her rooks tell her that a ramshackle hut sits again on the bones of a ruin at the edge of the village. She seeks out the magister (does he live forever?). For the girls he asks Leonore to sacrifice one hand and one leg, and she does not hesitate.

Blood and bone.

They cling to each other, Alice carrying a single boot and Brigit clutching a small locked chest. The twins wander to the cliff edge. Leonore follows them and gives them each a charm from her chatelaine, the boot and the chest.

The rooks pick the ashes for flesh and bone.

The magister stands before the great hinged box. The box glows with a pale blue light. It holds the parts of Leonore; it waits. He waits. He has waited for many years. Magic bides its own time.

His fingers are skilled at making. He can make mechanicals, unearthly creatures that are beautiful but dreadful. He adds the still-beating heart of a once-living thing to a clockwork creation that blinks and moves. He invents a creature made from tiny gears and pulleys and gives it a fleshy foot.

He ponders the capture of souls.

When he gave the new bride Leonore the chatelaine those years ago, he knew he had found an unwitting partner to aid him in practicing the blackest of magical arts. He is patient and waits for the right time. He knows the time will come when he can make something of dreadful beauty.

He will make life where none existed before.

With the charming of the twins, Leonore expands with happiness. She also bends with the added weight in her chatelaine, and about this she returns to the magister to ask.

"Souls," he answers. "That weight is the weight of their souls."

Leonore is staggered, sinking to the wooden stool.

The magister drones on, his back to her. Within her thirteenth charm she can hold twelve souls altogether. But oh so slowly, cautions the magister. Too many at once will weaken the magic. She must be patient, remain at the castle, and more children will come in time. And in time, when she carries all twelve souls, she will own a magic greater than love itself.

Leonore stares silently at the flames dancing on the magister's hearth. She carries the souls of four children in her thirteenth charm. She has watched as they cry out in pain and afterward go vacant. Was her lord right—has she become a witch?

But then she feels that bliss. She has lived long. She owns powerful magic. And she's saved them, those lonely children. She is heroic, for childhood is a terrible burden. Their souls lie within her thirteenth charm? So be it. She does, after all, sacrifice pieces of herself.

The magister does not tell Leonore what he does with her body parts.

The twin girls, together with Rose and Tim, for the next century and more, haunt the castle and the grounds and sing wordless songs. Leonore swells with the power she sucks from the souls of the four children. She later adds the fifth, the lonely cat-boy John, telling herself that this is good, this is right, this taking of children's souls.

Leonore is no longer fully human, but has become a witch and a monster (will she live forever?) made from the magister's superbly crafted mechanical parts.

19

Wish Upon a Star

THAT AFTERNOON THEY met their other instructors. The two new teachers took up residence in the castle on the second story with Mr. Storm and the Lord and Lady.

Miss Gumble taught grammar and literature. Mr. MacLarren was a red-cheeked Scot who taught maths. As they were introduced before lessons, Kat raised her hand.

"How do you know our father?" she asked them. "He said something about recommending you to Lady Eleanor."

Gumble and MacLarren exchanged a brief glance. "Your father gave a very interesting lecture on clocks at the university several years ago," Gumble said.

"We were quite impressed," said MacLarren. "So we invited him out to the pub for a bit of conversation."

"He's an interesting man," said Gumble, polishing her glasses.

"Quite," said MacLarren. "Now let's get on with your education, eh?"

Gumble was up-country English and reedy-thin, and spoke with such a monotone whine that it was hard to keep awake during her lessons. They were all provided with a book of grammar, a sentence diagramming primer, and a fat compendium of world and English literature, which, as Miss Gumble said, "I expect you to read each and every night, beginning at the beginning. I will assign pages. Take careful notes, as I will be examining you on the contents without warning." The younger children were given a shorter reading; even so, Kat saw that Colin's eyes were as round as melons at the amount of work.

MacLarren began with an exam, and then split them all into groups according to skills. Kat was alone in the top group, above even Peter and Jorry. She was pleased to see Jorry gape.

"You are quite skilled at numbers, eh, lassie? Well, don't be looking after my job." Mr. MacLarren grinned.

Kat wasn't sure what to make of him, but at least she knew exactly what to do with numbers.

During time off after homework she tinkered with the clock in her room, using hairpins and butter knives for tools, and got it running nicely. Many of the other clocks were stopped; she made it her personal mission to fix them all. She was sure Father would approve.

Kat wrote home to Mum:

> We're all fine. The uniforms are warm and
> the maid lays a fire every evening in our rooms
> while we are at supper. We've begun lessons,
> and I feel it's a relief, although Rob complains
> like crazy.

Kat did not mention the fencing, as she thought her mum
would worry—and rightly so.

And she did not mention the wireless, nor ghosts, nor peculiar Storm, nor evil nightmares.

She drank no more chocolate, and noticed that Peter didn't,
either.

It wasn't until Saturday that Kat and Peter had the chance
to revisit the hidden room. They found a place under the stairwell on the first floor where they could tuck in and listen, and
if someone made their way up the stairs, they could spy.

"Spying on the spy," Kat said.

They were there most of Saturday morning, and took a
break for lunch with nothing to show. They returned with several hours left until supper, so they made themselves as comfy
as possible and waited.

And waited.

It was the first time they'd been alone for a stretch of time.
Peter was very kind to the younger children and he didn't seem

to mind that she was good at maths, as some of the boys she'd met did.

"My father's abroad," Kat said out of the blue. She had to confide in someone. Peter, well, she trusted him.

"Is he fighting, then?"

"Not exactly. He works for MI6."

"So he's a spy." Peter whistled softly. "Do you worry?"

"Terribly," she said, and wrapped her hand around her watch.

"I miss home. New York," Peter said, sensibly changing the subject. He described his neighborhood and school, and Kat found herself wishing she could see the bright lights of New York City for herself.

After a moment's silence, Peter said, "I wonder if we'd be heroes if we caught a spy. I wonder if that spy would be executed. I don't know whether I'd want that on my conscience. Unless it saved lives, of course, catching a spy."

Kat thought about how she would feel if her father was caught, and her stomach was all at once tied up in knots. She hoped that two children on the other side weren't about to give Father away as he struggled to uncover secrets for his country, two children who would love to catch a spy. She squeezed the watch.

"You probably haven't seen that movie *Pinocchio*." Peter shifted his legs so they stretched before him. "I saw it last winter, before we left the States. 'Always let your conscience be your guide.'"

"What's that about?" Kat asked, peering at him sideways.

"It's one of the things the character Jiminy Cricket says in the movie. Let your conscience be your guide and you can't go wrong, is what he says. That, and he says, 'When you wish upon a star, your dreams come true.'"

Kat focused on the knot of her shoelaces, her fingers plucking it like strings of a harp. "I've made a wish. Upon a star." She shrugged. "It's silly. An old superstition. Dreams don't come true just for wishing."

"What did you wish for?"

"You know I can't tell you. Or that's what they say."

"Then I'm guessing it hasn't come true yet."

"No." Her wish hadn't come true. And she was so afraid it wouldn't ever come true. It was silly, wishing, and she chewed her lip, mad at herself.

"I understand," Peter said. "I have a wish like that." He knitted his hands together. "I didn't want to leave."

"Leave?"

"Leave the States," he said softly.

"Oh." His eyes were fixed on his fingers. Kat said, "But your dad, he came here to work?"

"Yes. But it was my mom, mostly. She wanted to be here for her parents and family. Dad's family are gone, so he took a job in London for her. And then the war really started, and here we are."

"That's thoughtful of him, though awfully bad timing."

He glanced up and then away. "Yeah. Thoughtful except

for me. I had to leave my friends, my school, even my dog . . ." Then his eyes lifted again. "But this is fun. This crazy, maybe haunted, maybe spy-filled castle in Scotland. An adventure. Right?" He gave her a quick smile.

She smiled back.

They fell silent and sat in the shadows for what felt like forever. No one had come up or down the stairs since they'd been there; the entire castle seemed drained and silent.

Kat thought back to a warm spring evening when she was out with her family and the air was filled with the sound of crickets. Mum walked ahead with Amelie and Rob, while she'd walked at Father's side.

"Look, Kitty," Father had said. He pointed to a star, the first to appear.

So she'd wished. *Star light, star bright, first star I see tonight . . .*

He'd smiled. "What did you wish?"

"You know I can't tell you," she said, and nudged him.

And then only a week later her first success, fixing a clock, and only a week after *that*, her failure, when she broke his watch by acting silly.

"I can't fix it, Kitty," he'd said, short, putting the watch aside. "Not enough time." He'd left it on his workbench.

And then he was gone.

Now she felt stupid, making wishes. She was only surprised that her father had encouraged her. He should have said, "If wishes were horses, then beggars would ride."

Kat's legs burned with cramps when she finally stood up to shake them out. Peter had closed his eyes and seemed to be asleep. She shook Peter's shoulder and his eyes fluttered open. "I think we'd better get going," Kat said.

"Right," he said, and scrambled to his feet.

They were halfway up the stairs when they heard it. A door on the next floor opened and closed, and soft footsteps came down the hallway in their direction.

There was no place to hide, no time to escape. They came face-to-face with the Lady.

She started and her eyes narrowed. "What are you children doing here?"

"We've come in from a walk," Kat said. "Lovely weather."

In fact, the day had gone from clear to miserable, and Kat now heard the beating of rain on the windows. "Well, it was lovely until a bit ago. So we were just . . ."

"Talking," said Peter, his voice firm.

The Lady's eyebrows lifted. "Since I am in the position of parental guardian, I will only tell you once that when you are not in the classroom or at meals you must remain on your corridor. I'm establishing a new rule: no wandering about the castle or grounds, even in pairs."

Kat chafed at the scolding and this irritating rule. Especially when Peter said, "Yes, ma'am."

Kat grew bold. "I've been wanting to talk to you, my Lady," she said. "I have questions."

The Lady's steely eyes locked on Kat.

Peter shuffled his feet and Kat was sure he thought she would give away what they knew about the wireless. But that was not on her mind.

She squared her shoulders. "What I asked about before. When we arrived here we saw a girl out in the garden wearing only a thin summer dress. It's far too cold for her to be dressed that way. I think she needs a coat."

The Lady raised her perfect eyebrows. "Really?"

"And we've seen a crippled boy who should be taken to see a doctor, because his deformity might be fixed. And speaking of doctors, I hear that there's another boy here, one who looks after the cats, and it sounds like he's taken ill." Kat's cheeks burned by this point and she could almost feel Peter's astonishment. "I wonder whether they are children of people who work here? Or are they from the village? Surely they aren't students. Are they? For they would be joining us in studies and meals and so on, wouldn't they?"

The Lady was silent; rain beat at the windows. Her eyes ran Kat and Peter up and down from head to toe. "You were outside? You don't appear to be wet."

They said nothing.

"Your parents have given me full charge of you. I don't suppose you should like to be locked in your rooms for a few days as punishment for wandering without supervision?"

Kat pursed her lips and Peter said, "No, ma'am."

She glared at Kat. "Your father said to be especially strict with you, Katherine Bateson. That you are immature and too sure of yourself and need a firm hand. I have no trouble depriving you both of a meal or two, if that will make you understand that I'm in charge."

Kat tightened her fists, and her mouth went dry.

"If I find you out like this again, I shall be forced to keep you under lock and key and let you go hungry. Is that clear?"

Peter nodded. Kat was furious. Father would never have said—

"Go," the Lady said, and pointed up.

Kat's face was on fire but she didn't move; Peter tugged her sleeve.

"Now," the Lady said, her voice a hiss.

They went.

Kat and Peter faced each other in the hallway.

"Why'd you have to make her angry?" he said in a harsh whisper.

"Peter, she was awful. Don't you see?"

"What I see," he said, his face red, "is that she's in charge and we'd better not cross her. Or we'll go hungry, or worse. Why do you have to be so demanding? She's just trying to keep us safe. Plus, I was afraid you were going to say something about the wireless. People have been killed for less, you know. Even children. There is a war on."

"What does it matter if I said something about the wireless? I thought you didn't believe she was a spy." She clenched her fists. "What are you really afraid of?"

He marched into his room and shut the door in her face.

Kat stood in the hallway, her blood pounding in her ears.

All she wanted was to keep her brother and sister safe from harm, and bring her family back together, and have the war done and Father home, and be away from this creepy castle.

Father. Her eyes burned. She couldn't believe he would have said that. She couldn't believe he'd have been so hurtful about her. Everything Kat did, she did to show him that she was his logical girl. The Lady was downright mean.

Unless . . .

Unless this business of not letting them wander about was to keep them out of the way of something evil. Maybe the Lady knew something terrible, and Peter was right, that she was trying to keep them all safe.

Kat didn't think the Lady would really starve them, or lock them up. Why, if their parents found out, they'd be furious. Father would never send them to such a place.

Except, maybe he would. To give Kat a "firm hand." She swallowed a sob.

She went back to her room and stood at the window. Rain streamed down in long ribbons. She leaned her forehead against the cool glass.

And then, Kat saw movement in the park below the window. She peered through the streams of rainwater. It was Jorry; she couldn't mistake his tall thin frame. He appeared to be at some form of exercise, jumping and bouncing.

Kat shook her head, thinking *honestly, he'll be in great trouble now if he's caught out,* when suddenly Jorry halted in midjump.

He started, his eyes widening. His left hand flew to his neck, and he held it there, palm tightening against his neck just under his left ear, where she'd seen his birthmark. His lips moved and he shook his head. His mouth curled in a sneer. He took something in his right hand—someone handed him something, Kat could see only a black greatcoat—and Jorry's sneer grew to a grin.

Then he lifted the thing, and Kat saw it was a chain, and she pressed to the window as he lifted it over his head and put it around his neck.

The rain came down so hard, she wasn't sure she saw right.

Jorry's eyes went wild and he clutched at his throat and ripped at his shirt, his mouth gaping in what looked like a scream, and then, lurching like a drunkard, he disappeared into the shadows and out of sight.

She pushed against the glass, but he was gone.

Kat stepped back from the window, uneasy. She might not like Jorry, but he'd looked so frightened. What had he seen, and who was he talking to? And his expression, that terrible expression, like he was being sliced open . . .

Hang it all. Her inner voice and her protective instinct drove her to try to find him, or at least find one of the teachers.

She knew if she was caught out now by the Lady there would be the devil to pay, so she slipped downstairs as quietly as possible. She took several wrong turns before winding up opening a door to a hallway lined with oil portraits. As she stood in the shadows trying to decide whether to go right or left, a small portrait hanging among others caught her eye, and as she moved up close to it her heart began to pound.

It was a painting of someone who looked uncannily like Kat, only a bit older. The girl wore antique clothing and sat with her hands folded, her long hair piled on top of her head, and a dog at her feet. And at her waist . . . Kat's breath caught and she pressed her palm to her chest.

Kat leaned close. It looked like Great-Aunt Margaret's chatelaine. No, it *was* Great-Aunt Margaret's chatelaine.

It's a family heirloom. Family. Of course. Father's Aunt Margaret was related to Gregor, so it was Father's family, and hers . . . and that girl was family, from way back.

But the thing that really took Kat's breath away, the thing that made her hands tremble, was that the portrait was cut, a long, thin diagonal cut from one corner to the other, a razor cut that sliced straight through the face of the girl.

Kat stepped away, shaking.

Somehow, she found her way back to their floor and to her room. She took out her great-aunt's chatelaine and sat on her bed, trying to sort through it all.

Three chatelaines—hers, the Lady's, and Storm's. Kat's portrait doppelgänger. Odd and mysterious children. Ghostly singing. A teacher who was plucked out of the sea like something from a fairy tale. The look of terror on Jorry's face. Shifty, confusing hallways and passages. A hidden wireless and maybe a spy. A mistress whose hands and eyes and heart were cold as ice.

Kat had tumbled down the rabbit hole into a realm of shadowy mysteries.

Something was terribly wrong in Rookskill Castle. Kat didn't know what it was yet, but some part of her couldn't help but wonder, against all her logical instincts, if this castle was possessed by something dreadful—something dark and grim—like magic.

20

Dark Magic

THE YEARS 1938 to 1940. Magic bides its own time.

When Gregor, Lord Craig arrives to his inheritance of title and lands, Leonore knows her time has come again at last. Gregor is the near image of her first lord, his ancestor. She remembers her brutal father and her heartless lord, who made her feel powerless, lost, broken, and unloved.

And war. She's seen it before. Dark magic grows out of the strife and misery and turmoil of war. Dark magic gathers beneath the thunderheads of war, the angry clash of red and black and dust and ash. Dark magic finds root in blood and bone, and with centuries of waiting Leonore's heart has grown bitter-dark. She wants more of the powerful magic she carries in her thirteenth charm.

Leonore comes out of the keep and calls herself Eleanor and enthralls and marries Gregor. She finds the magister again (it seems he will live forever), and the magister says yes, now is the time.

The magister tells Eleanor that she can now steal the remaining souls. Slowly, carefully, but yes, she may take seven more souls to fill her thirteenth charm.

"Remember," he says. "Take them slowly. Too many at once will weaken the magic."

As he speaks she regards him with veiled eyes. She now suspects he's used her. He says that once her thirteenth charm holds all twelve souls she will be more powerful than any mortal man. No one will use her again.

No one, she thinks. *Not even you.*

The adults around Eleanor each require different spells so that she can manage them, but they cannot stand between her and the gathering of souls. She spells her husband with illness, Marie with foolishness, Hugo with ignorance, and Cook with loss of memory. She fishes Mr. Storm out of the sea and turns his dreams to her own, casting a spell to shape him into a more useful form. She makes the school, the academy, a perfect pretense to bring the remaining children to her doorstep. She confuses Mr. Bateson and her teachers MacLarren and Gumble.

The children will be charmed, but they are too innocent to

be spelled like adults, so Eleanor must keep them from guessing her plan. Her clamor of rooks feeds her the news and secrets of war and the doings of all those within the castle.

Magic bides its own time. And there is always a price to pay for its use.

21

No Place for Holidays

THE RAIN CAME down with a vengeance now, and the wind battered the windows. Once Kat had been able to calm herself, she built a fire to warm the room and then sat on her bed cross-legged and fingered her great-aunt's chatelaine.

Pen, scissors, thimble.

She held it up, the chains moving, and the watery light from the windows and ruby light from the fire reflected off the three objects and flashed around the room.

Kat realized that it was possible Storm, too, had seen the portrait of her doppelgänger wearing her family chatelaine, and that was why he was so interested when she brought it up.

And the Lady's chatelaine—had Storm seen that?

And did old things really gather magic like they collected dust?

It couldn't be real. If her great-aunt's chatelaine could help her make magic, Kat would magic away this dreadful war. She'd bring her father home safe and sound from the dangerous mission he was on, and she and Robbie and Amelie would all return to London, to a peaceful, serene London, and to their mum and father and great-aunt. If Kat could make magic, she'd find the fishing girl and magic her a coat, and find the crippled boy and magic him whole, and find the cat-boy and magic him well. She'd even magic Peter back to America, if that's what he wanted.

There is always a price to pay for its use.

A dark shadow crept over Kat. What price would she have to pay? And, honestly: a pen, scissors, and a thimble. What in the world could they do besides the obvious?

She tossed the chatelaine back in her drawer and shut the drawer with a *thump*.

Sundays in Rookskill Castle were quiet days of "rest and contemplation," said the Lady at breakfast. Kat had little choice but to rest and contemplate, as the other children were not around. Rob was acting cranky and surly. Amelie was under the spell of her new friendship with Isabelle. Colin was busy with homework—stewing over it, in fact—and Jorry "has taken ill," said the Lady. "Marie is bringing him porridge and tea, but please do not disturb him."

Had Jorry been so terrified by whatever had happened that he'd gotten sick? Kat fretted. She wasn't sure whom to trust with what she'd seen, and Peter was still not speaking to her.

Kat finished her homework and paced in her room. She'd started a fire, but it wasn't enough to warm her mood. It was almost as if she could sense that something bad was about to happen.

So when the knock came on the door, Kat's skin crawled.

It was Marie. "Telegram up from the station," she said, handing it over before she walked off.

Telegrams were usually bad news. Kat closed the door and tore open the envelope.

**FRANCE HAS PROVEN NO PLACE
FOR HOLIDAYS STOP TAKE CARE OF
ROB & AME REMAIN SCOTLAND STOP
GREAT-AUNT M SAYS HANG ON TO HOPE
& DON'T FALL TO PIECES STOP LOVE M**

Kat sank onto the bed. That first line was code from Mum, their code phrase for news about Father. This news was bad.

Kat went to her window, staring out at the bleak mist, and winked back tears. Somewhere out there across the sea, somewhere in Belgium or France or maybe even in Germany itself, her father on his mission had gone missing. How was she supposed to hang on to hope here in Scotland?

She thought back to the day Father had left them, not long after her embarrassing babyish behavior. They'd all said their good-byes, and Father had gathered his luggage—including the short-wave wireless—in the front hall, but he'd forgotten something in his workroom, and Kat had followed him out into the evening. He was closing the door when she burst out.

"Don't go!" And she threw her arms around him, burying her face in his chest. "Please! Please don't go!" And Kat began to sob.

"Kitty, what's this?" He held her and petted her hair.

"Please stay." His jacket was wet with her tears. "I have a terrible feeling about it if you go."

"Now, Kit. I'd expect this kind of talk from Amelie, but you're my big girl. My logical girl. You have to be strong. Carry on."

"I can't." Her voice was muffled and she shook her head no.

He pushed her away gently and held her at arms' length. "You must. I'm doing this for you. For all of you. It's important."

"But . . ." She rubbed at her nose, the tears still running down her cheeks.

"You have to promise me you'll take care of them. Your mother, you know, she has her hands full. She can't manage without you. And I expect things from you."

He'd held her eyes with his. Kat wanted to protest, tell him she couldn't; but she would not let him down. She could not let Father down.

"All right then," he said. "Promise?" Kat nodded. She swallowed her tears. "Keep calm, Kitty. Carry on. And remember, no matter what happens, keep faith."

That was the last time she saw him, and the memory of being so weak shamed her.

After he'd left, she'd gone back out to his shop. The broken watch waited on the workbench. She'd strapped it onto her wrist and it hadn't been out of her sight since.

Now she gripped the watch face and then folded the telegram into little squares. Carry on, that's what she had to do. Take care of Rob and Ame. Do her best for her family's sake. For her father's sake. For her promise to him.

She looked at the clock on the mantle, still ticking away. She picked up her makeshift tools and knocked on Peter's door.

Peter wasn't friendly at first, but when he learned why she was there he gave her the clock, and then watched with curiosity as she opened the back.

"Can I help?" he asked, sounding shy.

She was glad to have him back as her one and only friend. She pointed out what needed to be done, and for the rest of the afternoon they worked side by side, first on his clock, and then on the one in Isabelle's room, and finally on one in an empty room down the hall.

"Funny that so many clocks aren't working," Peter said.

"They've been neglected. Maybe the Lord and Lady don't have time since he's taken ill."

"You're good at it," he said, pointing to the clock as she dusted her hands.

"Thanks," Kat said. "It's because my father taught me." And worry crept back in.

Maybe he was in some safe house, hiding; the resistance in France had a good reputation, and the members of the resistance there were growing in number. Maybe someone had taken him in.

Maybe there were no children there looking to catch a spy.

She decided not to say anything to Rob and Ame about their father going missing for the moment. She didn't want to worry them; though maybe it wouldn't be fair to them not to tell. She'd have to think on that.

"I have to tell you," she said to Peter as she set the clock back on the mantle, "something happened with Jorry." And she described what she'd seen.

"You don't suppose it has anything to do with this illness of his?" Peter asked.

"He looked so odd. Like he was in the midst of something really painful." She hugged herself. "Like he was being stabbed or torn to pieces."

"He's a stuck-up jerk, but that doesn't make any difference," said Peter. "What can we do?"

Kat twisted her watch. "I don't know," she said. "I just don't know."

It took her a long time that night to fall asleep, long after Amelie's breathing slowed and softened, long after the fire burned to glowing coals and the room grew cold and dark and still.

22

Knives

SOMETHING SLIDES THROUGH the dark until it stands over the bed Kat shares with Amelie. It hovers, a dreadful monster made of metal and wheels and gears, like clockworks, a monster that buzzes and clicks and reflects the moonlight that streams in through the unshuttered window. Instead of proper arms and legs it has limbs that are thin and shiny like knives.

It stands over the bed, eyes bright in a half-eaten skull, and strokes Amelie's cheek with a thin metal finger that sticks out from its hand like a crooked claw.

The finger runs down Amelie's cheek, down to her throat, and then to Amelie's heart. Kat tries to scream, but it's as if she's under water, as the claw digs into Amelie's chest and pulls out her heart and holds it up in the moonlight.

Kat keeps trying to scream, trying to fight her way up from sleep, keeps fighting to stop this monster, wanting to save little Ame, but she is helpless, helpless and rigid in the grip of some dark magic, until the nightmare fades.

After that she sleeps like the very dead.

23

Lost Souls

OH, THE TERROR!

The villagers speak of it in hushed whispers. Of the sounds of chains and wheels and machines in need of oil that come in darkness; the cries and the calls and the soft tuneless songs. The lost.

"It were the bogeys," say mams to their wide-eyed bairns. "You dinna go out at night, loveys, or your souls'll be snatched."

"Like them others," mutter the das. Among themselves, the das mutter their own thoughts about the castle and the things that go on there, but only among themselves.

No one knows for certain, and no one in the village is brave enough to ask.

The giant Hugo, who drives for the beautiful Lady newly

wed to Lord Craig, he sees. He sees the magister through the smoky glass window and has the vague memory that the magister does wonderful and terrible things. As he sits alone with his mug in the corner of the Rook, the giant is heard to say, "Those poor bairns. Whatever'll become . . ." He wishes he could help them, but something muddles his mind.

The wee ones, sleeping, hear it in their dreams—the mechanical whir, the clang and scrape, the soft cries—and they stir, restless and fearful.

Oh, the terror!

The charmed child Rose, who wears the small silver fish, has feelings, yes, but they're locked deep inside. And she has memories, too, of a small cottage with a mum who held her, and of the many sisters who scrabbled around fighting and bossing and laughing, but her memories are ghosts, wispy things.

Rose tries to catch her memories. The little pond in the garden is where she goes with a net she's fashioned from a tangle of wires and strings and strands of her long yellow hair. She sits at the edge of the pond and waits for a fish. A memory fish.

She is very patient, that Rose.

When she catches a fish and brings it up, she lays it on the stone edging and watches and waits. Will the fish give her back her past? What, little fish? You are opening and closing your mouth, but Rose can't hear you. She turns her head but hears nothing. Speak up, little fish!

When the fish's eyes are gone blank and staring, Rose carries the fish with her, carries it until it falls away in her pocket, falls to rotting pieces, until she's forgotten its purpose as she's forgotten so many things.

Tim, the hunchback boy, wearing the hunchback charm, knows how to polish, yes. He can't recall his name or the old priest or the chapel or the offering or the fair. But he remembers the polishing. It makes him feel special, though now he can't remember why. So that's what he does. He polishes.

Oh, but he remembers the saint, yes. The beautiful saint who gave him the polishing cloth he is holding now and the charm he wears, the saint who was followed into the woods by dark wings beating overhead, so she must be a saint. Yes, he felt a momentary pain in her presence, but wasn't that the pain of love?

Tim is in his private place, the place he's found at the bottom of the bottom, the place where he lies neither dead nor alive next to the furnace on a bed of straw. On occasion, when he leaves his place, he polishes things in the castle, things like mirrors and faucets and handles, as he was when caught in a bathroom by those children, who frightened him so that he ran back to his dark hideaway and shook with fear.

Arrayed around him now are the lovely, shiny baubles he has collected over centuries in this drafty castle, candlesticks and bowls, platters and forks. He breathes a sigh and takes his polishing rag and goes to work.

The twin girls, Alice and Brigit, with their wordless tunes, find their way to the top of the high tower, the keep, from which they can see the wide gray ocean, and they sing to the water, Alice still clutching her one old boot and Brigit still clasping her locked treasure chest, and the things that mimic their relics are charms that hang round their necks on thin silver chains.

Alice and Brigit sing to the sea, sing for the loss of their parents and home, and their voices carry down the allée of trees to the ocean's edge, carry over the water and back, some trick of the land and seascape that brings their voices back like a bird returning to roost.

The villagers, hearing the sad melodies as if they come from the ocean itself, believe in selkies, selkies with the voices of angels.

Cat-boy John, with his charm of cats, with the cats that come and go and follow and mew, was the fifth to be taken.

He will not be the last.

24

Lessons

THE FIRST THING Kat did when she opened her eyes in the early light was reach for her sister, taking her by the shoulder. Amelie grumped, "Quit it. Trying to sleep."

Kat lay back and took long shuddering breaths.

While getting dressed, as she fished in her drawer for her uniform sweater, her fingers landed on the chatelaine, and she lifted it out. Dreadful monsters? Dark magic? If Great-Aunt Margaret hadn't planted this fantasy in Kat's head, would she even think such things?

Kat grew angry, with her aunt, with herself, with her fears, and with the ridiculous chatelaine, and she dropped it on top of the sweaters and slammed the drawer shut.

After that she was grateful for the distraction of school.

Classes fell into their regular rhythm, with English at the start of the day, followed by maths and then history. The only thing missing was Jorry.

"Yes, he's quite ill after all," said the Lady, when they asked at lunch. "I've sent for the doctor. I think it might be a chill, and I'm hoping it's not influenza. Please do not disturb him; I can assure you he's being well tended, and I don't need his contagion spreading throughout the house."

Contagion, Kat thought.

English lessons were rigorous. Colin was not a model student: he fretted and worried, and Miss Gumble, though not mean, was not easy on him. Even Peter chewed his pencil and knitted his brows over her questions. Kat had to work hard to get all the readings done and the questions answered, and she wasn't looking forward to the long essay assignment that was due the following week.

In history Storm continued to query them on coastal geography, interspersing those "lessons" with recent history of the British Isles. Sometimes he would pause in the middle of some ramble as if he'd forgotten where he was. There were times when Kat wondered what he was playing at. He only mentioned the artifacts once in passing, and Kat swore Storm stared long and hard at her before he moved on to the geology of the Great Glen Fault.

Maths, of course, was Kat's favorite, and she quickly discovered that MacLarren was impressed she was so skilled.

"Perhaps I should be giving you harder assignments, eh, lass?" And he tossed out a long list of problems for her to do that night. When she finished them by the next class, he raised his brows.

"Showing off a wee bit, are we? Maybe they're not done right, eh?"

But they were. He doubled her assignments for the rest of the week.

It bothered Peter more than it did Kat.

"Why does he pick on you?" Peter asked after supper mid-week.

"Probably because it's easy for me," she said. "Maybe he thinks I need a challenge."

"Well, it's not fair."

She shrugged. "I don't mind." There were too many other things that weren't fair for her to worry over one mathematics teacher.

There was Jorry, for one thing. The Lady informed them that the doctor had visited and proclaimed him ill "but not in danger. But indeed contagious with influenza, and no one is to disturb him." He was confined alone to his room for the duration.

Kat still hadn't been able to bring herself to tell Rob and Ame that Father was missing. She kept hoping he'd turn up and she wouldn't have to say a thing.

By the following Saturday, however, there still had been no news about Father. Kat chewed her lip as she stared out the window into the highland hills. Today she could see the sea, a flat gray sliver at the far edge of the grounds. The gray clouds hovered like a blanket over the land.

And then, as she stared aimlessly out . . . there was someone striding across the grounds toward the allée of trees and the sea.

Whoever it was, he was draped in a long oilcloth coat as he made his way toward the water. Kat pressed her hands to the glass of her window as the figure grew smaller and finally disappeared into the woods.

Was it the wireless operator? Her spy? Maybe it was even someone taking a message to a waiting U-boat?

She opened her door. She couldn't go to Peter; he wasn't interested in making waves. She didn't want to risk making him her enemy again.

But she had to do something.

The corridors were empty and silent. Kat remembered then that Miss Gumble had offered to conduct a Saturday study hall for extra credit, and the other students must have gone. Kat didn't need the extra credit. What she needed was to find answers.

Kat slipped down the stairs, pausing on every landing to listen. By this time she knew at least one way down, though she almost wanted to tie a thread to her door in case she got lost. She most certainly didn't want the Lady to find her disobeying orders. She'd be punished for sure. Locked in her room with no supper, or worse.

As Kat passed by the secret room she paused, crept up to the hidden door, and placed her ear to the wall. Nothing. And then . . .

It began as a faint crackle. Then a voice hissing and spitting from over the wireless. She couldn't make out words; the volume was too low. Then a pause, and someone in the room was speaking back into the short-wave.

Drat this thick wall! Kat plastered herself as flat as she could, her ear right against the narrow crack. Again she couldn't make out words, but there was one thing certain: the voice speaking back to the wireless in the room was definitely that of a man.

She straightened and stepped away. There were only four men in this castle: the giant, whom she hadn't seen since the day they arrived; Lord Craig, whom she'd never seen; Mr. MacLarren; and Mr. Storm. Only four men—unless there was someone else here, another man, in hiding. And whoever she'd seen outside and the wireless operator couldn't be one and the same.

Kat pondered this. The castle was huge and rambling—more than rambling, it was a maze—and had many rooms. It would be easy for someone to hide. Unless she searched every corner—an impossible task—she'd never know.

It wasn't Lady Eleanor who operated the wireless. Kat pursed her lips. She still thought that the Lady could be using one of the men. Kat wouldn't let her off the hook. There was too much about her that Kat didn't like.

In fact, there was something odd about each one of the adults in this castle, except maybe—she hoped—Cook.

Now her little inner voice said, *Find Cook.*

Kat went down the stairs, but when she reached the lowest floor and started down the hallway, she promptly became lost.

"What is it about this place?" she muttered after a good ten minutes of wandering. The only thing to do was to make her way back upstairs and then find the kitchen from her room.

It was as if she was the only person in the entire castle and the castle itself was alive, with the moaning of the wind outside and the groans from the radiators. Kat climbed the stairs to her hall. She shivered as she peered back over her shoulder.

Which was why, when she turned the corner in the hallway to her room, she nearly jumped out of her skin.

"Miss Bateson!" Storm dabbed a handkerchief at his forehead, which was beaded with sweat. "Shouldn't you be in study hall?"

"It's—it's voluntary," Kat said, stammering. Then, "But what are you doing here on our hallway?"

The fear left his face, and Storm's eyes betrayed a glimmer of triumph. He stuck his hand in his pocket and drew up. "That's my business, Miss Bateson. Back to your room or to study hall at once, or I shall be forced to inform the Lady that you are wandering."

Kat pressed her lips into a thin line as he marched away down the stairs, whistling. *Peculiar.*

But she wasn't about to listen to Storm. Kat found her way past her room and down to the front entry. From there she made it to the great hall and, orienting herself, slid along the dark hallways to the kitchen at the back.

She made only a couple more wrong turns before she found the kitchen door. Comforting smells guided her.

She opened the door an inch at a time until she could peek inside. Cook bustled about the steamy room. Back and forth she walked, carrying great bowls and platters. She chattered as if the whole of London was there to hear her.

Kat pushed the door another inch, so that she could scan the room. No one. Nothing. Maybe Cook talked to herself. Maybe she was as odd as the others. Kat was about to push her way in when she saw them: a pair of feet in shoes with soles so thin, they were dotted with holes. She paused.

Someone was huddled on the floor by the stove, and Kat could see feet. Small feet. Someone young.

A cat trotted across the kitchen, and then another. The cats wrapped themselves around the feet, twining and mewing, until one dropped to a hunch on the floor by the feet and began to groom.

Cook was talking to a child who sat on the floor with the cats. Well, that meant Cook really was to be trusted, so Kat walked on into the kitchen.

With that movement she startled the living daylights out of a boy, handsome and dark-haired though thin, wraith-thin, huddled by the stove. Kat startled him so that he sprang up, his dark eyes blank and staring, ghostly, and he bolted out the back door into the miserable weather, cats on his heels, slamming the door in his wake.

25

The Sixth Charm: The Devil's Sign

OCTOBER 1940. The devil takes many forms.

Jorry carries a birthmark. He is the first of the academy students the Lady charms because there, under his left ear and just above his shirt collar, is a patch of red in the shape of a hand. A hand that holds up two fingers in the shape of horns, two fingers meant to ward off evil.

But Eleanor knows it can also be the devil's sign.

Eleanor finds him outside, exercising, alone in the sleeting rain, the peculiar boy. He needs her, doesn't he? Needs to be rescued from parents who would demand such behavior. Needs to be rescued from the curse of his birthmark. She stands in the shadows. She doesn't know that Katherine watches from the window above, but the Lady is hidden nonetheless.

"You poor thing," she says, touching his arm with her fine, delicate mechanical hand, hugging the black greatcoat with the other. The wind whips it around her ankles. "I hope you carry a token."

He stops moving. "Huh?"

"You must know, since you have the mark, that you also have need of protection."

He's puzzled. "Protection? From what?"

"Why, from evil," she says, feigning astonishment.

"What? Nonsense." He rubs his hand over his short wet hair.

"No one has ever told you? My, my." She pulls the hood of the greatcoat tighter about her face as she leans close to him, the rain a curtain between. "'Tis an old Celtic wisdom, that those with birthmarks are especially vulnerable to the ministrations of"—she lowers her voice to a whisper—"the devil."

Now Jorry touches his neck. Holds his hand over his birthmark. "I never heard the like." He snorts with derision, though his eyes betray uncertainty. "And there are no devils."

"Perhaps your parents were sparing your feelings." She leans so close now. "I can help. I have just the thing to ward away evil." He narrows his eyes now, and she shifts direction. "Of course, there really are no devils, as you say. A boy as wise as you are knows that. Why, look how clever you are, exercising despite the weather."

He preens, the rain in rivulets running over his face.

"And as clever as you are, you'll see that this charm I offer is pure silver. Quite old and valuable. I would give it to you because," she pauses, "you are the cleverest of all." She places the charm in his palm. "They'll know how clever you are when they see this about your neck. They'll know I favor you."

His smile becomes a sneer. "Silver, hey? A favor? I should wear it then. Thank you, my Lady."

"My deepest pleasure." The wind slaps her greatcoat against her shins as she turns away whispering the words, the foolish boy following, the chatelaine weighing against her hip.

He is the cleverest! Jorry lifts the charm in the rain as he walks. The devil horns. Huh. Whatever foolishness she says about devils and evil, he only cares that the charm is made of silver and is a favor for his cleverness. Besides, if she's right—though she couldn't be, but at any rate—then he's protected. He slips the chain around his neck.

He hears words but he can't make them out. They seem to come from the ground beneath his feet, rolling up from the ground like thunder, terrible, ugly, piercing. He tries to lift his feet, tries to dance away.

The agony that comes next rips deep, deep, tears something inside him, a knife-thrust to the gut, but he can't get the chain off, can't stop it, can't . . .

Your soul will sleep within its keep. It is your bane, this chatelaine.

26

Children

COOK DROPPED THE gleaming copper pot and it clanged on the floor as the remaining cats scattered, and Kat jumped nearly out of her skin with the noise and confusion.

Cook began talking in a rush. "There now, look what you've done. Scared me half to death! And poor boy. Poor little thing."

She went on, muttering as if to herself, "Just trying to lure him inside. Have to leave food out there, in that damp barn. Maybe they be ghosts and maybe not, but I never hear of no ghosts eating the scraps of food we leave." All the while she talked, Cook went to her knees, cleaning up the mess on the floor. "And here all this waste. I'll have to start these biscuits again, and just look at the time! Nearly supper! The Lady'll have me head."

Kat bent to help clean, but Cook straightened and looked her in the eye, stopping her. "Here, now, that's my job, and you poor children need feeding and education, not this wandering about frightening people." She peered at Kat. "What are you here for, anyway?"

Kat straightened. All the confusion had knocked the wind out of her sails, too. What was she here for? She cleared her throat and said, "I'm worried about the children."

Cook opened her mouth and then closed it again.

Kat blundered on. "The Lady doesn't seem too keen to give that girl a coat, the one I saw out the window. She was fishing but there were no fish. And that other sick boy, the crippled boy, who is taking care of him? And who was that boy here with you, anyway? Is he the cat-boy Isabelle talked about?"

Cook scratched her head, looking befuddled. "There's a good deal of confusion in my brain."

Kat reached out, touching the back of Cook's hand. "I want to help the children."

As if the touch of Kat's hand on hers did some good, Cook's face cleared and she eyed Kat. "I'll tell you what's what, as near as I can, though I confess that things get muddied in my mind. Right. There's things going on around here, and the village folk have been full of rumors, but I only know what I know, and that's that something strange is up in this house. I may not have been here as long as some others, but something's mucked up, for sure."

"But you've seen these other children, then? They are real?" *And not ghosts?* Kat thought, but didn't want to say out loud.

"They're as real as can be," Cook said, though she sounded doubtful. "Least, I don't think they're ghosts. Though they don't talk, mind you, and I haven't had the chance to touch one yet. I only lured that boy inside for the first time today, after much trying. They do eat, these ghostly bairns, aye. So they have stomachs. They're cagey and, well, they may be soft."

"Soft?"

"Touched, you know. Daft." Cook pointed one large finger at her head. "They don't seem all there." She paused, and then rubbed her forehead and murmured, "Not that I'm much here, meself."

"Are you caring for them, then?" Kat asked.

"If it weren't for Hugo and the warmth of the animals, they'd be froze to death, I expect. Although they've been here longer than me, and longer than he has, and there's been rumors about children being about the castle for ever so many years now, stories handed down, so I don't have a notion how they've fared before, unless with the aid of other kindly souls who have passed through the place. But yes, we feed them, we do, and give them warm things, though that's a secret, mind, and not for her Ladyship's ear. And that poor Lord Craig, lying up there, waiting to die but not dead, I take care of him, too. I don't know what she's . . ." Cook let her voice trail off and mumbled under her breath, as if she began to think better of voicing her thoughts.

"And you've seen the crippled boy, too," Kat said.

"Oh, yes, I've seen him, but a slippery one he is." Cook leaned closer to Kat. "The villagers, they thought I was daft to come work here. They say the Lady Leonore haunts the castle still, and a cruel ghost she is, which may be why my brain gets in a muddle. Only the lords and their ladies and bairns be living here, and even then they've not stayed long before being driven away or driven mad. No one stayed here long, not until this Lord Craig. I came here to work for him, oh, these two years past. He was trying to bring the castle up to date and all, and didn't take to these fairy tales, as he called them."

He sounded like a man after Kat's fashion. A logical man who'd be related to Father for sure. "And our Lady Eleanor?" Kat put in.

Cook folded her arms and looked cross. "Not much of a lady, if you ask me. Showed up out of the blue and he fell head over heels and married her before anyone knew the better of it. And then, poor man, taken sick not long after, and confined to his bed for these five months past. And now she's made up this school, this academy, and I don't know why . . ." Her voice trailed off and her face grew dark.

"And what about Mr. Storm?" Kat asked.

"Ach, she pulled him out of the ocean, where he'd been sailing and dashed upon the rocks. But there's more to Mr. Storm than meets the eye. Might be a magician or some such, the way he rattles on about one mysterious thing or the other that he's looking for. Questioned me up and down, talking of magic and wanting to find odd things. Something fishy about that one, let me tell you, and I don't mean because he was a sailor."

Kat hesitated. "Could anyone else be hiding somewhere in the castle?"

Cook's brow furrowed. "'Tis a big place, truly. More than once I've heard odd noises, I have. Not sure you should go about exploring."

Kat bit her lip; too late for that. "And what about Jorry?" Kat asked.

"Jorry? Don't know about him." And she grumbled under her breath, "Another sick bairn? Not right."

"Thank you for taking care," Kat said, and reached for Cook's hand and squeezed it. Kat believed she'd found a grown-up ally, even if Cook was somewhat confused. "Thank you so much."

Cook blushed and then hid her face, turning away. "Here, now, it's almost supper and I shouldn't spoil your appetite, but I have tea and toast and a gooseberry jam that's dying to be eaten . . ."

Kat took a piece of toast and was about to ask Cook again about the cat-boy, and who was Hugo, when the door opened and the giant entered the kitchen, a brace of pheasants hanging from one large hand.

Hugo and the giant were one and the same, Kat learned when Cook said his name as she ushered him inside. He nodded to Kat, but remained silent as she finished her tea. He hovered in the corner, shifting from one large foot to the other, his cheeks flushed, one hand rubbing his nose as he tried not to meet Kat's eyes, until Kat excused herself and left.

She slipped upstairs and back to her room. Hugo was a kindly soul if Cook was to be believed, as he was looking after the children, not letting them freeze or starve. Still, Kat harbored a suspicion of everyone except Cook until she sorted out who was using the wireless. And until she understood the terrible things happening to the others.

Before breakfast the next morning, Isabelle tugged at Kat's sleeve, and she and Peter huddled with Isabelle in the hallway near their rooms.

"Marie, she has told me Jorry is very, very sick."

"Yes, we heard," said Kat.

Isabelle went on, "But he is very contagious. With spots. We must keep away, Marie says." Isabelle shuddered. "I've heard that the Germans, you know, they may spread illness. That they have diseases. We must be careful if Jorry has spots."

"Spots?" said Peter. "I thought it was flu."

Isabelle shrugged. "This is what Marie tells me. Spots all over, and itchy."

"But what's the truth, then?" asked Peter. "Is it flu, or is it spots?"

Kat rubbed her forehead. "I think we need to find out."

"I'm not sure we should be bothering him if he's sick," Peter said.

Kat pursed her lips. "Don't, then. You can stand way over there."

She knocked on Jorry's door but got no response, though she thought she heard a whimper and a shuffle from inside. She tried the handle, but the door was locked.

Isabelle raised one eyebrow. "I don't much like him"—she pointed at Jorry's door—"but no one should be left all alone with itchy spots."

Tension filled the air at dinner. Robbie glowered at her when she asked if he was wearing padding while at fencing lessons, and snapped, "I'm not an idiot. Quit telling me what to do." Isabelle and Amelie whispered together throughout dinner, and even Colin pushed his food around without eating much.

And the Lady—she seemed harder and colder than ever, her smile a thin line.

As they went up to bed, they paused before their doors, and Isabelle said out of the blue, "Can Amelie sleep in my room tonight?"

"I don't think that's a good idea," Kat said, thinking of her nightmare. "I don't want you staying in someone else's room."

Amelie huffed. "You're being mean. And you aren't Mum."

"Ame, what's gotten into you?" Kat said.

"You're a bossy-pants, always saying no," Ame grumbled. "I'm staying with Isabelle tonight." She glared at Kat, giving her a look she'd never seen on Ame's face, angry and mean.

"Fine," Kat said, giving up. "Just do your homework."

Kat hadn't yet shared her experience with Cook and the cat-boy and the giant with Peter, but when she went to talk to him he, too, seemed out of sorts, and retreated to his room, saying with a sharp note, "Not now."

Everyone was cranky and angry, and Kat was sure it had to do with Jorry's unexplained illness. Or so she hoped. She hoped that her night terrors and dark worries were not shared by the others.

At bedtime, Marie came up, as usual, bearing a tray with steaming mugs of chocolate. They each came into the hallway and took a mug, chattering and horsing around while Kat pretended to drink. Whyever they were being drugged—*if* they were being drugged—it seemed important that she stayed awake. But also important that she not expose the others to her sleep-depriving nightmares.

Sure enough, within fifteen minutes the others were nodding and stumbling into their rooms, so Kat pretended the same.

As she closed the curtains in her room, she caught the gleam of the new moon on the water, and her heart went out to her father. She wished she could be more like him, steady and sure.

All she knew now was that they shared this: they were both alone and friendless and in the grip of war. And, Kat thought, her heart sinking, she and her brother and sister might be in the thrall of forces even darker and more evil than war.

27

Howl

WHEN KAT HEARS the clock chime midnight, a low howl comes from outside her window, the moaning howl of a pressing wind, and the glass panes rattle. Rain patters at the window and she misses Amelie's warm body.

And then a new noise, a rasping, wheezing noise, emerges from the wall behind her bed. She shuts her eyes tight and clutches her sheets, and a lead weight settles on her limbs and she's drowning in a half-sleep, locked in a horrific nightmare that is much too real.

Something moves into the room, shuddering and clinking like metal chains, a monster made of pins and cogs and long thin blades.

The clicking and rasping slides to her bedside and hovers,

and she's so cold, so cold, and then it slips past her bed and out again, and in her petrified stupor she's sure it moves right through the wall into the next room, where Isabelle and Amelie sleep drugged as Kat lies helpless and rigid as stone in her locked room.

Kat comes out of the stupor but remains still and silent, trying to calm her pounding heart.

Yes, her heart is pounding, and not only for fear; it's pounding out of guilt, too. Had her door been unlocked, she isn't sure she would have gone next door to help Isabelle and Amelie. She isn't sure she's brave enough to protect them from whatever it is. And she doesn't think she'd go help Peter and Rob, either. Father asked her to look after them, and she can't. She lies stiff in her bed, hiding, fearful, and ashamed.

No, there's no sleeping for Katherine Bateson this night, though by morning her memory is cloudy and she can't be certain of anything.

Except for a sense of guilt. That is clear as glass.

28

Tim, and Kat's Chatelaine

TIM IS IN the room when the big man enters, so he hides.

Tim's only come back for his polishing cloth, the one he lost when the children surprised him in their room. He doesn't like this big man named for nasty weather. This Storm.

Tim peers through the crack in the door. He watches as Storm searches the room. He's terrified Storm will search the bathroom, too.

But Storm doesn't need to search for long. He finds what he wants when he opens the dresser drawer. He holds it up, and Tim's breath snags in his throat.

Storm dangles the silvery thing, and his wide mouth opens in a terrible grin as the silvery thing begins to glow with a strange blue light.

Oh, it is so beautiful!

That's why Tim follows Storm, follows the man to his room, watches where Storm puts the thing, watches as Storm leaves the room, then takes the silvery thing for himself.

Yes, Tim has it now. He polishes it with reverence. After all, it doesn't belong to Storm.

Tim loves the chatelaine so much, he thinks he will give it to the beautiful lady saint who watches over the children.

Yes. He holds it up in the candlelight. He will give this chatelaine with its three dangling charms to the Lady.

29

Exhaustion

"HAVE YOU SEEN Colin? I haven't seen him since lunch."
Robbie stood splay-footed, facing Kat with glowering eyes, as
if the fact that Colin was missing was her fault. It was Friday,
and Storm had let them out early, thank goodness, for it was
the end of another very long and tiring week, a week in which
Kat had gotten little sleep.

The only saving grace with her nightly hauntings was that
the memory of them faded with the dawn, so she remembered
only snapshots—a blade, a grinding noise, the stench of something rotten . . . and a gnawing fear.

She couldn't help her temper. "I haven't seen him, and you
don't need to suggest it's my fault," she snapped. "Honestly,
Rob, I don't know what's gotten into you lately."

"We were going to have a go at swords today, me and Colin," he said. "You don't like me playing at swords, do you?"

"Not when you could kill someone," she shot back. "It's not play, Robbie."

"When did you get so mean?" he said. "You're lucky Father isn't around. You're a mean monster." Robbie turned on his heel and stormed away.

Kat leaned back against the wall and wrapped her hand around the watch. Maybe she *was* lucky Father wasn't here to see her act like this. After all, Rob was learning a skill and loving it. Amelie and Isabelle had become fast friends, sharing Isabelle's room now. None of the others seemed to be having nightmares, thank goodness. Her brother and sister were safe, and wasn't that all Father had asked of her?

Yet everyone in the castle was on edge with exhaustion. For the past week the students, minus the still-missing Jorry, had been in the classroom all day, with breaks only for meals. Kat had turned a corner after breakfast yesterday to find Gumble and MacLarren huddled together in conference, and they scuttled away from her acting fearful that she'd overheard them. Storm grew increasingly strange, as if he was drinking some of their hot chocolate or too much claret, and had begun lecturing on random historical half-truths.

She couldn't remember when she'd been so tired before. She pushed away from the wall and climbed the stairs, her feet feeling like they were encased in lead.

Each morning, after a sleepless night, her clock was stopped, and she couldn't seem to figure out why, which added to her frustration. And Amelie was behaving more and more like a spoiled child, while the Lady Eleanor prowled around like a thief.

Just the day before, as Kat made her way alone back to her room after lunch, she turned a corner to spy the Lady alone with Amelie at the foot of the great stairs. The Lady spun around, as if Kat's sudden appearance was an unpleasant surprise, and clutched her fist to her chest.

"What are you doing wandering about?" she snapped at Kat.

"I'm going back to my room," Kat answered.

The Lady opened her mouth, then hesitated, and smiled. "Yes. Of course you are. Amelie and I were having a chat. Weren't we, my dear?"

Amelie said nothing, confusion in her wide eyes.

Kat and Ame walked upstairs together, the Lady watching them. "She was about to give me something," Ame said, grouchy now. "A treasure, she said, for when Issy and I play dress-up. You spoiled it. You're always spoiling things."

Kat wanted to tell Ame to stay away from the Lady, that she was a bad influence, but she held her tongue.

Now, Kat thought about Peter. They hadn't had a chance to speak, but she assumed from his deepening dark circles that he, too, shunned the chocolate and lay awake hearing . . . what?

Her throat constricted at the thought.

She reached their hallway and found Peter's door and knocked.

"What?" came a shout, and a few seconds later the door flew open.

Kat stepped back. Peter looked like he would bite her head off. Tears started to her eyes. "You don't need to be rude," she said.

His eyes softened and he ran his hand over his unruly hair. "Sorry. Since you told me about the chocolate, I haven't been drinking it, and I haven't really been sleeping. I'm about out of my mind I'm so tired, and I lay down and thought I might take a nap—"

"I'm sorry," Kat blurted, interrupting him. "I'm sorry about the time we met Lady Eleanor on the stairs. I didn't mean to get her riled up against us."

The corners of his mouth lifted in a smile. He shook his head. The lock of hair fell across his forehead and he leaned against the door frame. "You remind me of Dodger."

"Who?"

"My dog. The most scrappy, stubborn mutt you've ever seen. But smart as a whip. I swear he could do sums in his head. When I counted he'd nod along."

"Oh." Kat tilted her head. The sadness of his loss was

palpable. "Is he the one you had to leave behind in America?"

Peter looked away. "Yeah." He scuffed his feet. "So."

"So," she echoed. Kat twisted her watch. "I've heard noises in my room. Though I can't remember much about them, it feels like I'm having a whole string of nightmares. They started when we left London."

"Yeah," he said, and his shoulders slumped. "Last few nights, I've been having weird dreams, too. I think this place is haunted. I think I've been seeing that Lady Leonore."

"Everything here is wrong. The hallways that seem to change. The children who wander about. Storm and his artifacts. The noises and nightmares. It's all making me feel . . ." Then Kat straightened, as a new thought came to her. "Crazy. That's it. That's what she's up to. She's making us all crazy."

"Who is?"

"The Lady," Kat answered stubbornly.

"Why would she bother?" And Peter laughed. It was good to hear him laugh. And it felt even better to have a good, clear reason for all this peculiar stuff happening.

"Be logical for a minute," said Kat. "It's perfect, don't you see? If we try to report to the authorities or our parents that we think there's a spy here, we'll all sound completely mad and they won't believe a word we say. Ghosts and sleeping potions and crazy nightmares and magical artifacts and a hidden wireless and mysterious illnesses . . . It would make us sound loony." Kat took a breath. "It does sound loony, don't you think?"

"Yeah. But how would someone go about making us crazy?"

"By putting something in the food? We might not drink the chocolate, but we have to eat. Why, that would even explain why Storm is so odd and getting odder."

Peter chewed his lip. "You've got a point," he murmured. "Maybe there is something planned to all this."

"It makes much more sense than evil magic or ghosts," Kat said, feeling better and better. Logic. Things that made sense.

Not magic. Not like Great-Aunt Margaret had said.

Which made her think, *I should check on the chatelaine. Make sure it's safe.* It was a precious gift, after all, even if her aunt was a bit confused about it.

But she didn't have the chance, not then. She and Peter heard Robbie coming from a mile away. He ran thumping up the stairs, so he was breathless and panting hard when he reached them. His face was beet-red, and his eyes were wide with fright.

"Take your time," Peter said, patting his back. "That's better. Now, what's wrong?"

"Colin's gone. Gone. Completely missing. And Isabelle and Amelie, too. I lost them in the old part of the castle. In the keep."

"You lost them?" Kat asked. Her heart hammered, and she didn't think she could breathe.

Rob nodded. "And, and—" Robbie stopped and swallowed. "I've seen a ghost, a real one, a real honest-to-goodness ghost for sure."

30

The Keep

"SLOW DOWN, ROB," Kat said, her hand on his trembling shoulder. "Try again."

It turned out that the three of them—Robbie and the girls—believed that Colin had wandered into the old part of the castle, and they had tried to find him. Robbie had been the leader until the three had gotten lost in one of the odd passageways, and when they were separated and Robbie was alone he'd come face-to-face with "a ghost, I swear. He was tall and pale and had this awful look in his eyes and . . . and he *moaned*."

Robbie was a great storyteller, but he was white as snow and shaking so badly, his teeth chattered. This was no story. Kat went down on one knee before Rob, trying to make sense of things.

"And Ame and Isabelle?" she asked, her heart pounding. "Tell us again where you lost them."

"I don't know. They turned a corner and vanished, like that." He snapped his fingers. "And I tried and tried to find them, and kept hearing them calling, but they were always on the other side of the wall, a wall with no doors, and then I saw the ghost and I ran. I just ran."

He said the last with such a miserable tone that Kat knew he felt bad. Even so, she was furious with him.

"I don't even know how I found my way back. It's so dark and twisty in there, and there were all those noises and that, that *thing* . . ."

"Honestly, Rob," Kat said. "You shouldn't have led them in there."

Robbie's face flushed. "We were trying to find Colin, remember? It's not like you'd have done it. You're too scared to admit you're scared."

Heat flooded her cheeks.

As if Robbie could read her mind, he said, his fists clenched, "I'm betting you don't even want to go after them now."

That did it. She had no desire to go into the scary old keep, especially since she'd only barely convinced herself that there was a logical explanation for everything. That there were no ghosts. But she had a responsibility to Ame. She stood up and exchanged looks with Peter.

Peter nodded and said, "We're going to need a good flashlight."

"Cook," she answered. "I'll bet she'll have one. Or at least candles."

"I'm taking a sword," said Robbie, sounding stouter again.

Cook was not in the kitchen. A stew bubbled gently on the stove, fragrant and rich, but they didn't want to wait for her to return. They searched the kitchen and came up with two candles and some matches, and then Peter discovered a flashlight in a cupboard. He turned it on, testing.

"Batteries are low, but between this and the candles at least we'll have some light."

"Lead the way, Rob," Kat said.

As they passed by the great dining hall, Robbie stopped and took a broadsword from the grip of a knight's fists. "This is the one I've used," he said, and he hefted it with two hands.

Kat was impressed he could lift the thing, much less wield it. "Just be careful you don't point it in the direction of any of us."

"It's for the ghost," he said, but he sounded as if he'd like to use it on Kat.

"Don't think a sword will do much against a ghost," Peter murmured.

Kat didn't want to even acknowledge the possibility, but she said, "Whatever you saw is probably something worse than a ghost, like a crazy villager holed up against the cold."

"Wait till you see him, Kat," Rob said. "You'll see how wrong you are."

The old and new parts of Rookskill Castle were joined by a long, crumbling, covered-parapet walk. Through the narrow windows they could see the courtyard, or bailey, below on their left. Dusty cobwebs draped the corners and what remained of the roof. The furnishings, if there had been any, were long gone, and the walls were exposed stone, cold and damp to the touch. Kat wished she had her coat, and the thought of Amelie and Isabelle shivering in this chill made her pick up her pace.

The ancient keep was as big as the new part of Rookskill Castle. It was a tall, odd structure. From outside it looked rectangular. But inside, as they found now, it was all stairs and angles and rooms and hallways jutting off into nowhere, and they'd open a door from one hallway to find another blank hallway, or worse, to find open air in a windowless shaft. Like the newer part of the castle, there was something at work inside this keep that made no logical architectural sense, a complex network of passages and stairwells.

More than once Peter grabbed Kat's elbow, or Kat snagged Robbie's shirttails, in the nick of time, before one of them fell into darkness.

"Ame!" Kat yelled into the hollow space, and heard only echoes. "Isabelle!"

"I wouldn't do that," said Robbie, his voice low. "That's how I saw him—the ghost. Because I was yelling like that."

Kat turned. "Rob, please. Quit talking about ghosts."

"You know what?" he said. "I can't wait until you're scared out of your wits." He held the sword pointed tip down in front of him, his knuckles white.

Peter panned the flashlight from corner to corner. "Rob, do you have any idea which way they might have gone?"

"There was this one stair, and we were going up because we heard something and thought it might be Colin, and that's when it all happened. I think it started when we went through this door." Robbie gestured. A crest carved into rock formed the keystone of the door arch, and Rob nodded. "Yeah. See that nick in the crest? That's it, all right. Come on."

Robbie impressed Kat with his bravery, but then, he did have a sword.

They stepped into the stairwell. Peter moved the flashlight up and then down. And then they heard it.

Singing. Wordless, sweet, voices that wove threads of tunes in and out together. Kat would have thought only angels could make such music.

"That's the sound," whispered Rob. "That's what we all heard. Right before they disappeared."

Peter and Kat exchanged a glance in the shadowy light. They'd heard that singing before. It sounded exactly like the voices that came from the sea. Only now the singing came from above them, no question.

"I'll lead," Peter said.

"No, let me," said Rob. "You can shine the light from behind." He started up the steps.

The steps themselves were crumbling beneath their feet, chunks of old stone breaking and cracking, and the tower almost felt alive, as if it was heaving and sighing with their presence, and it was so dark, the light from the flashlight was swallowed up ahead in the shadows. The singing drifted down from above them, drawing them on.

And then several things happened at once. The singing stopped. A new noise filtered through the stone wall to their left, the sound of voices calling, as if from a great distance. Girls' voices: Amelie and Isabelle.

Then the flashlight died. But before everything went black, something floated suddenly in the gloom ahead of the tip of Robbie's sword, and Kat saw it, suspended as though disembodied: a white face, a man's face, framed with dark hair, and eyes that glittered blue and blank and lost.

Kat screamed.

Robbie let out a mighty yell, and Peter grabbed Kat's arm. It was black as pitch, but she heard Robbie's sword clang as he must have flung it back and forth at the ghostly face and the sword ricocheted from left wall to right. Kat staggered back and, trying not to run over Peter, fell hard against the wall on her left.

Which gave beneath her weight.

Kat almost screamed again, but this time she swallowed it as her eye caught the sight of light: a thin bead of daylight now sliced vertically along the wall just where she'd fallen against it.

"Robbie! Peter! Quick!" Kat pushed against the wall and the bead widened to a crack, and then she could see it—the outline of a door.

Peter was beside her, and he said, "Push!" and they pushed together, and the door slid open with the harsh grating sound of stone on stone.

The light that flooded into their dark hallway blinded them. Kat covered her eyes and squinted. She turned back and saw Robbie's pale and sweaty face, and Peter's.

There was no sign of the ghost.

"You see, Kat?" asked Rob, panting a little. "I told you!"

Kat couldn't get words out, her chest was squeezed so tight, but she nodded, meeting Rob's triumphant look.

There was no logical way to explain what she'd seen.

The three of them pushed through the door and landed in a chamber filled with windows. Even though it was gray and cold outside, the dim light, by comparison to the dark hall, was most welcome. They stood rubbing their eyes, and then Kat heard a familiar squeal.

Isabelle and Amelie threw their arms around Kat.

"We were lost!" Isabelle cried. "We couldn't find Rob, and this place is so confusing." Amelie stuffed her face into Kat's stomach and held her tight. Then she pulled away.

"Did you see him?" Ame asked.

Kat stroked Ame's hair and scolded, "You shouldn't wander off alone."

"Let's get out of here, okay?" said Peter. "Where does the stair go?"

"We only went partway down," Isabelle said. "You know what they say when you're lost in the woods, that you should stay put, yes? So your rescuers can find you. That's what we did. *Mon dieu,* what a time we have had."

"How did you get in here?" Kat asked.

"There was a door and a hallway, and we slipped through, and it closed behind us as if someone pushed it . . ."

And as if the walls had ears, the door through which they'd just come slid, grating, shut.

"Magic," whispered Amelie.

"Interesting," said Peter.

"Most likely a counterweight," Kat said, "that worked when we stopped pushing. Clever." Peter gave her an odd look. "We'd better find out which way to go."

"I think those stairs," Peter said.

"I'll lead the way," said Robbie, lifting his sword.

Kat went to one window of the tower and looked out. They were not at the top of the keep; she reckoned they were about halfway up. That was the good news. The bad news was that she couldn't see the bailey from this lookout. Their balcony—that's what it was—seemed to jut over the old castle entrance and the ruined drawbridge and moat.

"Down it is," Kat said.

Rob led the way down; it grew darker as they left the windowed aerie, so Kat and Peter lit the candles. The steep winding stairwell was only wide enough for one at a time. Kat kept one hand on the wall and counted the number of steps as they went.

"Stop, Robbie," Kat said. "I'm betting we should be at the level of the parapet." In fact, they had arrived at a landing barely large enough to hold them all.

They clustered together. The stair went on down, but that wasn't the way Kat thought they should go.

"How do you know where we are?" asked Peter.

"Each step is about twenty centimeters, so it would take us twenty steps to cover the distance to where the parapet meets the tower. I was counting."

By the light of their guttering candles Kat could see something of Peter's expression. His eyebrows were up and his mouth formed a small "oh."

"But there's no door," Isabelle said, a wail creeping into her voice.

"Let's try the walls," Kat said.

"Right," said Peter. "If there's one hidden door, there are bound to be others."

They spread out along the walls, pushing, until sure enough, Peter found the opening, right into the covered parapet back to the new castle. It opened with their combined effort, and shut behind them on its own, just as the other had.

They made their way back through the parapet. The familiar passage, cobwebs or no, was a great relief.

By the time they reached the entry into the new castle, Isabelle and Amelie were practically running.

"Hold on, you two," Kat called, but it was no good. They were weary of being trapped in the crumbling old keep.

And Kat was weary of having to chase them down.

"Well, that's turned out all right," said Robbie, stopping and wiping his brow.

"It did this time, but you should never have made the problem in the first place." Kat let her worry out on Rob. "Don't be going off alone again."

Rob stared at her. "You've got no right to boss me. You treat me like I'm about five years old. I'm not a baby. Plus, we haven't found Colin, you know. There's still that." He paused. "And there's the ghost. I was right about the ghost."

"That doesn't matter," Kat said. "You were wrong to lead Ame and Isabelle into that old keep."

Rob's face darkened. "I'll do what I want, and if Ame and Isabelle want to go with me, they can. Don't tell me what to do!" And he thumped off, sword in hand.

Kat looked at Peter. "What?" she asked.

"You may be able to do sums in your head, but Rob's got a point."

Her cheeks grew warm. "But he was the one to cause the trouble in the first place. The Lady told us not to go exploring."

"Trouble?" Peter's brow furrowed. "It was you and me who went off exploring and got caught, remember? Not Robbie. And I saw that face, too, and I'm convinced it was a ghost." He paused and chewed his lip. "Something is going on in Rookskill Castle. I know it sounds ridiculous, but I think those hidden doors and passages in the keep appeared and disappeared. No," he said, shaking his head, "I'm not sure this whole place isn't haunted, like the stationmaster said."

Kat's cheeks burned. "Thank you for that analysis, Peter Williams, but here's what I think. Someone in the castle is a spy, and there are odd things about the old keep, which also happens to be filled with strange secret passages made by some clever person hundreds of years ago."

"Stick to that if you want," Peter said. His face was dark

and his eyes narrow. "But the truth might not be so obvious." He marched off in the direction of their rooms.

Fine, Kat thought irritably. *Fine.* The problem was, what she'd seen in the keep had no logical explanation. In fact, it had scared her silly.

Despite her best logical intentions, Kat had to admit that it was possible. No, even worse. Kat had to admit that something haunted Rookskill Castle—something very like magic.

31

Hidden Magic

LADY ELEANOR PAUSES before the fire in her room. Something feels off. Something is wrong.

With each charming, Eleanor has become more and more sensitive to magic of any kind. She knows that dark magic spreads like mold across the war-ravaged fields of France. She tingles with the ancient magic that lies buried in secret hollows of the highlands.

Since charming Jorry, she senses that a magic not of her making has appeared in Rookskill Castle.

Magic not of her making?

She's tired of the magister's warnings to go slowly. She's tired of the magister, period. She wants another soul. The power that has grown in her with time and each charming, she will not lose it. She will not return to being a helpless girl forced to suffer bruises, and worse. And, after all, she's saving these children not only from the Blitz but from the ravages of war.

Yes, she's saving them. But she's done with pretending that this is for the children. She's impatient, and hungry for more of the dark joy that burns through her with each charming.

She pauses before her embroidery box, opens the lid, and takes out her silver thimble. She rubs her fingers over the engraving: *Leonore. You have my heart and soul.* Her first husband's gift, and his lie.

She tried to catch Amelie's soul, but was interrupted by that irritating Katherine, who reminds her of someone she hates. So she'll try again, even though she must grit her teeth to beg the magister to fulfill his part of their bargain.

Eleanor grips the sporran that hides her chatelaine and narrows her eyes at the low flames of her fire. Whatever and wherever this other magic is, she will find it, yes. She'll take it for her own.

And then she'll no longer need the magister—or any man—at all.

32

Punishment

AT DINNER, EVERYONE was even more out of sorts. The faculty were grumpy, and the students pushed their food around without enthusiasm. The Lady shot dagger looks in all directions. Storm muttered under his breath, searching his pockets and mopping his brow in a worried gesture. Icy rain beat at the windows, and the wind howled so badly that occasional puffs of smoke belched from the fireplaces, so that a sooty pall rose to the high ceiling and hung over them like a cloud. Marie went from one end of the room to the other, stoking and putting on more wood in an effort to increase the draft.

As Kat listened to the howling wind, she was grateful that at least their uniforms were wool and their jackets were thick.

The faculty had donned robes, probably as much for warmth as out of tradition. But the Lady wore a ridiculous gown again— diaphanous and pale icy blue—which Kat was sure would not be warm enough except in this fire-stoked room, and was made odder by the sporran that hung from her belt.

And what in the world was wrong with Mr. Storm? He cast looks in Kat's direction as if he suspected she was up to some-thing. And he not only acted different, he looked different.

Had his hair always been so dark? It had grown, that was certain. But his shoulders—they seemed less broad. Maybe it was just that his jacket, underneath his robes, fit better; it did look like a new jacket, much more suited to dinner. He didn't slurp so much, or show his teeth as he ate. Did his face seem more angular? His cheekbones were prominent in a way she hadn't re-membered. He reminded her somewhat of that face they'd seen in the keep . . . Kat shuddered. Perhaps it was shadows.

The only good thing was that Colin reappeared before they sat down at the table. He'd been missing because he was clos-eted all afternoon with Miss Gumble, who was kind enough to spend time helping him with his homework, which might have accounted for her cranky mood, and his miserable one.

"I don't read fast," Colin lamented. "I can't understand these long words. And my writing is terrible. I don't understand why the subject and verb have to match. If Miss Gumble hadn't been willing to help, I don't know what I'd do. But by the end she was mad at me. She rapped my fingers with her pencil." He plopped his chin on his fist.

"I can give you a hand," Kat said. "I'm not the best writer in the world, but I can help with the reading."

"Oh, could you?" He sounded plaintive. "That would be so kind."

When the Lady stood and left, even before the sun was down, she wore a strained expression, and Kat thought perhaps there was indeed some illness about, and the Lady didn't want them to know. Maybe Jorry did have a terrible disease, like a pox or measles or polio, and they'd all been exposed, and the Lady didn't want their parents to take them away because she didn't want to lose the income.

Kat pushed the food around on her plate; her stomach was in knots. She was relieved when dinner was over.

Nobody spoke all the way up the stairs. It wasn't until they reached the hallway to their rooms that Robbie said, "I don't believe her. About Jorry. I think there's something else going on." He glanced darkly at Jorry's door.

For Robbie this was something. He'd had an obvious crush on the Lady from the start.

They stood in a circle in the hallway.

"I agree. It's odd," said Peter.

"And the ghosts, and the noises," said Isabelle, and sniffed. "Very peculiar."

"It's magic," whispered Amelie.

Magic. The shiver went right up Kat's spine.

Kat woke the next morning even more exhausted than usual. It was Saturday, so no lessons, and as she pulled the curtains aside she saw a fresh, thin blanket of snow covering the land-scape. Dread filled her, though she couldn't say why.

After breakfast, Peter disappeared, Amelie and Isabelle tucked into Isabelle's room, and Rob and Colin made off with swords to swing. Kat, back in her room, stared out the window at the new snow. Tracks patterned the garden—maybe a fox, she thought, or one of the cats—and that gave her an idea.

Maybe the new snow would tell other tales. Maybe she'd find child-sized footprints, or something more sinister. But something she could follow, so she could learn what was really going on at Rookskill Castle.

She pulled on her warmest sweater and headed down the stairs. She'd no sooner reached the great hall than a knocking rattled the front door, sending a drum-hollow echo throughout the castle.

Kat froze as Marie appeared, hastening down the corridor. She saw Kat and said, "Whatever are you doing here? You're lucky the Lady doesn't catch you. Go on, be off, back to your room."

Kat retreated. But she stopped on the landing above and ducked around the corner as she heard Marie open the door.

"Telegram," came a familiar man's voice. "And since I were up this way, brought someone along who wanted to pay a visit to her Ladyship."

"Her Ladyship is not receiving visitors," said Marie, her voice crisp. "She's running an academy."

"Yeah," said the man, sounding hard and determined. "But this is the mother of one of her Ladyship's students."

Kat crept back down the stairs to catch a glimpse, her heart pounding. Could it be her own mum, come to take them home? She peered around the corner.

The man was the dwarf—the stationmaster—wearing a different cap today, showing his service as a telegraph officer. Behind him Kat could make out the form of a woman, and her spirits fell. It wasn't Mum, but a thin woman dressed in a tweed coat, a warm cloche, and practical Wellies.

The woman pressed forward, elbowing past the small man. "I'm looking for my son Jorry," she said. "He promised to write, and I've heard not a word for over two weeks. I've come up from London expressly—"

"Thank you, Marie." The Lady emerged from one of the side parlors as if lifted out of the shadow itself. "I'll take it from here."

Kat stepped back behind the wall so she could just see

below. Marie, as she turned away, handed the Lady the telegram. The Lady glanced down at it before slipping it into her pocket.

The Lady walked across the hallway slowly. But her bearing was rigid and regal, her hair shining like the snow, and she wore a slim white dress with a white jacket that fell below her hips. The dwarf's jaw dropped. Jorry's mother froze in place.

"Jorry is most remarkable," the Lady intoned. "He is an intelligent boy, one of my favorites of all the children." Her smile was so bright, it seemed to glow.

"Oh," murmured Jorry's mum. "Oh. Well, he would be," she finished more certainly.

"He's doing extremely well with his studies and has made many friends here at the academy."

Kat barely held back a snort.

"Yes," said his mum, less sure. "I can see he would." She nodded, head bobbing.

The dwarf gaped like a fish, his mouth opening and closing. He mumbled, "Yer Ladyship . . ." and "Humbly sorry to disturb . . ."

The Lady walked forward, and the dwarf, still in the doorway, stepped back into the snowy world outside as Jorry's mum almost imperceptibly leaned away.

"Thank you for coming," the Lady said, her voice a silk ribbon. "I don't want to distress the students who have adapted so well, especially your talented son. I'm sure you understand."

"Well, yes, of course," Jorry's mum said. "But you see, I've come up from London—"

"And I hope you have a pleasant journey back."

In her astonishment, Kat had moved out from her hiding place to stand on the landing with her fists clenched as the Lady shut the door on the two blank faces. Not a single mention of Jorry's illness! Not even letting his mother see him?

And then the Lady turned, and she saw Kat, and her ruby lips curled away from her shining teeth.

"Katherine. I thought I told you not to prowl the castle. You must be punished." The Lady lifted her voice. "Marie?"

Marie appeared.

"Take Katherine to her room. Lock her in for the remainder of the day. She is to have no supper."

Kat backed up the stairs, retreating. "You can't—" she began.

"Indeed I can," the Lady said.

Marie caught Kat's elbow. "You best come along now," she said, low, "or it will be the worse for you."

Kat had no choice.

They'd reached the next landing when the Lady called up. "Why, Katherine, this telegram brings news for your ears. It's from your mother." Kat stepped back where she could see the Lady, so pale in her white dress and her shining hair that she seemed to glow in the dark hallway. "Your father, I'm afraid. They fear he's been captured by the Germans."

Kat's knees grew weak.

"The Germans are ruthless," the Lady continued, looking up from the telegram and shaking her head. She sighed. "I imagine he'll be executed. And he was so helpful to me." She turned away, letting the telegram flutter to the floor.

Kat waited until the Lady disappeared into the parlor again and shut the door before she sprinted down the stairs, ignoring the hiss from Marie, and snatched the telegram, running back up the stairs with it clutched in her fist. The eyes in the huge portrait of Leonore burned into Kat's back.

Marie took Kat by the wrist and pulled her along the corridor and into her room, then left, locking the door behind.

Kat let the hot tears run down her cheeks as she read the telegram over and over and over. Mum hadn't even bothered with a code; Kat could feel the worry in those few words of the telegram:

TAKEN BY GERMANS M

Father. Alone in some dark and terrible corner, a prisoner, with evil all around. She'd been right, what she felt before he left, and he should never have gone, and for the first time her fear for him spilled over into anger at him.

If he hadn't gone, they wouldn't be here, in this castle haunted by ghosts and worse. Evil was not only on the battlefield.

Anger burned through Kat, anger at Father, anger at useless wishes, and anger at the cruel Lady who held all the children completely in her power.

33

Magister

KAT MAY BE asleep, or maybe not. Her room is cold and dark and the clock reads half past five. The others must be at dinner. At the thought, she's aware of a gnawing emptiness in her stomach.

If only she could sneak down to the kitchen . . . but her door is locked.

And then she remembers the crippled boy. He must have come into her room through a hidden doorway, like the one they'd stumbled upon in the keep. She knows there has to be one in her room somewhere. How she'd love to get back at the Lady by finding a secret way out.

She feels her way inch by inch along the walls, searching for a crack, and then she has it, right along the side of the fireplace. She pushes, and it opens with a low *shush* into a narrow stairway.

She lights one of the candles she'd found in the kitchen and steps down, down, until she's sure she's on the ground floor, and, sure enough, there's another door, the handle on her side. With the candle in her left hand she pulls it open with the right.

It opens on tight hinges—she can feel the counterweight—a heavy door of brick. She holds up the candle and she's in a large, dark closet. She lets her eyes adjust, and all of a sudden another door opposite her opens.

It's all a blur. It may all be a dream.

Kat starts, her right hand still on the door frame, as a very surprised Hugo steps into view, and then the wall of rock behind her closes, the counterweight working its brand of magic, the brick wall closing on her fingers.

The pain in her hand is excruciating, so terrible she can't scream. Hugo moves faster than she would have dreamed for his size, and he heaves his body against the door to free Kat's hand. When she looks at it, some combination of the terrible pain and the sight of her mangled fingers causes her to fall in a faint.

She's back in her dark room, and the clock reads eight thirty. Eight thirty on Saturday evening, it must be. She doesn't remember how she got back there, or very much about the two and a half hours she's lost. She'd heard Hugo muttering something like "must take her to the magister," and she had the image of a hut with a glowing fire, and a wizened man holding her damaged hand as Hugo begged him to do something, as it was "my fault, all my fault"—which, of course, Kat knows it wasn't.

She sits up and switches on the electric light. Her hand is perfect. Her fingers are intact, not crushed. She seems to recall white bits of bone and lots and lots of blood. But here it is, unmarked, unscarred, and unbandaged. And something more.

Kat clenches her fist. Her hand feels powerful, better than ever. It's marvelous. And delicate, and super-sensitive. Her clock-mending skills will be superior. She might even be able to fix her father's watch.

It can be nothing but magic.

This magister must be a doctor of extraordinary skill. She doesn't remember the surgery. Except for the strength of her hand, it might never have happened. No, the whole thing is a dream. In fact, there is no magister. Her hand is a normal hand, flesh and bone, no more.

And yet.

By the time someone knocks on Kat's door at eight forty-five, she feels as though she's just awakened from a long sleep and a most bizarre dream. But, dream or not, one certainty fills her.

Magic not only haunts the shadows of Rookskill Castle.

Magic is a real and solid thing, and lives inside her, as real as blood and bone.

34

Missing

ᗰARIE KNOCKED, THEN unlocked Kat's door and slipped her a package "from Cook. Do not say anything to her Ladyship." Inside was a Spam sandwich, which Kat sat right down and ate in the hallway, though without enthusiasm. Her mind kept turning toward her father, lost somewhere on the continent.

The other children, as they came out of their rooms, gave her sympathetic looks.

Peter said, "We thought you were taken ill, too, at first."

Amelie leaned her head against Kat's arm. "I'm sorry I've been so mean to you. The Lady is wicked."

Kat patted her sister's head.

Rob said, his voice low, "Good thing you aren't ill, since you're the sensible one." Kat smiled. She knew that took a lot, coming from Rob. "What did you do, Kat," asked Amelie, slipping her hand into Kat's, "when you were all alone and hungry, locked in your bedroom? Were you lonely?"

"I'm fine," said Kat. "I was fine. I've been doing a lot of thinking. Yes, the Lady is mean. But she's more than that."

"What are you saying?" Peter asked.

"There's something about her that . . ." Kat paused. Everyone's eyes were on her. It was one thing to think it and another to say it.

She finished eating and balled up the wrappings, then stood and dusted off her hands. "I'm going to try to break into the hidden room with the short-wave wireless."

"What hidden room?" asked Isabelle.

"There *is* a hidden room!" said Colin, wide-eyed. "I knew it!"

"There's a short-wave wireless?" said Rob, leaping to his feet. "You mean, where we heard the noises, there's a wireless? Why didn't you say so?"

"I want to get into that room so we can use it to get away. To get word to our parents, I mean. Listen."

She told them about seeing Jorry's mother, and how it was wrong that the Lady didn't let her in. Kat said, "We're trapped here. Our parents don't know a thing. Have any of you received letters from home?"

Silence. Peter shook his head, and Isabelle tugged on her curls.

"The only thing I've heard is through a couple of telegrams, which makes me think the Lady has been confiscating our letters," Kat said. "So we're on our own. Plus," she added, "we're all at one another's throats. I think we're being divided to make us easier to control."

"But," Rob asked, "why?"

"One possibility that Peter and I came up with is that the Lady might be hiding a spy."

Rob whistled.

"And if she is hiding a spy here that would explain a lot, including the short-wave wireless," Kat said. "And it would mean we're prisoners. Or hostages. In danger at any rate." She paused. "But it could be something in addition to a spy. In fact, I'm pretty sure now that there is something else here. Something worse."

"What's worse than a spy?" Colin whispered.

"Dark magic," said Amelie, her voice soft. "Something evil."

A chilled hush settled over them all.

"Or some*one* evil," Kat said, "like the Lady." She plunged on. "I've had the worst dreams. Nightmares. Ever since leaving London. There's something about each dream that feels like a message. Sometimes I don't really remember them. But they're telling me something, and . . ." Kat hesitated. "Ame, you may be right."

"You mean," Ame said, "you believe now that this could all have to do with magic? Dark magic?"

"Dark magic," Colin echoed, his face drained of color.

"Yes, Kat. Do you?" said Peter. "Do you believe in magic?"

Ame and Isabelle both stared intently at Kat.

Kat nodded, her lips a thin line.

Ame's eyes widened, and Peter cleared his throat and scratched his chin. Isabelle made a murmuring noise. Colin looked like he might cry. Rob whispered, "If stodgy Kat believes, that's, well, scary."

They were so quiet for a few minutes that Kat could hear the wind moaning around the outside walls.

"Well," said Rob at last, in a bright voice, "whether it's a spy or dark magic, I'm game for going after the wireless." He squared his shoulders, but his eyes read worry.

"Okay," said Peter. "Hang on." He stepped into his room and came out with the fireplace poker. He raised it up and grinned. "In case we have to really break in."

"Right," said Rob. "And I've got my sword."

They all made off together toward the stairs and secret room. Kat hoped Marie wouldn't arrive—or worse, the Lady—and find them all out of their rooms.

As it turned out, they had no need of the poker or the sword. For the first time the door was ajar and no one was there. The room was small and windowless and hollowed out under the stair.

It was also empty.

Kat sagged against the wall. "Blast."

A single lightbulb with a long chain pull hung from the ceiling. A desk hugged one wall, and a chair lay on its side on the floor. Old linens were stacked on a shelf along the back, as if that had been the original purpose of the room.

But there was no wireless. There were no papers, no electric cords, nothing to indicate what had been in the room when they'd heard the noises.

"Now what?" asked Peter.

Kat shook her head. She was fresh out of ideas.

Peter broke the chain pull and wrapped the broken half around the inside handle, tugging the door shut with the end of the pull outside. "In case we need this room."

"Wow," said Colin, squinting at the door. "With that fancy wallpaper you can't even see it when it's shut."

They trudged back upstairs. A heavy weight pressed on Kat's chest. No wireless, no way to contact their parents, no escape. They were trapped.

Trapped in the terrible castle Father had found for them. Father, who might be lost to her forever.

As they passed Jorry's room, Kat paused and pressed her ear up against his door. "Jorry?" she called.

Nothing this time. Not even a whimper. She tried the door, and to her surprise the knob began to turn.

"Here, what are you up to?" It was Marie, once again appearing as if out of nowhere. "Why are you all loitering about in the hallway? It's time you were in your rooms. Off with you." She carried the tea cart with the chocolate; Kat didn't even pick up a mug tonight. "And stay away from that room, hear? Doctor's coming tomorrow to take that lad away. He's a terrible contagion."

Kat hugged her watch. *A doctor is coming.*

"This is great news," Kat whispered to Peter. "Not that Jorry's ill, if he is in fact ill, but that a doctor's coming."

Peter nodded. "If we can get the doctor to see what's happening and take word back to our folks . . ."

"If he believes us about the spy," Kat said, her hope fading. "Without the wireless we have no proof."

"No," Peter agreed. "No proof of anything."

As they were making off for bed, Kat pulled Rob aside. He was already yawning. She spoke fast, whispering to him about their father.

The news that Father was captured snapped Rob awake. She watched him take it in, trying not to cry.

"We've got to figure out who was using that wireless and where it went," Rob said. "For Father's sake."

Kat put her hand on his shoulder, glancing at Amelie, who was now settled permanently in Isabelle's room, the two of them tottering off to sleep. "Let's not tell Ame about Father yet."

He nodded. "Kat, what do you think the Jerries will do to him?"

"Maybe they'll keep him a prisoner. For, I don't know, a prisoner exchange or something."

"But Father's a spy. Don't they execute spies?"

They'd never before admitted to each other what their father did. When Rob said it, the truth settled on her like a terrible weight. Their father was a spy for their country. And execution was how the enemy dealt with spies. She swallowed the lump in her throat before saying, "Let's hope they don't."

Rob yawned again. "I'm always so tired at night. Must be all this schoolwork."

Kat turned away, then paused. "Robbie, don't drink the chocolate. I'm pretty sure it's been tampered with."

His eyes grew wide as he realized what she meant. "So that's it. Now I really don't like this place."

"There's something else," Kat said. "Someone who wears a black greatcoat is wandering the grounds. I've seen him heading toward the cliffs. I think whoever it is might be connected with our mysteries, but I don't know how."

Rob chewed his lip and nodded, but said only, "Night, Kat." He turned away, then turned back and gave his sister a quick hug, the first in many months.

"Night, Rob."

Kat closed the door to her room and leaned back against it.

When the doctor came for Jorry, she'd beg him to take them all away, get them out of this nightmare. She'd see her mum again and her great-aunt Margaret. She'd return her great-aunt's chatelaine and pretend that she'd never believed magic to be real.

As she was closing her dresser drawer, she paused. The chatelaine.

Of course.

Of course! If dark magic was real—and Kat felt sure now that it was, although she still wished it wasn't—then the magic her great-aunt had given her would be real, too. That was what Great-Aunt Margaret was on about. She wasn't loony. She was trying to prepare Kat to use good magic, magic that Storm had said collected in certain old things like dust.

Kat's heart rose, and she couldn't wait to hug her great-aunt. Kat would figure out how to use the chatelaine, how to turn its good magic against the dark, and they would all be saved.

She couldn't help smiling.

Kat reached inside the drawer and felt around. She brushed her hand back and forth. All right, then. Where was that blasted thing?

She put both hands in the dresser, rumpling the neatly folded sweaters and socks, ruffling them with more and more anxiety, pushing and pulling, searching.

Where was Great-Aunt Margaret's chatelaine?

Panic filled her throat as a knotty lump.

She pulled the drawer fully open and dumped the contents on the floor, tossing things left and right until she'd sorted through it all once, and again. She peered under the bed. She searched the bathroom. She lifted the corners of the curtains and lay flat on the floor to feel underneath the dresser.

There was no trace of her great-aunt's chatelaine.

Kat's heart pounded, and she found it hard to breathe as she sat on the floor among the scatter of clothes. Why hadn't she looked for it before this? When was the last time she'd seen it? Was it a week? She seemed to remember seeing it a week ago on Saturday. . . .

Kat hugged herself and rocked back and forth.

If only she'd believed in it sooner. She'd been too logical. Too stodgy. Her stomach ached with realization.

If her great-aunt was right, the chatelaine in Kat's keeping was the one thing that might protect them from the dark magic of Rookskill Castle.

And Kat had lost it.

35

The Cave by the Sea

KAT WOKE TO the sound of the lock clicking open; it was barely dawn. She waited, stiff as a board, fearful, but no one entered. She heard then the slashing patter on the windows and a howling wind whistling through the cracks. A great storm must have blown in off the North Sea.

Her first thought went to the missing chatelaine. She swallowed hard. How could she protect her brother and sister without it?

And then she remembered the doctor. He would come. They'd be saved. But Kat would have to explain the lost chatelaine to Great-Aunt Margaret. Well, she'd take that responsibility, as long as they could all get away from this terrible haunted place.

She left her warm bed and went to the window, staring into the gray dawn. The weather alternated ice and rain, and Kat hugged herself and shivered as the wind found its way into the castle. The snow was all gone.

Kat washed and bundled into her uniform and opened her door. The passage was silent and dim. She might have roused Peter and Rob, but it was so early.

Find the doctor. Then, she hoped, find the chatelaine.

She slipped down the stairs, heading for the kitchen. She hoped she'd catch Cook readying breakfast. Readying things for the doctor.

The castle was dark and her footsteps echoed, even as she tiptoed. When she reached the kitchen it was cold: no cheery fire, no pleasant smells, silent as a tomb. She stood in the semi-darkness and chewed her lip.

Kat went to the door to the kitchen courtyard and eased it open.

The wind blasted her backward, and she held the door to keep it from banging wide. It was the devil to close, and she had to put her shoulder to it. But before she shut it she saw the headlights of the Lady's motorcar coming in through the back gate, the lights in the gray rain bouncing from wall to wall in the close kitchen yard. Kat watched until the car pulled to a stop inside the garage bay across the court.

The giant heaved himself out of the driver's seat and closed the garage door behind. Kat started. He wore a long black oil-cloth greatcoat.

She closed the door tight and leaned back against it, rubbing her forehead.

Wait, she thought. He must have gone to fetch the doctor. Brought him in by the front door. Yes, that had to be it. Hugo wasn't the enemy, despite that coat.

And the doctor was here. They were saved! The thrill of knowing that soon they'd all be off and home filled her heart. She could stand up to any number of thumpings from the Nazis, just to be back at Great-Aunt Margaret's again with her brother and sister and Mum. Her great-aunt would understand about the lost chatelaine, as long as they were all safe and together.

Kat would wake the others and let them know. They'd need to be ready to leave. Joy surged in her. Home. They were going home!

She ran back upstairs to Peter and Rob's door.

She didn't dare pound, but she knocked as loud as she could and whispered, her mouth right against the jamb, "Peter! Rob! Wake up now!"

Within a minute the door opened. Peter held the door, still in his pajamas and scratching his head. She could see into the room, the two empty beds. There was no sign of Rob. She looked away, blushing at the sight of Peter in his pajamas. "Where's Rob?"

"What?"

"Where is he?"

"Hang on," Peter said.

She closed the door to an inch and heard Peter scrambling around the room. When he came back to the door he was clothed and finishing buttoning his shirt. His eyes were wide and his face ashen. The metallic taste of fear filled Kat's mouth. He held a piece of paper in his hand, a note in Rob's wobbly scrawl.

"Rob?" Kat asked, trying to calm herself, her heart racing so that she thought her chest would explode.

"He's gone."

Kat paced. "Out alone on the cliffs?" She wanted to kick herself. How she wished she hadn't mentioned the black-coated figure to Rob.

Rob had written: *Up early and saw that black-coated spy heading toward cliffs. Back soon.*

"I don't know how he snuck out without waking me." Peter pursed his lips. "At least he took his sword. And his coat."

Peter was trying to be comforting, but it wasn't working.

Kat prayed Rob would show up for breakfast, but, no, and Cook was not at breakfast, either. Marie brought out some cold meats and cheeses and bread. Peter told the Lady that Rob didn't feel well and was sleeping in, at which the Lady grew furious and left the dining hall. The five remaining children huddled together, whispering.

"*Regardez*," said Isabelle as the door slammed shut behind the Lady. "She is angry about something. Something is amiss."

"Yes, what's amiss is Rob," Kat said bitterly. And her chatelaine, but Kat couldn't worry about both at once.

Storm was missing at breakfast, too, but MacLarren and Gumble kept a wary eye on the small band of students. Peter said, "We're going to have to keep up the pretense for Rob's sake, until he shows up."

Colin said, "What if he's, you know, like Jorry?"

"*Oui*," said Isabelle. "Ill with spots."

Kat's throat burned. There was no going away with any doctor without Rob.

"Off you go," said Marie, who came to clear the table.

"Did the doctor come for Jorry?" Peter asked her.

Marie stared at him. "Why, no. I don't think so. At least . . ." She paused, rubbing her hand over her forehead. "This is a very confusing morning."

Well, that settled it. No doctor. No rescue.

They went back to their rooms and Kat tried to finish her homework, but her mind was on Rob.

At lunch, Cook was back, and Kat felt a small glimmer of relief. But when Cook saw that Rob was not at the table, she set her lips and murmured to herself.

After lunch Kat ran for the kitchen, the others right behind.

Cook sat at the kitchen table, shaking her head. "I knew when her Ladyship sent me out early to the train but nobody was at the station that, well, something was not right. And then me getting stuck in the mud in the wagon and Hugo not around neither to pull me out until forever. It's good I got back here at all." She sighed. "All right. When did you last see him?"

Peter explained while Cook listened and Kat paced back and forth.

Cook leaned back on her stool. "So he's gone wandering down toward the coast. I'll fetch Hugo. He knows these cliffs and wastes like the back of his very big hand."

Kat was certain that Hugo was not their enemy. Someone else must also wear a black greatcoat. When Hugo came in, Kat explained again about Rob.

"Ach." Hugo rubbed his chin. "Well, now. Where to begin, that's the question."

"I'd begin with coats," muttered Cook.

"Aye, too right. Cook, you are a smart one." He dropped his voice and leaned over the children. "Where would we be without Cook, eh?" He raised up again. "Everyone fetch your warmest coats and hats and mittens, and we'll meet back here in a jiff."

A fog was starting to settle, dripping chill on brown grass. Kat was so anxious, she walked ahead of the others with the giant, who led them down the allée of trees.

"Don't think he'd strike out across the moorlands," Hugo said. "There's naught between Rookskill Castle and the islands but hills after Dunraven, and the moors are no place to go, bleak they are, with naught but rocks and heather, and they say these wastes are full of the ghosts of highlanders. But the seacoast, now, he might be looking after ships and the like, what with all that's going on these days and the waters filled with ships of all kinds."

They reached the cliff edge. The water struck the rocks below them, pounding, pounding; seagulls wheeled and called, mournful; the sea gave up its salt smell in the mist around them.

"Ach!" said Hugo, going down on one knee. "Look here." He lifted a button from the dense turf.

Kat's heart kicked up. It was definitely one of Rob's coat buttons; she recognized the lion's head stamp. Hugo began walking north along the cliff, head bent as if he was tracking.

Hugo muttered to himself as he walked, and he picked up the pace, striding out with his giant's reach. "Used to spend me time as a lad up here. Still remember these crags." Kat now had to run to keep up with his long legs.

Kat and Hugo pulled away from the others, and her heart beat harder as a shaft of sunlight broke through the line of clouds, the sun now low on the horizon. How much time before dinner, before the Lady returned and caught them out? The useless watch weighed heavy on Kat's wrist.

Then Hugo stopped, so abruptly that she ran smack into the back of his legs. The cliffs had lifted beside them so that they stood on a high point of land, the ocean to their right. Before them the slope dropped steeply to a deep ravine that released a narrow stream of water into the surf, and beyond the stream, a swath of green woods, and beyond that, Kat spied the high rolling rocky hills of the moors, glinting with low late light.

"Right here," Hugo muttered. He raised his hand and pointed. "That's Fairnie Burn, there," he said, indicating the stream, "and that's Dunraven Wood. So that means that right about here . . ." And he went to the sheer edge of the cliff and leaned over, looking down.

"Ho!" Hugo called into the salt air. "Ye found it, did ye?"

Hugo could reach his long arms down over the cliff face just far enough. By the time the others had caught up with Hugo and Kat, Hugo had hauled Robbie up and over the edge, where he lay panting and dirt-smudged, staring up at the sky.

"I know that ledge well, lad," said Hugo. "Used to sit on it when I wanted to be left alone."

"I couldn't climb back up," Rob said, wiping his forehead on his sleeve. "I thought I'd be there forever." Then he sat straight up. "But I found the spy. And the wireless. Although there's more than a wireless there. There's another machine there. Something weird."

Kat didn't care about machines. She knelt down and wrapped Rob in a bear hug.

"Please, Kat," Rob said, pushing her away, his cheeks turning pink. "For heaven's sake don't sniffle."

She rubbed her eyes. She couldn't help the tears. It had been a dreadful day. She wouldn't scold him, grateful as she was that he was all right.

Peter pointed to the west, where the sun shot a last ray through the low clouds. "We've got barely enough time to get back."

Rob filled Kat and Peter in as they ran back to the castle. Hugo carried Isabelle on his back and Amelie in his arms and he lumbered at a fast pace.

"I followed him," Rob panted. "Your black coat fellow. Followed him, then hid in the trees and saw him disappear over the cliff and then climb back up and make for the castle. I waited till he was out of sight, then thought I could go down like he did and get back up again, but he's taller . . ."

They tumbled into the front hall, and Hugo put the girls down. "I'll be leaving you bairns. Be quick about it, now," he said before trudging away. They threw off their coats, stashing them in a pile in the closet, and made a beeline for the dining hall.

Rob continued in a coarse whisper, "I got down to that ledge, and that's when I found the cave."

"Cave!" said Peter.

"There's a cave there, right in the cliffs. And, well, that's where I found the machines."

The six of them surged into the dining hall, where the teachers and Lady waited at the head table. They stopped in a rough heap, trying to smooth ruffled hair and rumpled clothes.

The Lady drew herself up, examining them all, but especially the dirt-smeared Rob. "You are late."

They ate in silence. Kat stole glances up at the head table. MacLarren and Gumble were stiff and careful; Storm looked odder than ever, thin—yes, thin!—and drawn, muttering to himself and glancing through narrowed eyes at everyone around him. The Lady seemed shrouded in a dark cloud.

When they finished dinner, the children trooped upstairs and gathered in a circle in the hallway. Kat asked Rob for more details.

"I know it was dumb to go alone," Rob said, "but when I woke up and looked out and saw that guy in the black overcoat I remembered what you said and I had to follow. Especially since the wireless was missing and all. I thought maybe I was onto the spy. And I was, wasn't I?"

"I'm just glad we found you in one piece," Kat said. "And really, Rob, I should be mad, but I'm proud of you."

Rob looked surprised, and then gave Kat a big smile.

She asked, "But what's this other machine you saw?"

"I don't know," said Rob. "It's like a typewriter of some kind. It has a keyboard and it was inside a wooden box with a lid, and above the keyboard were wheels and gears with numbers, and I couldn't see where you'd put in paper like in an ordinary typewriter."

Peter let out a low whistle and Kat rocked back. She knew what that machine was, and clearly Peter did, too. "An encryption machine," she whispered.

"What's that?" asked Colin.

"It's a code machine," Kat said. "Spies use them to translate things into code. So they can send information back."

"Could it be that the spy, he is on our side?" asked Isabelle.

Peter shook his head and said, "Not likely. Why hide it in a cave? No, it's probably the enemy. Kat, you were right all along. The Germans do have a spy here."

Kat shivered. Somehow, she didn't feel happy she was right.

"If you ask me," said Robbie, "a Nazi spy is worse than a ghost, any day. But at least I can truly use my sword on a spy . . . Oh, no!" Robbie's eyes grew round and he stood up.

"What, Rob?" Kat asked.

"My sword," he said, his voice expressing his horror. "I left my sword—the castle's sword—in the cave. The spy will know someone from the castle has been there."

They all exchanged wide-eyed glances.

"We'd better get back there tomorrow," said Peter. "We'll want to get at that code machine anyway."

"A code machine," said Amelie. Her round cheeks were pink, her eyes bright. "A machine that makes new words and sends them away over the air. That sounds like magic."

Kat stared at her sister. A mathematical device that translated letters into numbers and was made of pins and cogs and wheels, that was magic? "Well, until you unravel the secrets, I guess it is magical, a bit, Ame. But it's really only a big and complicated puzzle. Once you figure it out, it's not so magical after all."

Amelie shook her head, curls tumbling. "It turns shadows into light."

Kat opened her mouth and then closed it again. She was beginning to realize that there were times when Amelie spoke the truth. Kat leaned back against the wall. Was Rob right? Was a Nazi spy worse than some evil monster possessed of dark magic? That's what she'd thought, at the beginning. Now she was not so sure. A spy was solid, real. Magic, well, that was still something slippery to Kat. Solid things first.

Solid things including her missing chatelaine. First thing in the morning she'd begin a concerted search.

If Kat had known that something in Rookskill Castle stole the souls of children, she might have changed her priorities.

36

Ice

KAT IS DRIFTING into sleep when they arrive: grinding, moaning, shivering sounds, slithering from one side of her bed to the other, and she lies still as death, trying not to cry out, trying to keep her face a mask. As the monster slides away she hears the soft *shush* as if a door closed.

She doesn't move for what seems hours. And unlike the other times she'd heard the noises and thought she might have dreamed them, she does not fall asleep, but lies awake.

Moonlight streams through the curtains. The clock on the mantle, the one she has fixed and restarted so many times, has stopped again, the hands poised at ten past midnight.

Whatever that thing is, it has the power to stop clocks.

And the room is frigid.

37

The Seventh Charm: The Dog

THE LADY ELEANOR of Rookskill Castle catches Colin out before breakfast. She will not be interrupted this time, as she was with little Amelie. Eleanor, done with pretense, finished with kindness, won't be stopped or delayed any longer.

"*Tsk*," Eleanor says to Colin, scolding. "You know the rules. You've seen what happens. You should not be wandering about."

Colin's face drops; Eleanor is pleased. She's planted such perfect seeds. "I was only . . ." His voice trails off. His eyes study the ground. He waits.

"There, now." She pauses. "I think I have a suitable punishment. Do you like dogs?"

Colin's face lifts again. For a moment he looks suspicious, and then his eyes brighten and he nods so hard, he might rattle apart.

"My favorite hound has whelped and her pups need attention. You can take care of them."

It's clear that this is anything but punishment to Colin. He dances around her as they walk. The chatelaine thumps against her hip; she has the dog charm clutched in her fist, ready.

Eleanor pushes the barn door aside, then closes it behind. "This way," she says. She leads him past the empty stall to where one is dimly lit. Cats scatter into shadows as they pass.

Colin jumps and skips. To him, the barn smells of damp and hay. Maybe they were wrong about the Lady, if she loves dogs.

As they step around the stall door they see the slender hound and a pile of mewling puppies.

Eleanor reaches down and lifts up a puppy and hands it to Colin. She wipes her hand on her black coat, disgust filling her. To her, the barn smells of feces. The hound bares her teeth but doesn't dare bite her mistress, a mistress now made more of metal than of soft flesh, metal that would cause great pain to the hound and her babies.

Growl at me, you filthy cur, thinks Eleanor. *You'll be sorry when I throw your pups into the well and turn you out into the snow.*

But Colin is in heaven, cuddling and cooing. The pup's eyes are still closed and it's a small brown-and-white ball in his arms. Colin turns his bright eyes to Eleanor, talking baby talk to the wee thing.

It's perfect: she slips the silver chain with its small dog charm over Colin's head and whispers the accursed words.

Your life will linger dark and deep.

She's seen the change six times before: the cry of pain and then the jaw gone slack, the eyes that dull, the vacancy as the boy's soul leaves his body and becomes hers.

Hers.

Her chest grows tight and she closes her eyes. The boy's soul is joined to her thirteenth charm, held there with a bond formed of dark spells. Eleanor swells with the power of it, feeling the bliss surge through her as it has before, each time more strongly, and she tilts her head back and laughs out loud.

Her laughter rolls through the barn, shrill and piercing. The living things scatter before the sound as if it contaminates the very air.

The hound bares her teeth again and her throat fills with a growl, as the boy Colin sinks to his knees, clutching the pup, sinks to the mother and her other babies, and becomes one with them, acting like a whining, whimpering puppy, accepted by the hound as another of the forlorn creatures of the barn.

Eleanor draws herself upright, her metal arm's gears whirring and clicking. She points her claw finger at the hound and says, "I will take care of you before the end."

Her thirteenth charm now carries the weight of seven souls, and Eleanor bears it, limping, staggering, bending, but also with dark joy.

38

The Cave of Plato

"JUST WHAT YOU'D expect from a ghost," said Rob when he and Kat and Peter gathered in the hallway before breakfast.

"I don't want to scare them," Kat said of the younger children. "I don't want them to know."

Peter and Rob, who didn't drink the chocolate either, had heard it in their room, too. "Pretty awful," was Rob's understatement.

"It makes me feel like I can't move," said Peter. "And I don't want to open my eyes. And it gets so cold in the room."

"I think it's using secret passageways," Kat said.

"I know what I have to do," said Rob, straightening his back. "I've got to go back for my sword."

And Kat had to find her chatelaine. She'd had time when

waking up to take her room apart piece by piece. But after a fruitless search Kat sank back on her heels, exhausted. Her room was a shambles, all of her and Amelie's clothes dumped on the floor and the bedclothes rumpled and every object turned upside down or inside out, and still no chatelaine. She wanted to cry, but that wouldn't do any good.

Stolen, was her next thought. Someone must have taken it from her dresser. But who? And did they know that it might contain magic, and how to use it?

As they sat down to breakfast, Rob asked, "Where's Colin?"

"In his room?" Isabelle said hopefully.

But after breakfast he didn't answer the knock on the door, and his room was locked.

"He must be here," Kat said, a knot of worry forming in her stomach. "Maybe he's getting some extra sleep." They were all exhausted.

Miss Gumble told them they were taking a test and had to compose an essay on the spot, and she handed around a paper with a question at the top. Kat hoped she had enough energy to write something decent.

And then she read the question: *Compose a three-page essay on the Allegory of the Cave in Plato's* Republic, *and, using examples, relate the allegory to your own efforts to distinguish between reality and fantasy.*

Kat sat back in the chair. This question was far too close to her recent experiences. Was it coincidence? She looked up at Miss Gumble and was met with a hard stare.

"Miss Bateson, do you have a question?" Miss Gumble asked.

"Um," Kat said, "well, I guess that I'm surprised, because we read that section about Plato's cave a while back."

"And?"

"I just thought . . ."

"You thought I was going to test you on more recent reading. As in something you should have read last night." Miss Gumble seemed to be trying not to smile. "You all need to think about deeper meanings. Plato, of course, in Aristotle's voice, was addressing ideas about illusion. What might be real and what might not. That seems to me a worthy exercise. Now, please begin your essay with a précis." Miss Gumble picked up a book and buried her face behind its covers.

Kat and Peter exchanged a glance; the others were already writing. Kat set to work, and decided not to hold anything back.

In maths MacLarren changed focus entirely from what they had been working on for the past weeks.

"Something a bit different today," he said. He handed each of the children a stack of puzzles, of varying degrees of difficulty according to each student's abilities, and asked them to solve the puzzles during class.

The puzzles he'd given Kat were difficult mathematics equations that worked on permutations of numbers to letters. The question posed on each of the five puzzles was the same: *Given the variables, how many different solutions are possible?*

MacLarren stood over her with his hands clasped behind his back. "Yes, lassie? Are we having difficulty?"

"It's just that this looks like, well, it's a bit like . . ."

"A code?" he prompted, his voice unnaturally soft. He'd leaned over her so that none of the others could hear.

She nodded.

"Then best get to it, eh?"

She nodded again.

Kat finished in record time, and she approached the desk where MacLarren sat with his feet propped up, his head back against the chair, and his eyes closed. She coughed.

He opened one eye. "Let's see, lass." He reached out his hand.

He took her papers, glanced through them, and nodded. "Care to try the next step?" he asked.

Kat lifted her brows and smiled.

The next step was a translation exercise involving one of the puzzles. Kat was given a key and had to create the algorithm that would translate the numbers to letters.

She didn't move away from MacLarren's desk this time, but pulled a chair up and created the equation while he watched.

"Good," he said softly. "Very good." It was the first time he'd praised her skill. He raised his voice, the old MacLarren back in full force. "Now, lass, go work on those algebra problems you got wrong last week."

Kat smiled to herself as she returned to her desk. One small victory in the midst of confusion.

"They know," said Peter. "Gumble and MacLarren. That's the only explanation." Peter and Kat had lingered behind the others after lunch. "It's like Gumble knows we're trying to work out what this terrible dark magic is."

"And MacLarren has some idea there might be an encryption machine," said Kat. "Father suggested them to the Lady. Maybe they really work with him."

"With him? What, MacLarren and Gumble, spies?"

Kat chewed her lip. "Even if they aren't, they seem to be on our side."

"Wonder what they'd think if they heard those sounds," Peter said with a shudder.

"I wonder what they think of Lady Eleanor."

Peter grabbed Kat's elbow and gave her a look.

From behind her Kat heard, "You two. Don't you have another class?"

The Lady. Kat and Peter hustled to the classroom.

"How prone to doubt, how cautious are the wise!" Kat heard her father's voice in her head, repeating one of his maxims. He would then put one finger to his forehead, while pinning Kat with his stare. "Caution, my dear. Keep calm."

In history, Storm acted as if he was tipsy. He staggered from topic to topic, lecturing randomly, referencing everything from the Napoleonic Wars to the Russian Revolution. Kat stopped taking notes when she could no longer make sense of the line of discussion. Storm walked back and forth, faster and faster, sweating. He'd lost so much weight in only a few weeks, and he was pale, and even his hair had changed, now dark and sparse. He paced and wheeled and paced as the sweat dripped from him; at one moment when his back was turned, Isabelle, who had been sitting in the front, moved into a seat a row back, as if fearing that he might drip directly onto her.

"Disgusting," Isabelle muttered, wrinkling her nose.

"The artifacts!" Storm said abruptly. He stood still, his eyes darting from one corner to the other. "Where did it go, that chatelaine?" And he glared at Kat so fiercely, she shifted away from his glance.

Kat waited for more, but with a blink Storm looked confused, and then moved on to some obscure and random historical details.

Except that when his gaze had stopped on Kat, she'd remembered, a sudden sharp realization. She'd seen Storm in the hallway outside their rooms, and wasn't that just after she'd last seen her chatelaine?

Could Storm—a treasure hunter, according to Peter—have stolen her great-aunt's chatelaine?

When the children were dismissed from history, they had about two hours before dinner. Kat, Peter, and Rob made for the kitchen.

"Don't know where Hugo went," said Cook. "It may be that her Ladyship went off on one of her errands in the village and needed him to drive." As she said this, Cook's face went dark.

Peter asked for some rope, and Cook bustled out to one of the storerooms.

As the three of them left the kitchen, Peter said, "I think I'm tall enough to get down that cliff face and up again."

Kat hoped Peter was right.

He was.

Peter's long arms were just long enough so that he could lower himself over the edge of the cliff onto the ledge.

"Wow! What a cave." Peter's voice came up as a thin echo. "It would be a great hiding place."

"No time to look around," Kat called. "Get those things out so we can get back."

The hard part was hoisting the two machines up the cliff, but Cook had given them stout ropes.

Kat and Rob pulled the first box over the edge. It was polished oak with brass hinges and latches, and she had to open it. Inside was an encryption machine.

She could have run her fingers over the mechanism for hours, but there was no time. The wireless came up next, and then the sword, and then she and Rob had to lie on their stomachs to help Peter gain footing so he could climb back up.

They'd also brought a pair of backpacks, and were able to shove the encryption device and the wireless inside. Rob carried one backpack, and his sword, and Peter carried the other.

They bolted across the landscape, already shadowed with the approaching sunset.

"We're late," Peter panted. "And we've got to hide these before we can get in to dinner."

Rob stopped abruptly. "What's that? It's not Colin, is it?"

Kat and Peter drew up, Kat squinting against the shadows and the setting sun. Rooks circled high above them, calling, *Off, off, off!*

At the far end of the allée of trees someone—something?—was moving back and forth, directly in their path, and dancing like the devil.

"What *is* that?" Kat whispered.

"I think . . . " Rob began, his hand shading his eyes against the red strip of sunset. "No, it can't be."

"What?" Kat pressed. She wanted to run backward, away. Whatever it was, it was moving, agitated, like a puppet, shadowed black against the light.

"It looks like Jorry," Rob said.

"Jorry!" said Peter. "Jorry? After all this time? But what in the heck is he doing? Dancing?"

Kat moved forward, toward Jorry. The boys followed her. "I think he's exercising. But it's a weird form of exercising. Like he's a puppet. You know, like he's hanging from strings."

"Hey," Rob called out. "Jorry?"

Jorry froze, midleap, one foot still up. His head swiveled in their direction.

"You all right?" Peter called. "You're not sick anymore?" He dropped his voice so that only Rob and Kat could hear. "Something's not right. He is sick. And it's not spots or influenza."

They'd drawn within a few yards of Jorry, where they paused.

Jorry was definitely not all right. His eyes were blank, black holes. His face was a mask. His mouth formed an *O*. His right foot was still suspended in the air, as if he'd been frozen in place.

"Oh, my," said Kat.

"He's a ghost," said Rob.

Kat did not contradict him.

Without warning, Jorry turned and ran, fast, across the expanse of lawn toward the old keep, speeding away in the blink of an eye and disappearing into the shadows.

They couldn't chase after Jorry; they were already late.

The three made for the kitchen. Cook was not about, although some things were laid out for dinner, ready to be taken to the table. They stashed the backpacks with the wireless and encryption device in the pantry, in one of the low cupboards that held large flat baking pans, shoving the packs and the sword into the corner.

"Jorry couldn't be a ghost," Kat said, panting. "He just couldn't be." *That would mean he was dead,* Kat thought but couldn't say out loud.

"Whatever he was, he wasn't himself," said Rob.

They ran back to the main stairwell so that they could enter the dining hall in the usual way.

"We're ten minutes past time," Peter said, glancing at the great clock on the mantle. The eyes in the painting of the Lady Leonore glared at them as they passed.

As they came in, everyone went still. Dinner had begun. Silence settled over the room, broken only by the crackling of the fires.

The Lady rose from her chair. "This lateness is intolerable. This is a school, not a playground. Lessons must be learned. I believe a punishment is in order."

Kat's heart pounded in her ears.

"Marie?"

Marie appeared out of nowhere, standing before them.

"Take them upstairs," the Lady commanded. "Lock them in. No supper."

Rob groaned. Marie began to usher them out.

"And Marie?"

They stopped.

"Move one of the boys. Separate rooms tonight."

From where she stood, Kat could see the Lady's cold smile.

On the way up the stairs, with Marie leading the way, Rob whispered, "Colin still wasn't there. He wasn't in the dining hall."

Kat and Peter exchanged a glance. "I'm sure he's here somewhere, Rob," Kat said in a low voice. "He turned up the last time, remember?"

"Yeah, but—"

"Enough chattering," Marie called. "The Lady'll have my head if you go on scheming. You're lucky it's just supper."

At that moment, Kat didn't feel lucky.

39

Hand

WHEN THE NOISES come, the room grows so cold that Kat shivers even under all her blankets. If only she had her great-aunt's chatelaine. She lit a fire in her fireplace before climbing into bed, but it goes out with a *snuff* as the shadows begin to descend. The only light comes from the waxing moon.

She's pinned to the bed, her legs and arms useless dead weights, her right arm trapped outside her blanket. The smell of cold steel rubbing against cold steel fills her nostrils.

She has a hard time keeping the tears from filling her tightly closed eyes.

She imagines Rob, in a separate room, alone. And Amelie and Isabelle, oblivious. *Keep calm.*

Something scrapes along her cheek, something smooth and

sharp, so sharp she doesn't dare move for fear of slicing her cheek open, her eyes shut tight. And then it scrapes down her right arm to her hand, where it stops.

Her right hand makes an involuntary fist, and she can hear wheels turning and gears meshing, and she realizes with a shock that those noises come from her.

And then she hears an intake of breath, as if whatever is hovering over her has seen her hand and expressed surprise. She cannot open her eyes.

The monster hovers, and then cold steel presses on her right hand, and then with a hiss and growl the monster moves off and leaves Kat alone with her fear and her spinning mind.

Kat flexes her fingers without opening her eyes and hears it again. Feels the strength of her hand, an unnatural strength.

What is inside her hand that sounds so much like the monster itself? She opens her fist, and there it is yet again, the faintest sound of cogs and gears.

Is this something growing inside her, a disease? What has she become?

And then anger surges. This is Father's fault. If he hadn't gone, they never would have had to leave London, despite the Blitz. If he hadn't suggested Rookskill Castle, they would not be here. How can she protect her brother and sister from something that might eat them away from the inside? That may already be working inside her like a poison?

Is she, Kat, turning into a monster?

The tears stream down her face as she chokes back sobs. What should she—what *can* she—do? Her chatelaine . . . If only she hadn't lost her chatelaine.

"One must be prepared," Great-Aunt Margaret had said, "with appropriate countermeasures."

What countermeasures can I take now, without the chatelaine?

Sleep comes over her suddenly and without her will, like a drug.

40

Lost

TIM HAS NOT seen the lady saint in a long time, but he so wants to make a gift to her of his chatelaine that he ventures out at night, hoping to find her. He doesn't like the dark of night, but he's willing himself to search the castle for her even so. He's holding the chatelaine in his fist when he wanders into an empty room on a high floor and hears a noise.

Tick, tick, tick.

Tim shakes all over, for he thinks he knows that noise, that terrible clockwork noise, that nightmare noise he has heard only in the black of night. He does not link that noise with the saint but with a dreadful monster. After all, how could a saint make such an evil sound?

Tim goes rigid until his slow mind twists and he sees the

clock upon the mantle *tick, tick, tick*ing, something it has never done before in his long memory of Rookskill Castle.

He flees the room, running silent in the inky dark until he reaches his safe corner, until he can grab his polishing cloth and polish until his heart stops thumping in his chest.

A clock ticks on the mantle. Children sleep fitful, nightmarish.

A shiny silver chatelaine with a pen, scissors, and a thimble lies forgotten where it fell.

41

Porridge

KAT HEARD THE click of the lock and was awake at once. And she looked at her right hand.

It looked like a perfectly normal hand, and felt perfectly normal, and now in the daylight she heard no sounds. It was a normal hand, except... it was exceptionally strong. She crushed the bar of soap in the bath to powder.

It was her hand, but it was not.

She dressed, feeling alien to herself. She couldn't tell the others about this, not yet. Maybe it was happening to all of them, each one of them, bit by bit, that they were all becoming monsters. Maybe that's what had happened to Jorry. She couldn't frighten the others with this idea.

It was past time for breakfast. When Kat opened the door to her room she saw Rob slumped against the wall in the hallway.

"Rob!" She hurried to his side, kneeling. "Rob?"

He jumped. "Sleeping," he mumbled.

She sat beside him. "Bad night?"

He nodded, eyes closed. "Really bad."

"Me too." Worse than bad. She swallowed hard so she wouldn't cry.

Peter stepped out, or rather, stumbled out, rubbing his face as if to rub away the memory.

Rob said, "The others have gone down already. I waited for you."

"Let's go, then," said Peter, lending a hand to help up Kat and Rob. "I'm starved."

"Before we go down," said Kat, "I want to see if Jorry's in his room."

Rob sighed, but he and Peter waited while Kat knocked at Jorry's door.

By now, they should have been used to Marie appearing out of nowhere, but Kat still jumped at the sound of Marie's voice. "Here, what are you lot up to, now? It's past time to go down for breakfast."

Kat was so exhausted and hungry and startled, she spoke before she thought. "We need to see Jorry."

Rob tugged at Kat's sleeve. "Food," he hissed. "We'll starve if she locks us in again."

But Marie shook her head. "Too late. The boy's gone."

"What?" Kat stepped back out of sheer surprise.

"Doctor came yesterday, took him away."

"Are you sure?" After having seen Jorry she'd stopped thinking of him as ill, unless he was ill in the head.

Marie frowned. "Quite sure."

"But we saw him last night."

Marie scratched her head, an odd expression crossing her face. "I don't know. Funny, that. Sure it was yesterday. Sure it was the doctor. Funny."

Kat went to Marie and stood right up close. She'd never much liked Marie, but now she saw something about her. Kat asked, "What's funny?"

"Don't know," Marie said. "Can't remember." Now that Kat was close up, she could see that Marie's eyes were glazed and her pupils dilated. Kat's practical side kicked in again. There was definitely something wrong with Marie, and it was not natural.

"Okay," Kat said, trying to sound light. "No problem. We'll head downstairs."

"Yeah," Marie said. "You do that, won't you?" And she ran down the stairs ahead of them as if she had the devil on her heels.

As soon as she was out of earshot, Kat whispered to Rob and Peter, "She's been drugged. Or hypnotized."

Peter said, "That would explain her confusion, but what about Jorry?"

"And Colin?" Rob said. "What about him?"

Yes, Kat thought, *what about Colin?*

They'd reached the dining hall and the smells of the break-fast were overwhelming. Cook stood off to the side, preparing to serve. Rob almost ran to the table.

The Lady sat with the teachers at the head table. She rose as the three children entered and watched as they seated themselves. Cook approached the table with a platter of eggs and sausage.

"Stop," the Lady commanded.

Cook halted midstep.

"They can have something cold. I prepared porridge for them last night. You'll find it on the sideboard." She sat again. "This will teach them to be on time in the future. There are many lessons to be learned here in Rookskill Castle."

Cook grumbled, but she turned away and fetched the porridge.

It was sticky and tasteless, like gluey cardboard, but Kat was too hungry not to eat. Rob looked sick and Peter picked at it.

When the Lady suddenly left the dining hall clutching her chest and looking like she might be ill, Kat felt no pity.

"Evil," said Rob, heated. "She's evil. And Colin's still missing."

"The Lady, she was wearing the devil's sign," Isabelle said to Kat with a knowing look. *"Sur sa châtelaine."*

At the reminder, Kat felt the tears well in her eyes. She had to find her own chatelaine, but where to begin? If Storm had it, could she break into his room to search?

In English class, Miss Gumble brought in a small tray. When she lifted the towel, there was a fresh-baked and still warm loaf of bread underneath, and a slab of butter, and she placed the tray on a desk in front of Peter, Rob, and Kat. Kat had never been so appreciative of a teacher.

When Rob, Peter, and Kat had finished eating several slices, Gumble said, "Let's continue to discuss the real and the fantastic from yesterday, shall we? Let's begin with ideas from ancient civilizations. What do you know of how the ancients viewed the concept of magic?"

Kat knew now. She knew. There was magic in the world, and she'd been stupid enough or stubborn enough not to believe it until now. There might even be magic in her missing chatelaine, but she'd been a careless guardian.

In maths, Mr. MacLarren posted a large chart on the board. "This is a representation of the Rosetta stone," he said. "It contains a simultaneous translation of ancient and Demotic Egyptian hieroglyphs and ancient Greek, and so is a key to the interpretation of ancient Egyptian language."

MacLarren tacked another chart on the board. "And this is an encryption key used in one German code that was discovered last year in northern France. As math algorithms are used in the interpretation of codes"—and here MacLarren stared straight at Kat—"I've decided to let you all play with the hiero-glyphs and this encryption key, to make your own code today."

He turned away. "Oh, and I've got something here." He reached into his large pockets and pulled out five apples, laying one on each desk.

After morning classes, Kat, Peter, and Rob went straight to the kitchen. Cook bustled about.

"Here, you lot, go to the dining hall. I've prepared a special lunch, I have, since her Ladyship has gone off for the rest of the afternoon and you've been near starved to death."

"We need to fetch something we've left here," Kat said. She showed Cook the backpacks they'd stowed in the pantry. She didn't seem surprised to see them there.

"You might want to leave them be," said Cook, "in case."

Kat exchanged glances with Rob and Peter. "In case?"

"Your rooms may not be the safest," she said, without meeting Kat's eyes, "if you get my meaning. There's always some-thing prowling about."

Rob took his sword because, as he put it, "I won't spend another night without it." They left the backpacks right where they were. "They're not in my way," said Cook.

"I'm going looking for Colin," Rob said.

Kat nodded. *And I'm going looking for Great-Aunt Margaret's chatelaine.* At this moment, that chatelaine and its promise of magic offered Kat her only hope.

42

The Perfect Heart

THE LADY ELEANOR is gratified that the three children don't seem to like the porridge.

Porridge is something Eleanor remembers well. She ate
much at one time, when she was a girl—it was all they had. The
very smell of it conjures a vision of her father's fist, the pain of
a swelling bruise on her cheek, the prison of her helplessness.
Eleanor hates porridge even more than she hates her loveless
father and heartless first lord.

Now Eleanor's eye stops at Katherine. Katherine so reminds the Lady of her first lord's new wife, the young wife he
took after he drove Eleanor to the keep, the young wife who
became mother to his only child by blood. Eleanor knows from
seeing it last night that the girl has been given a hand, perfect,

mechanical. Could it have been a gift from the magister? It horrifies her that Katherine Bateson might be the magister's new pet, and her heart clutches.

And then she realizes—the magic she's felt, the magic she doesn't yet control, that magic is somehow linked to this girl. The pain in Eleanor's chest becomes unbearable.

The Lady places her hand on her chest, her fingers gripping the beaded fabric, and she sucks in air with a wrenching gasp. The teachers look up in confusion. The children, too, lift their eyes to her and stare, some eyeing her fearfully, some surprised. She stands, the gears in her legs whirring to life; had she been still made of flesh she is sure her legs would tremble.

"Excuse me," she says, and leaves the hall, fast but stately, her hand still clutching her chest. The hand, all steel and moving parts, that has the strength to rip her heart right out of her chest. The strength to rip out Katherine's heart if need be.

The Lady is still able to shed tears, and one strays now from her right eye. She brushes it away, angry. Angry that Katherine should remind her of the past. Angry that she should see in Katherine the form of something—of someone—she hates. Angry that Katherine may have received the gift of a perfect hand from the magister and may have access to any kind of magic.

Katherine—and all the children—will give up their souls. Eleanor will hold power over men like her heartless lord and her cruel father, even over, she thinks, the magister.

She smiles grimly at this thought as she clutches at her heart. The rooks follow, circling, as she guides the wheel of her motorcar, this time leaving Hugo behind.

"All?" the magister repeats. His hut is exceedingly warm.

"Yes," she says, seething with impatience. "All. And at once. I must be able to use the chatelaine as I see fit." *To control even you.*

"You must not take them too quickly," he says. "The magic—"

"Yes, yes. The magic will weaken." She dismisses his caution. She is tired of the power of others, including the magister, tired of being told to move slowly.

"Giving all will require a complete sacrifice." He does not face her; he is busy stoking his fire, an unnecessary gesture. When he turns and lifts his eyes they are birdlike, button-black. "You will no longer be human."

She doesn't like being human. It's far too emotional, too messy, unpredictable, uncontrollable. Being human means wanting things like love. She's been human for long enough. She clutches at her chest, and her words form a snarl. "You will take my heart as well?"

The magister grins; his teeth are sharpened to fine points,

like the spikes on a saw blade. "Yes, my Lady. I will have your heart. And I have for it the most magical replacement."

As he holds up the mechanical heart, the perfect shape of a heart even as it clicks and whirs with precision, gears and wheels turning on tiny pins, it beats with such a calm and steady clockwork regularity that Eleanor knows it will be glorious.

43

Sisters

STORM HAD DISMISSED the children long before class should have ended, collapsing in the chair at the front of the room and mumbling to himself while waving his hands about as if fending off a swarm of bees. He no longer looked anything like the Storm Kat had met only a few weeks earlier.

As she left the classroom she overheard him muttering about "finding all the artifacts," and he repeated one word again and again: *chatelaine*.

Kat was certain now that Storm had stolen her chatelaine. But how was she supposed to get it back? Was she brave enough to sneak in and search his room?

Kat dropped her books on the dresser and stood in the hallway in front of her door. Amelie and Isabelle, playing in Isabelle's room, squealed with laughter.

No one else even knew of the existence of Great-Aunt Margaret's chatelaine. Kat chewed her nails. Maybe it was time to enlist help. She started down the hall to Peter's room.

As Kat passed Isabelle's doorway, she glanced inside. And she was not prepared for what she saw there. Her cheeks went hot and shock gave way to anger mixed with extreme relief.

"What are you doing?"

Both girls stopped and turned. They were dressed up in some of Isabelle's fancy clothes. Smaller Amelie wore a long slim skirt that dragged on the floor, and her curls were pulled up in a messy bun.

And around her waist was a wide leather belt from which hung Kat's chatelaine.

Amelie grinned. "I'm pretending. See?" Amelie pointed at Kat and lowered her voice. "And you shall eat porridge for the rest of your life!" Isabelle rolled on the floor with laughter.

Kat took two fast steps across the room and grabbed Amelie by the wrist while she unfastened the belt with her other hand.

"Ow! Kat! That hurts!"

Kat snatched the chatelaine from the belt and clutched it tight, and only then did she let Amelie go. "You had no business taking this from my drawer!"

Tears rolled down Amelie's cheeks. "I didn't take it! It's Isabelle's."

Kat rounded on Isabelle. "Then you stole it."

Isabelle stood up straight and tall. "I did not. I found it this morning. It was lying on the floor outside one of the empty rooms. I did not know you had a chatelaine." She folded her arms across her chest and narrowed her eyes. "I did not know you carried such a . . ." And she paused before saying, with a dramatic flourish, "such an artifact."

Then Amelie took a big, gulping sob. Kat had grabbed Ame's bare arm with her right hand and squeezed hard, and Ame's arm was already turning black and blue. "Oh," said Kat, her breath a little puff. "Ame."

Kat's strange and transformed and monstrous right hand had hurt Amelie terribly. Kat reached for her sister, to stroke her hair.

Amelie howled. "Don't touch me! You're wicked and evil!" And she began to cry hard. "I want Mum. I want to go home."

Isabelle went to Ame and gently took her arm, examined it, and *tsk*ed. "It might be broken." She narrowed her eyes at Kat. "I do not know how you could break her arm."

Kat's knees went weak. "I'll take her to Cook for a poultice."

"No!" said Ame through her tears. "Don't touch me!"

"I shall take her," said Isabelle, and, holding Amelie gently around the waist, pushed past Kat and out of the room.

Kat sat on the floor of her room. She played with the chatelaine, working it around and around in her fingers. The fingers of her right hand, a hand she hated, moved with precision.

If her great-aunt's chatelaine, recovered at such great cost, had magical properties, she couldn't tell at this moment.

And how had it come to be on the floor down the hall? Had Storm dropped it there? He was certainly confused enough.

She held it on her open palm. An heirloom. *Quite magical. Keep you safe.* The chatelaine hadn't kept Amelie safe from Kat and her terrible right hand. What kind of magic did she possess with that hand? Was it good? Or was it something evil and dark?

Could an heirloom—an artifact—that Kat now believed was "magical" be made evil, just by Kat's actions?

Peter knocked on the door, and Kat jammed the chatelaine into her pocket. He said, "I ran into Isabelle and Amelie. Isabelle told me what happened." He paused. He wasn't judging Kat, at least. "Ame's wrist isn't broken, and Cook bandaged it up. She'll be okay."

"Is Ame still angry?"

He shrugged. "She's scared. Said you were so strong. Like your hand was made of iron or something like that." He stared at the floor.

Kat slumped a little. "I didn't mean to hurt her. I was . . . upset." She was relieved to have the chatelaine back, but still . . .

Torn, scattered, her mind was all in pieces, her heart aching.

"Yeah." Peter ran his hand over his hair, pushing it off his forehead. "Well. I think you're right. We're being made crazy by the stuff in the castle. Whether it's ghosts or magic or spies or whatever it is. Anyway, I came to ask. MacLarren's down in the library off the main hall, alone. What do you think? Time to share what we know with the two teachers we think we can trust?"

Kat and Peter found MacLarren hunched in one of the huge leather chairs next to the fire.

MacLarren lifted his eyes over the top of the book in his hands. "Yes?"

"Well, sir," Peter began, "we've discovered some things here in Rookskill Castle that seem a little . . . off."

"Off?"

"Yes, sir." Peter cleared his throat. Kat stirred, impatient.

MacLarren put the book aside and folded his fingers over his stomach. "Can you be more specific, Williams, lad?"

"Well, it's just that, um, we think . . ."

Kat blurted, "We believe there's a spy in residence. A German spy."

His face darkened. "Do you now?" he said softly.

Kat's heart pounded.

Then MacLarren seemed to retreat, and he began to talk

to himself. "Just as he feared. Involving the children, too. In which case, it's double the difficulty here." He rubbed his chin, looked between Kat and Peter with bright eyes, and lifted his voice. "And what's your evidence?"

Kat and Peter exchanged a glance, and they went for it.

Taking turns, they told him the entire spy story: the hidden room with the wireless, someone sneaking around in a black overcoat, Rob's discovery in the caves.

MacLarren's eyes grew brighter still and he leaned forward as Kat described the code machine.

"As suspected," he muttered, standing and pacing the room, his hands clasped behind his back. "Jack was right. Must report he sent good information. And the details. Well, well. We'll find them now."

His reaction made Kat feel instantly better. They could trust MacLarren. And it sounded like he wasn't entirely surprised, maybe even expected it.

He looked at Kat and Peter. "I'd like to bring Miss Gumble in on this, if you don't mind," MacLarren said. "She's gifted with languages and might be a help. And good work, you two. I could tell you were clever bairns."

Kat sensed Peter stood a little straighter. She did, too.

MacLarren looked around the library. He lowered his voice. "We'd best not meet here, or in any of the public rooms, for that matter. I think your headmistress doesn't like your wandering about untethered, eh?" He grinned. "You know a private place we could have a look at your findings?"

Kat and Peter exchanged another glance. Kat said, "What about the secret room on the landing, now that it's empty?"

MacLarren rubbed his chin. "The secret room, eh?"

"It must have served as a linen closet at one time," Kat said. "Now there's a table and wiring. And it's very hidden."

"Just the ticket," he said. "Tell me how to find it."

Kat and Peter went off for the backpacks while MacLarren went to fetch Miss Gumble. The children had to evade Marie by hiding behind a column, but there was no sign of the Lady.

"What do you suppose he meant, double the difficulty?" Kat asked as they waited on the landing. She shifted the pack on her shoulders. She carried the encryption device, and it weighed a ton.

"What?" Peter said. He'd been bent over, tugging on his chain, opening the hidden door.

"MacLarren. When we told him about the spying he said, 'In which case, it's double the difficulty here.'" She'd dropped her voice to sound like their teacher.

Peter stared at her. "You have a memory like that, do you?" He shook his head. "I had a friend back home with a photo-graphic memory. It was uncanny what he could recall. He told me there are people who have memories like that but for the things they hear. You have that, don't you?"

Kat blushed. She shrugged best she could under the weight of the pack.

Peter said, "I don't know what MacLarren could have meant. Except it sounded like he wasn't really surprised about the spying."

Kat said, "And I wonder who Jack is."

"Who?"

"He said, 'Jack was right.'"

Peter nodded. "Jack might be a code name."

Kat turned that idea over. "A code name." She shuddered. A code name for a spy, like her father. If Father had been captured, why, he might already be dead. She'd been angry at him last night. Now the anger was gone, replaced by longing and worry and fear and anger at herself. He was doing what must be done. Kat swallowed hard as her throat and eyes burned.

"It seems to me," Peter went on, oblivious, "MacLarren is already pretty well informed."

Kat swallowed again. "That's true," she said. "I wonder if we should have mentioned the ghostly things. The magic." Her right hand—her transformed hand, her terrible hand—went into her pocket and found her great-aunt's chatelaine. She pulled it out, lifting it up between them.

"What's that?" Peter asked.

"It's a chatelaine my great-aunt gave me. She said it was magic."

"A chatelaine? Like the thing Storm has been going on about? Is that what you and Ame fought over?"

She nodded, miserable.

Peter reached for it, but before he touched it they heard a noise. Someone was coming up the stairs, and Kat and Peter were in the open on the landing. They exchanged a glance; Peter's eyes grew round and he put his finger to his lips.

"How do we know it's them and not *her*?" Kat whispered.

"We don't."

Up, up, up came the footsteps.

"We should've arranged a signal," Peter whispered.

The footsteps were two turns below them now, and still coming.

They had no choice: they slipped into the hidden room and shut the door as quiet as could be. They couldn't be caught out, especially not with the code machine and wireless in their possession.

Kat still clutched her chatelaine in her fist. From between her fingers she saw it: a blue glow.

44

Spies

IT WAS VERY dark inside the hidden room under the stairwell with the door closed. Kat opened her fist, and the chatelaine shone with a soft blue light. Kat's eyes met Peter's as his grew round.

Was this magic?

Scuffling noises filtered through the wall from the landing. Kat pressed her ear up against the thin crack that outlined the door. Someone coughed outside on the landing, and then they heard the gruff voice: "Lassie?"

Relief surged through Kat, and as she stuffed her chatelaine back into her pocket, Peter opened the door to reveal a startled MacLarren and Gumble, who were looking almost everywhere but at them.

"That is a hidden room, for certain," said Gumble, tucking stray strands of gray hair back into her bun. She ran her fingers over the door frame, as if measuring the wall. "Quite nicely done."

Peter fumbled for the overhead light chain and the four of them shut themselves inside the small room. Kat and Peter emptied their packs, placing the wireless and code machine side by side. MacLarren murmured in appreciation as he examined the code machine.

"'Tis a remarkable device, is it not?" he asked. "What do ye think, Beatrice?"

"I don't see how we can use it. We must have the key."

"Ah," he said, "but we do. Thanks to Jack, before he was picked up. This came today." He pulled a thin sheet of paper from his pocket.

"That Jack," said Gumble. "He is a credit to our nation. Pray that he returns to us safely." She glanced quickly at Kat and then away.

"We can make sure of that now we have this machine," MacLarren replied. "I think we can fool them on the other side into thinking—"

"Angus," Miss Gumble said, her voice a warning. "I suppose the children ought not hear every detail."

Kat spent half a minute thinking about her instructors' first names and their familiarity with each other, and another half a minute thinking about the suggestion that they knew something about spying. And then she focused on the key.

Kat asked, "You have the key? Isn't that all we need?"

"'Tis a start," MacLarren said. "Now we must crack the code, by finding the correct solutions." He raised his eyebrow at Kat.

"May I see?" Kat asked, reaching out her hand.

MacLarren grinned and handed her the paper. "I was hoping you would want to tackle it, lass."

Kat examined the key. It was a complex algorithm.

"So we can send a message, then. Falsify something," murmured Gumble, tapping her lip with one finger. "That might help Jack as well as our side."

"The double agent strategy, perhaps?" said MacLarren.

"Yes. Good one. And the short-wave, too, we can use that."

"Aye. But the first thing is to discover this object they seek. If Godfrey is correct, it may be a powerful weapon, this artifact . . ."

"Careful, Angus," Gumble interrupted, eyeing Kat and Peter.

But Kat started. *Artifact? Weapon?* What did Gumble and MacLarren know?

"We're not going to say anything," said Peter, who seemed not to have heard. "We're patriots. I mean, I'm American, but us Americans, we're on your side. Even if we're not in the war, but, still."

"'We' Americans, Mr. Williams, not 'us' Americans," said Gumble.

"Yes, ma'am."

For a moment Kat thought about mentioning magic and artifacts, and felt the weight of her chatelaine in her pocket, but something held her back.

Gumble said, "In any case, we must get this information and these pieces of equipment to Godfrey, and then hope they can fill in the blanks for us."

MacLarren said, "I'd like to spend a few days with the encryption machine before we send it on, since we have the key and all. I'd like to give this girl a chance to crack the code. That all right with you, Beatrice?"

"Well," Gumble murmured, "I don't—"

"Lass," MacLarren said, interrupting Kat's thoughts, "what do you think, eh? Think you might be able to break it?"

Kat glanced from the algorithm to MacLarren's face and back again. "Yes," she said. "Yes, I think I can."

Peter and Kat hid the machines back in the kitchen right before supper. They didn't dare leave them in the room on the landing, fearing the spy would return there to look when he found them missing from the cave. It was raining hard now, coming down in sheets against the great windows. As Peter and Kat went back up to their rooms, Kat's earlier misery crept through her again. She flexed the fingers of her terrible right hand.

She found Amelie in Isabelle's room. Both girls stiffened and looked away when Kat stood at the door.

"Ame, I'm so sorry."

Amelie's arm was wrapped in a tight bandage. She didn't look at Kat as she lifted her shoulders in a shrug.

"I didn't mean . . . " Kat said. "I was upset."

Amelie lifted her face. Her eyes were red from crying. "You hurt me."

"I know. I'm really, really sorry."

There was a long silence, and then Ame rose from the floor and flew across the room and into Kat's arms. Her words were muffled because her face was buried against Kat's stomach. "I love you, Kat."

Kat stroked Ame's hair, unable to speak. She hugged her sister tight.

Isabelle stood up and said, "Well. Apology accepted."

Colin's empty place at the dinner table next to Jorry's was like a dark omen.

It was Peter who ventured at last, raising his hand as Marie brought in the dessert, a berry compote. "My Lady, where's Colin?"

Lady Eleanor peered at him as if she could not see him well. "Who?" she asked.

Both MacLarren and Gumble turned to look at her; Storm stared at his plate, muttering darkly.

"Colin," Peter repeated, louder, and he pointed to Colin's empty chair.

"Ah," she replied. "He has decided to return home."

"No he hasn't," said Rob loudly. "We were having a fine time. He would have said something."

The Lady stood. With a start, Kat realized that she leaned as if her hip was out of joint.

She gave Rob a long, cold stare. "Colin has left. Now you will excuse me," the Lady said, and she limped down the hall and out the door.

"He hasn't left," Rob repeated. "He would have said."

No one ate the dessert.

Kat, Peter, Rob, Amelie, and Isabelle sat on the hallway floor.

"One by one," Peter said, echoing Kat's thoughts. "Something's happening to each of us, one at a time."

"Colin wouldn't leave like that," said Rob. "Not without saying good-bye."

"The Lady has to be in on it," said Kat.

"Perhaps Colin is a ghost now, too," murmured Amelie. "Like the fishing girl, and the crippled boy."

Kat shivered. "Cook said something about someone hiding

in the barn. We can't go there now, but maybe in the morning."

"And the keep," said Rob. "There's lots of places to hide there."

"We haven't really looked through the entire castle," said Peter. "I say we work our way through everything."

Kat stood up and brushed her skirt. "We're in for the night, so it'll have to wait." She sighed, biting her lip. "Well, I'm going to play with math."

"Play with math?" Rob snorted. "Good one, Kat. I'll be worrying about Colin, myself."

"So will I, Rob," Kat said, touching his arm. "So will I."

For the next several hours, Kat sat on her bed and worked on the algorithm. She created several tables and found one string that seemed to work, but ultimately she had to abandon it. Still, she felt she was closing in on the solution when she looked up and realized that it was nearly midnight.

Kat put her papers aside and crawled beneath the covers. Her great-aunt's chatelaine was clutched in her fist. A glowing fire burned in the hearth.

As she lay in her bed, she thought about poor Colin. Such a sweet boy. Whatever was happening to the children of Rookskill Castle, it was now circling closer and closer to Kat and her brother and sister. Maybe instead of searching the castle grounds she and the remaining children should run away.

But that was hopeless. They were stranded in the bitter and desolate Scottish highlands.

She drifted toward exhausted sleep, and without prompting her father's voice echoed in her head. *Keep calm.*

And carry on.

Yes, that's what she had to do, despite the fear, the cold, dark magic, the spies, and despite her terrible self-doubt: carry on.

45

The Eighth Charm: The Bell

THE LADY STANDS in the dark, frigid room, surveying. The clock has stopped; the fire is cold ash.

The Lady taps her metal finger against her lips. Raw energy courses through her. She likes it, the strength of the body the magister has made for her, now that it is complete, and she stretches her arm over Isabelle and Amelie, who lie breathing deeply side by side. The gears in her arm whir and sing and she flexes her clockwork hand and smiles.

She leans over Isabelle.

"Belle. *Belle* means *beautiful.* Like you are, *ma petite belle.*"

Isabelle's eyes flutter open.

"Hello, Isabelle," she says, so soft it is like rose petals falling on the coverlet. "May I call you Belle?"

The girl nods, eyes open in wonder. Perhaps she thinks she sees an angel. Amelie sleeps on.

"I have something for you. Something that is a token of your name. Something that will echo your beauty." The Lady holds up a silver charm on a silver chain. "You see? It's a bell. A bell for Belle."

Isabelle's eyes grow wide.

The Lady leans close. "But shh. You mustn't tell her. You must not tell a soul. It's our secret, yes, *ma Belle*?"

Isabelle's hand lifts off the coverlet, reaching for the charm.

"Oh, no," whispers the Lady. "Let me put it about your neck myself."

Something crosses Isabelle's face then, some note of alarm, and she withdraws her hand as if remembering something, something to do with charms and necklaces and children, and it is not nice, not nice at all . . .

The Lady watches this mental transformation, and she moves swiftly. As Isabelle opens her mouth to scream she also sits bolt upright, and the charm is over her neck and the cursed words spoken, and Isabelle gives a cry and then is lost, and she sinks back into the bed while Amelie whimpers in her sleep and turns away.

The Lady lifts Isabelle from the bed and seeks the hidden door in the wall. Oh, how strong and beautiful her arms are now, so that she can carry this child, Isabelle, as if she weighs no more than a feather! Soon she'll discover the other magic in the castle that has something to do with Katherine, but still eludes Eleanor. Eludes her for now.

The Lady leaves Amelie behind. But not for long.

46

Spies and Magic

"AMELIE, WHAT DO you mean, she's gone?" Kat thought she might be sick.

Amelie's eyes were bright with tears. "When I woke up. Isabelle's gone and I can't find her."

"Like Colin," Rob said.

The four of them stood grim-faced in the hallway in the dim morning light. It was snowing, and the wind rattled the panes.

"Right," said Peter. "That's it, then. We've got to get out of here. I say we head for the train station at once."

Kat nodded, grateful. But then, "But what about the spy? I've almost cracked the code."

"The spy's the least of our worries," said Peter. "How does

a girl like Isabelle disappear from a locked room in the middle of the night when Amelie is right there with her? First Jorry, then Colin, and now Isabelle. And we've seen what happened to Jorry."

"Downstairs, now," said Marie. Once again she appeared out of nowhere. "Breakfast." She folded her arms and waited until they began to move.

Peter whispered to Kat, "We're getting out of here."

Kat nodded, but she chewed her lip. She wanted to finish the algorithm. She wanted to catch the spy. For her country. Father would want her to make a difference, just as he was trying to make a difference.

If the children weren't uneasy enough, breakfast made them even queasier.

Neither Mr. MacLarren nor Miss Gumble was present.

The Lady wore a gown utterly inappropriate for daytime that made it look like she'd stepped from a medieval tapestry.

Mr. Storm, too, was changed, but not in his manner of dress. He was skinnier and darker-haired than ever, with caved-in cheeks and pallid skin.

They ate in silence. Kat kept stealing looks at Mr. Storm. One moment she could see the old Mr. Storm, and then he'd turn his head or take a bite, and it was as if he'd been replaced by someone entirely different.

And the Lady was dressed to the nines in that odd gown

and wearing a great, gem-studded belt that held her sporran.

The places where the others had sat—Colin and Isabelle and Jorry—hadn't been set. After a few minutes, that was enough for Kat to lay aside her fork and say without permission, "My Lady, what happened to Isabelle?"

"Isabelle?" The Lady's voice sounded like metal grinding on metal, and Kat flinched.

"Yes, my Lady. She wasn't in her room when we woke up."

"Yes, I know." The Lady heaved a melodramatic sigh. "The doctor took her away. Fortunately, it seems that she and Jorry will now be fine. They are in good hands."

"So she was taken ill? In the middle of the night?"

The Lady sighed again, with more impatience. "We caught her out sleepwalking, with a raging fever. Marie must have forgotten their lock."

Ame murmured something Kat couldn't hear.

Kat pressed on. "If that's so, then what about the rest of us? Shouldn't we see the doctor? Be checked for whatever it is?"

Mr. Storm sat up, suddenly interested. "The doctor? There's a doctor about?"

"My dear Mr. Storm," said the Lady, "you needn't concern yourself."

"But I do," he mumbled. "I should like to have a word with a doctor. I'm not feeling myself lately."

"Is it contagious?" Kat asked.

"What?" The Lady peered at her with sharp eyes.

"Is whatever they have—Jorry and Isabelle—is it contagious?"

"Not any longer," she said. "They've been taken off."

"And where are Mr. MacLarren and Miss Gumble?"

"They are indisposed. Perhaps a touch of this illness." She smiled, a stiff smile that showed too many teeth. "You must stop worrying, Katherine. I can see that you are a born worrier. That's why your parents wanted you out of London, I'm sure of it. I imagine all those bombs were making you quite anxious." She narrowed her eyes. "Speaking of parents, I'm terribly sorry about your father. Perhaps by some miracle, he'll survive."

Kat's blood turned icy.

"I'm afraid the Nazis will not treat him kindly."

"Nazis?" said Storm, rising out of his chair. "Where? I must speak with—"

The Lady put her hand on Mr. Storm's arm. "I'm sure you have some lessons for the children today, don't you, Mr. Storm? You will take the morning classes, since our other instructors are absent."

Yes, where were MacLarren and Gumble?

Mr. Storm looked confused, but then said, "Why, yes. Good idea. Lessons. Hunting lessons. Maybe we should all go hunting. Hunting is an English sport, is it not? We could hunt Englishmen." He began to laugh, that dreadful laugh that Kat found so unnerving. And then, abruptly, he stopped.

Silence filled the hall. Then Peter said, "Excuse me? Did you say—"

The Lady leaned over, interrupting Peter. "I think you meant they should all hunt English history. In the classroom."

"Oh. Yes. History. Classroom. Yes." Then he said something else, even more cryptic: "But what about my mission?"

"Mission?" the Lady said through her teeth.

"Yes. Mission. Artifacts. Scope out. Search for. Send back . . ." He sat up, abruptly looking very Mr. Storm-like. "I had one, for a time." He glared at Kat. "I'll get it back. Meanwhile, I must get to my short-wave."

"His short-wave!" said Rob with a hiss. Peter, Kat, and Rob exchanged a look.

"The children need their lessons, Mr. Storm." The Lady raised her voice. "Time for you to help these children forget their troubles."

"Time for me to report in," Storm said, looking even more like himself.

But only for an instant. He was shifting back and forth between his former self and his more recent self. Kat thought she was dreaming until she heard Peter whisper, "Do you see that?"

"I see it," said Rob loudly. "I see this is all unnatural and . . . and . . . un-English."

"Mr. Storm," the Lady repeated. "It's time for lessons." Her voice pricked the air like a thousand needles. The Lady's hand tightened on Storm's arm until her knuckles stood up, sharp, her eyes fixed on Kat.

Mr. Storm shook his head, once again not looking himself. "Lessons. Yes."

Kat sat still as the others trailed out. Ame was last, pausing before Kat. Ame said, "Father's in danger, isn't he?"

"Yes, I'm afraid so."

"But he'll be all right. Won't he, Kat?"

Kat hugged her sister hard. "I'm sure he will," she said, like a prayer, over Amelie's shoulder.

Kat remained behind alone, staring into space. There was no helping her brother and sister and the other children if she couldn't keep calm.

Mr. Storm wasn't any more Welsh than the rest of them. Mr. Storm was a bloody German spy. The Lady was harboring him, even if she was making a bodge job of it. And he was ridiculous if he was a spy; why, there was no way the Nazis would win this war with spies like Storm. That was Kat's only comfort.

She waited a long time before leaving the dining hall. Then she went into the kitchen to find Cook. Maybe Cook would know where MacLarren and Gumble had gone.

Cook was not there. The food was there, the kitchen had been used, but there was no sign of Cook.

Kat and Peter whispered to each other as Storm prepared his lesson.

With this confession of Storm's, Peter agreed they should stay in the castle long enough to find the other teachers or Cook or Hugo—some adult who could turn Storm in to the authorities.

"Besides," Kat said, "we can't just abandon Isabelle and Jorry and Colin. We need to find out where they are and what's happening to them."

Peter nodded. "You're right. But I have to admit I'm scared."

So am I, Kat thought.

During the entire rambling history lesson—which seemed to drag on and go nowhere—Kat worked on the algorithm. Storm certainly wouldn't have noticed her not paying attention, even if he wasn't out of his mind.

The others couldn't take their eyes off of Storm, and occasionally Kat, too, watched him, fascinated. It was like watching water: he shifted and changed with each step he took, from light hair to dark, from heavyset to thin, from a bulldozer build to hunched shoulders, morphing in and out and back again. She shook her head and went back to work.

And suddenly, the solution. Brilliant, simple, clear. Kat let out an involuntary shout. Everyone turned in her direction.

"Miss Bateson?" Storm asked, and licked his lips. "You, ah, have something . . ."

"No, sir, sorry, sir." She covered the math with a blank sheet of paper.

He strode to her desk, looking more like the old Storm, and without hesitation plucked the papers off her desk before she could react.

He stared at the algorithm for a long time, flickering back and forth between old Storm and new Storm. Kat's heart pounded in her ears. What if he deciphered what she was doing? "There's something familiar . . ." he began. "I've seen this . . ."

"It's just a math problem I've been working out," Kat said, keeping her voice steady. "Homework." What if he should take it away?

He began to walk back toward his desk, and it was all she could do not to rip the pages out of his hand.

"I think . . ." He shook his head, and then he was the new Storm, thin, dark, and bent. "Keep your math work to math class, Miss Bateson," he said, and he turned and dropped the papers back onto her desk.

Kat released her breath.

Directly after the class was done, Kat said to Peter, "Stay with the other two, won't you? I've got to try to find MacLarren. I've got the solution. We can use the encryption machine."

Peter nodded, giving her a quick smile.

"Promise me you won't leave them alone," Kat said. "Ame and Rob."

"Cross my heart."

Kat raced to the library. MacLarren wasn't there.

She snuck through the halls to the hidden room in the stairwell, but he wasn't there, either.

Nor was he in the small parlor on the first floor, nor in the dining hall.

She even ventured to stand behind a column and peer as far down the second-story hallway as she dared, fearing the Lady, or worse, and having no idea which rooms belonged to Gumble and MacLarren. Kat's only hope was to find Cook and ask for her guidance.

Kat went back to the ground floor, tiptoeing from dark corner to dark corner. She was in one of the narrow passages leading to the kitchen when she heard muffled voices.

She slipped into the shadows and waited, listening.

It wasn't the Lady; it wasn't Storm. It sounded like Miss Gumble and someone whose voice came from a distance.

Kat edged down the darkened passage toward the voices.

"Drat." It was Gumble. "Let me try this one, an oldie but a goodie. *Open sesame.*" Silence. "No good. How about, *The art of healing starts with an open mind.*"

Kat heard mumbling from somewhere. Was it MacLarren? What in the world was Gumble doing?

"Wait," said Gumble. "Something from Miss Emily Dickinson. *Not knowing when the dawn will come I open every door.*"

Kat heard a *snap*, and then, "Well, finally!" It was MacLar-ren. "I thought ye'd never get me out of there."

"Whatever is going on here, the work is of the highest level," said Gumble. "Extraordinary. I've never seen anything quite like it."

"I wouldn't have believed it meself, if it hadn't happened to me," said MacLarren.

"What did happen to you?" asked Kat as she stepped from the shadows.

"Good Lord, lassie! I nearly jumped out of my skin!"

Gumble and MacLarren stared at Kat as if they would bore holes right through her.

"Just how much did you hear, Miss Bateson?" Gumble asked.

"Enough to know what it sounded like," she answered.

"Which is?" Gumble asked.

"It sounded like . . ." Kat hesitated. Then she took a deep breath. "Well, to be honest, it sounded like Mr. MacLarren was locked in that closet, and you had to use a spell to get him out. It sounded like you were using magic."

They were part of a team recruited by MI6 to explore some of the less ordinary ways to defeat the Nazis.

MacLarren was an expert in puzzles, patterns, encoding, and encryption. Gumble was practiced in the occult. MacLarren, searching the castle for evidence, had been locked inside with a locking spell, and Gumble had to find the right disenchantment. Gumble was also an expert in what she described as "paranormal activities. Things like psychic abilities. Telling the future. And magic."

Kat rubbed her forehead hard.

"Between the two of us," Gumble said, "we've studied the kinds of things the Nazis might use that are out of the norm. Things like artifacts that may or may not have powerful properties."

Kat said, "Did you say artifacts?"

"I know it's a lot to take in," Gumble said. "I'm sorry we didn't tell you sooner, but I'm sure you can understand why."

"Our superiors thought that Rookskill Castle would be the perfect place for a base of operations," said MacLarren. "Your father proposed it, since he had the connection. And rumors have begun to swirl that Rookskill Castle is home to magic. That's where we come in, Miss Gumble and I."

"We were to discover whether the rumors were true," said Gumble. "And if they were, we were to prevent any of this magic from falling into the wrong hands."

"We all think Storm is a spy," Kat said.

"We know," said Gumble.

"And he was going on and on about artifacts that had magical properties." Kat's hand closed around the chatelaine in her pocket.

"Was he, now?" said MacLarren, exchanging a look with Gumble.

"But why did Father send us here?" Kat asked. "He sent us right into the thick of things. Terrible things."

"Ach, but he didn't know that, lass. None of us knew just how powerful a magic it was about this castle. We're in a wee bit over our heads, I'm afraid. We're not at all sure how it works yet."

Gumble murmured, "I sense a spell of confusion about the place. Like a fog."

"Aye," said MacLarren. "And don't be too hard on your father, lass. He was supposed to be here, too. Thought he could protect you, right here."

"Father? Here?" Kat swallowed hard. "But he didn't protect us. Jorry, Colin, and Isabelle have all disappeared, although we saw Jorry and he was, he was . . ."

"Ill?" Gumble asked.

"Like he was enchanted. But he ran off and we haven't seen him since," Kat said. "And there's something wrong with Lady Eleanor." She didn't say *evil* out loud.

Gumble peered at Kat. "The Lady does seem odd, does she not? There is something about her . . . but it's confusing."

MacLarren stared off into space before he murmured, "A bit like seeing someone through smoky glass."

"As I said," Gumble finished, "a spell of confusion. At the very least."

Kat pursed her lips. The only confusion she and the other children experienced had to do with the shifty castle itself. Maybe the adults were more susceptible to certain spells.

"So we've got two problems, eh?" said MacLarren, interrupting Kat's thoughts. "There's confusing and perhaps dangerous magic, and there's Storm the spy. Though he's not much of a spy, if you ask me."

"I almost forgot why I was looking for you," Kat said. "I've solved the algorithm."

MacLarren rubbed his hands together. "Why didn't you say so? Good lass. Well done. Let's get that encryption machine, shall we?"

Kat and MacLarren fetched the encryption machine while Gumble went to find the other children. They met in the hidden room on the stairs.

Kat spread the paper with her solution out on the desk while MacLarren set up the device. Everyone gathered around and watched. A copy was generated as MacLarren typed. It looked like gibberish, but Kat knew it was not. The cogs and wheels turned as the letters and numbers rotated into position.

"Complicated," whispered Peter.

"It looks like magic," said Amelie. Miss Gumble patted her head.

"What message are you sending?" Kat asked.

"I've told them that Jack is a double agent and must be released so that he can complete the mission."

"What mission?" asked Rob.

"Ah," said MacLarren, leaning back with a gleam in his eye. "That's a mystery we have yet to solve. But this is the first step."

Lunch was cold leftovers laid out on the sideboard. Neither Storm nor the Lady was there. The children and MacLarren and Gumble ate quickly, and after, MacLarren and Gumble told the children that they should go to their rooms and stay put.

"We must go to work," said Gumble, and she placed her finger alongside her nose, a gesture so much like Great-Aunt Margaret's that Kat was startled. "Mr. MacLarren and I will not be here the rest of today, so you should stay safe on your corridor. For heaven's sake, don't go accusing Storm of being a spy."

"And try to avoid Lady Eleanor," said MacLarren. "Something's up there, but we've yet to sort it out."

Kat nodded. She wanted nothing to do with the Lady.

When they reached their corridor, the four children agreed not to close the doors to their rooms. Ame wanted to be in Isabelle's room, "in case Issy shows up." It was a faint hope.

47

Dreaming

KAT'S ROOM IS so cold. She can see her breath. It floats above her head as she lies on the bed.

Lies on the bed?

She sits up so fast, her head spins. A dull gray late-afternoon light washes the room. The clock on the mantle is stopped, the big hand at half past, the small hand past the one.

Is she dreaming?

A rook lands on the sill outside her window. One beady eye regards her through the glass. Then it caws, three times, *Lost, lost, lost,* bouncing on its spindle legs before it flies away.

Kat goes to the window and sees them crossing the snow-covered grass. Amelie and Isabelle hand in hand, wearing no coats, walking away from the castle and toward the sea. And with them, holding Ame's other hand, is the little fishing girl.

A stabbing fear slices through Kat's heart. She is not dreaming.

48

The Ninth Charm: The Pearl

THE LADY STANDS before Amelie's prone figure, dangling the chain. It has become such an easy thing, this. Taking the children one at a time.

Ah, but now: the pearl for Amelie. The child is too sweet for anything else. Sweet and sensitive. Eleanor recalls trying to spell this child a few weeks ago, when that dreadful Katherine interrupted her. She stares down at sleeping Amelie, whose golden curls tumble across the pillow. For an instant the Lady Eleanor remembers . . . something about love.

I'll charm a child to call my own.

"Child?" Eleanor says.

Amelie wakes, eyes open, and sits up, fearless and comprehending, and Eleanor drops the chain over her head.

"Witch," Amelie says, before she is rendered speechless by the charming.

The Lady shudders, an icy fear traveling through her mechanical body. This child is different. A portent? The magister's words return: *Take them oh so slowly, or the magic will weaken.*

When Eleanor finds and takes that other magic, there will be no weakness in her ever again. She pushes aside her fears as Amelie's soul enters her thirteenth charm, the ninth soul of the twelve that will make her collection.

And then the Lady sets in place the spells to frighten the remaining children. She will wear them out now, one by one.

49

Wolves

KAT SHOOK ALL over as if she stood in a freezing wind. She couldn't keep the tremor out of her voice. "I know Gumble and MacLarren said we shouldn't leave our rooms. But still."

"I've got my sword," Rob said. He and Peter had also fallen asleep, and their clock had stopped, too. Rob looked ready to burst, his cheeks were so flushed.

"We'll get her back," Kat said, making fists of both hands. "Don't you worry. We'll get all of them back." She wished she believed her own words.

Kat clutched her great-aunt's chatelaine. Peter carried a sword of his own. Wrapped in their warmest clothes, they set out after the girls.

Once outside, they ran. It had snowed only an inch, but it

was a wet snow and Kat's feet were numb within minutes. They saw no sign now of the girls, and they could find no tracks.

The chill wind cut right through their clothes. Gray clouds spat freezing mist, and even as she ran toward the sea Kat could see the whitecaps kicked up by the early winter wind. If she was this cold, those girls were in danger of freezing. She sped up, and the boys followed.

They reached the cliff edge, but still there was no sign, so they turned north along the cliffs, running toward the cave.

They stopped, panting, at the high promontory above the cave. Waves crashed below and the gulls keened above. Then Robbie pointed down to the stream that cut from the moors above to the sea.

"Look! There they are!"

Below them, all the way at the bottom of the cliffs, Kat could see the three girls entering dark Dunraven Wood.

"Well done, Rob. Let's go!" she called, and scrambled down the path toward the woods.

How the three small girls managed to be so far ahead and to get down without incident, Kat couldn't imagine. By the time she, Rob, and Peter reached the bottom, where Fairnie Burn flowed over rocks and gravel on its way into the sea, Kat was covered in scrapes and bruises. Her hair was disheveled and her shirt untucked, and her right stocking sported a large hole where she'd caught it on a thorn. If the skirt and blazer hadn't been woven of strong Scottish wool, they, too, would have been in shreds. All the way down she could hear Peter's and Rob's swords as they battered the cliff face.

They crossed the burn, splashing carelessly through the icy water, and made for the woods. At the edge, Rob stopped.

"I don't know, Kat," he said.

The wood was already shadowed, and small things skittered among the brush and dead leaves, crackling and snapping dried branches.

Kat steeled herself, then turned and plunged into the wood.

It was dreary, dank, and dark within. The trees, bare, stretched above her like so many bony fingers. The wind whispered at the tops, and cold dripped through the bare spots so that she was even more chilled than before. She stopped, wondering which way to go.

Rob brushed past her. "Well, if Stodgy Kat is going for it, so am I. Even if it seems we're chasing shadows." Then Rob shouted, "Look!" and began to run.

They pressed through the woods, the branches tugging at Kat's hair and jacket, snapping and popping as they broke through, and all of a sudden they came out of the wood and onto the highland waste.

The sun sat watery and low in the west, gray folds of clouds wreathing the late yellow glow. The moors, where they were not snow-covered, were shadowed with purple, rocks rounding skyward, and here and there an orange or yellow patch of late autumn color glowed in the lee. The rolling hills stretched to the ends of the earth.

Nothing moved on the landscape save the gorse and bracken that were stirred by the chill wind and three rooks that circled silently overhead.

Rob flanked Kat on one side, Peter on the other. After a moment Kat spoke, her voice broken. "They're gone. They've flat-out disappeared."

Rob let out a deep sigh.

Peter said, low, "If they were ever here."

"That's the problem," Rob said. "Even though we saw them, there were no footprints in the snow. I kept having the feeling we were being led on."

The three of them exchanged a glance.

"But where are they? Ame!" Kat called, desperate. "Isabelle!"

The first howl drifted on the bone-chilling wind.

The sun set so fast, Kat thought it was being pulled down to the horizon. A second howl, and a third, came with the lengthening shadows.

"Wolves are extinct here," Rob said, his voice a coarse whisper. "They haven't been here for decades. Killed off. I mean, there might be one or two, but . . ." Another, distinctly different, howl.

"I would bet," said Peter, "that these are no ordinary wolves. Just like those were not Amelie and Isabelle."

The hair on the back of Kat's neck prickled. More howls.

"We've got nothing but your swords," Kat said. "No matches, nothing."

One howl from the left, and then one from the right, quite close, and then a third from behind. Kat squinted. She saw movement in the long shadows made by the rocky outcrops. The boys pressed close.

"We need to be back to back," said Peter. "We might need to stand all night."

"Why don't we run?" said Kat.

"Because, Kat, if they are real, or even if they are magical wolves with real teeth," said Rob, patient but also quivering, "then they'll figure we're food and chase us down and kill us and eat us."

"And if they aren't real," said Peter, "nothing we do will matter."

Another pair of howls, terribly close.

"All right then," Kat said, "let's at least try to get back to the castle before it's really dark. Without running."

They had already formed a rough triangle facing outward. "That's not a bad idea," said Peter, who began to edge back the way they had come.

"Unless you like being in the woods when they attack," said Rob. "I'd rather take my chances out in the open, where I can swing my sword, thank you."

Several howls, too close. The boys stopped moving and

braced and raised their swords. Shadows, shifting back and forth, closed on them.

Her fingers were stiff with cold, so Kat jammed her hands into her pockets. And there she found her great-aunt's chatelaine.

A rook wheeled. *Out, out, out.*

She lifted her right hand, the chatelaine glowing a faint blue in her fist. She let it dangle from her fingers, and at once blue light shot from it as if from a brilliant lantern.

"Whoa!" shouted Rob. "What is that?"

"Is that the chatelaine thing?" yelled Peter.

Gumble had used spells and Great-Aunt Margaret had given out quotes, so without thinking why, Kat cried out, *"How could they see anything but the shadows if they were never allowed to move their heads?"*

Silence. The chatelaine pulsed with blue light. A thin band of yellow sat on the western horizon. The rooks wheeled away inland. The sea pounded and the gulls keened, but there were no more wolf calls.

"Plato," whispered Peter. "Good old Plato."

"That was Plato? From that cave story? The one Gumble had us writing about? I'm going to study harder from now on," said Rob. "Nicely done, Kat. You've got to tell me how you knew."

"Come on," said Kat, breathing hard. "We've got to get back before it's really dark and we can't find our way."

By the time they reached the castle it was dark. Their only guiding light was the chatelaine, which glowed stronger with the deepening shadows. Kat held it before them as a lantern. They heard no more wolves.

They went to the dining hall, but no dinner had been laid; the fires had never been lit and the luncheon had not been cleared. The three of them snatched up bits of food—dried-out bread, fruit, chunks of cheese—eating as they moved. They tried the kitchen: also dark. There was no sign of any adult—not Cook, nor Hugo, nor the teachers. And, thankfully, no sign of the Lady or Storm.

They made their way up to their rooms, and, after changing into dry clothes, gathered in Peter and Rob's room.

"I wish I knew where she was," Kat said, and winked away tears.

They sat in a half circle after building a fire in the fireplace, warming their hands and feet. The chatelaine sat on the floor in the middle.

"It wasn't Ame," Rob said. "It was a figment. A shadow." He paused. "Like in Plato's Cave. It wasn't her, but I just know she's all right. She's all right, and real, and warm. And with all the others."

"That's good, Rob," Kat said. Somehow hearing him say it made her feel better.

"If you don't mind staying here tonight," Peter said, "I think we should stick together."

Kat said, "I wouldn't be in my room alone tonight for anything."

The chatelaine now glowed faintly.

"So, Aunt Margaret gave it to you," said Rob. "And she told you it was magic. But you didn't believe her."

"Not at first. But I do now," Kat said. "It's all different now." She thought, but didn't say, *I've found my way out of Plato's Cave.*

50

Talisman

THE LADY FEELS irritated. She paces, gears grinding.

The wolves hadn't worked, so her rooks have told her. She had wanted to lure the three children out to the moors, make them fearful, separate them, make this last bit go easy. But the girl carries a talisman, something that sheds a brilliant light, though it's so bright the rooks cannot make out what it is.

She knows now that this is the magic she's been sensing. She can feel it, back in the castle, with the girl. It's powerful enough magic that Eleanor must proceed with caution, take the girl Katherine last and alone.

Eleanor smiles. That will be a pleasure.

51

Gregor, Lord Craig

THEY SLEPT FITFULLY, but there were no nightmares, no nighttime visitors, and the fire never died, since one of them was up at all hours to make certain it was fed.

When they woke it was already light. Marie was nowhere to be found. Kat changed into her own clothes—no need for uniforms—and splashed water on her face, and then the three ventured down through the dark, silent castle.

The dining room was just as it had been the night before, and there was still no sign of Cook, or anyone else. They picked at whatever remained of the food, cold and stale as it was.

"MacLarren and Gumble might be trapped again, caught by some spell," Kat said. "They wouldn't just leave us."

Peter and Rob still had their swords. The two boys with

their weapons and grim faces looked more and more like they belonged in this old place. *Rob got his wish,* Kat thought. *They are knights in training.* She couldn't help noticing how much older both Rob and Peter looked.

"You do realize that it's All Hallows' Eve?" Rob asked.

"Perfect," murmured Peter. "Just the day for a haunting."

Kat shivered. She wished she still didn't believe in ghosts and dark magic; it would be easier to be brave.

They started their search in the attics. They weren't the kind of attics Kat remembered from Great-Aunt Margaret's house, with decaying storage and rotten furniture and trunks of old linens and papers; here were a series of little attic apartments with tiny windows. Kat assumed they'd served as servants' quarters back when the castle could afford such a thing. The rooms were all unlocked.

Their own floor was next, and they entered all the rooms they could; Jorry's room was locked. In Isabelle's room, the last they searched, they looked for a hidden passage. After all, whatever or whoever had stolen Isabelle had likely stolen Amelie, too, and now they all knew something about hidden passages.

They pushed and pulled on every corner. Peter even crawled under the bed. It wasn't until Kat lifted a tapestry and shoved her shoulder against the wall that they found it: a very well-hidden door.

"Do we go down?" Peter said, his voice low.

The wall opened into a chilly, dark passage. Stairs wound down, tight against the wall. They couldn't see beyond a few feet.

"I have my chatelaine," Kat said. She took a deep breath and stepped forward, holding the glowing blue chatelaine high.

But once again, Rob stopped her. "You hold the chatelaine so I can see," he said. "I've got the sword. I'll go first."

"Or I could," said Peter, holding up his own blade. Kat had to smile. Rob let Peter go first this time.

It was a small passage, and curving. Kat had to turn sideways once or twice to get by. Again she counted the steps. Rob wisely wedged the door so it couldn't close behind them.

"I think we've reached the next floor," Kat whispered.

They knew what to do now—each of them pressed against the nearest wall.

Peter found the door. He pushed it open an inch and then signaled the all clear, and they found themselves looking into the second floor hallway, by the main stairwell. In the dim light they could see that the hall was empty.

They exchanged uncomfortable glances. This was where the Lady had her rooms. Kat didn't fancy running into her.

"We have to search, or we'll never know," said Peter.

"Who would build such a place, with all these secret passageways and hidden doors?" asked Kat.

"They weren't uncommon in medieval castles," Rob whispered. "I wasn't surprised to see them in the keep. They were good hiding places during a siege. But someone must have really liked having them to build them in the new castle, too."

"Yeah, and this castle is . . . well, it's almost like it's *alive* or something," said Peter.

Kat shivered.

They tiptoed to the far end of the winding corridor, stopping at the last door. Kat put her ear against it, but all she could hear was the pelting rain against the window, barely drowning out the thumping of her heart.

She shrugged to let the boys know she couldn't tell anything. She tried the latch. It gave.

The room was large—twice as large as any of the other bedrooms they'd seen so far—but the air was close and musty, and the light was low, gray from the gray weather outside. The windows, slick with rain and sleet, looked out toward the sea, just as Kat's did. To their left was an enormous bed with four great corner posts and a canopy hung at the head with red velvet drapes. The bed was rumpled. They froze, fearing someone was about.

But it was silent as a tomb, and after a minute or so Kat decided that it was merely an unmade bed. After all, there was only Marie to do all the housework. And she wasn't anywhere to be found today.

They moved farther into the room, Peter going left and Rob to the right. Kat made for the bed itself.

Just as she reached it, the coverlet moved, and her hand flew to her mouth. She'd learned not to shriek, but she couldn't help saying it aloud, gasping.

"It's . . . the ghost!"

Lying against the pillows was the pale and wan face they'd seen in the keep.

The blood roared in Kat's ears as her heart pounded, but she could still hear the man when he spoke. In weak tones but with a thick Scottish brogue, he said, "Ghost, is it? Well, lassie, I'm not m'self, that's sure, but I'm no' dead yet."

"I'm Gregor Duncaster, Earl of Craig," he said. He was thin, and Kat couldn't tell how old, and his face had a deathly pallor, but he was able to pull himself up against the pillows and assume a lordly manner, even as his voice quavered. "And you are?"

"I'm Katherine Bateson, my lord, and this is my brother Rob and our friend Peter Williams." Kat made as grand a curtsey as she could manage, since it seemed only fitting, especially after she'd called him a ghost. And since this was his castle, and he was a lord, after all.

"Well, Katherine Bateson, I don't know what you three are doing in my bedchamber nor in my home, nor do I understand why the two young masters with you are bearing swords that look uncanny like my own arms." He stopped and took a breath. "But you all are right welcome nonetheless."

No doubt about it, the Earl might be ill and wobbly and short of breath, but his mind was sharp. Both Peter and Rob held their swords down and shuffled in embarrassment.

"Now what are you lads and lass about?" he asked. "And why are you in my chamber?"

"We're looking for the others," Rob piped up.

"The other whats?" Lord Craig asked.

"The other children, and the teachers," Kat answered. She saw his puzzled expression. "You do know, don't you?" She wondered if perhaps he'd been too ill to be informed, so she said, "We're here taking refuge from the Blitz. From London. The Lady, um, her Ladyship, she's running an academy for us refugees." She paused. "An academy of sorts."

"Is she now?" And his eyebrows shot up. "Blitz? Don't know that word. From London? Teachers? Refugees?" He shook his head. "The Lady Eleanor, is it? Not the type to look after those in need."

Kat wondered whether she should tell him that the Lady Eleanor was harboring a German spy.

"We were told you were terribly ill," Peter said.

"Were you now?" He shifted. "Well, that's true enough. Until quite recently, I was a bit under the weather. Things are looking up, with Deirdre on the case," he added, pronouncing the name *Deer-dree* and leaning back into his pillows. "She's been wondrous good."

Kat exchanged a look with Peter. She imagined he had no more clue how this sick man would have made his way out to the keep than she did—if Lord Craig was indeed the person they'd seen there, the ghost.

"Sir, have you been wandering in other parts of the castle recently?" Peter asked.

"It's a confusion," Lord Craig said. "At one point I went out to the old keep. Felt like I was called there for something. Felt like a bad dream. It wasn't an easy thing to get there and back again." He sighed. "I wore myself right out."

"Well, that's a relief," Peter whispered to Kat. "Not a ghost."

No, thought Kat. But maybe Lord Craig was magicked to the keep to scare the devil out of the children.

Lord Craig said, "Now what are these bairns, these children, you're looking for?"

"The other children who've gone missing," Kat said. "And the ones we've seen from time to time but can't find again."

"This must be what Deirdre meant," he said to himself. "I didn't know what the blazes she was on about. But now I see. There's evil afoot."

"Please, if you have any idea—" Kat began.

He lifted his hand. "The only idea I have is that her Ladyship is not what you think. And those bairns, I fear . . ." He broke off.

Silence filled the room.

"Who's Deirdre?" asked Rob.

Lord Craig's eyes grew bright. "She's the only reason I'm alive."

Something in his expression niggled at Kat, had begun niggling at her the minute she saw him, and now it came clear and sharp. "Why, you and Mr. Storm!" Kat said. "At least, you and the new Mr. Storm. You're nearly identical."

"Mr. Storm?" said Lord Craig. "Whatever are you on about?"

Peter and Kat exchanged a confused glance. "It's just that you look so much like someone else, or someone else has begun to look a lot like you," she said, musing.

"Puzzles within puzzles," Lord Craig muttered as he leaned back and closed his eyes.

They waited. Silence. For a minute they assumed he'd gone to sleep, and then Kat fretted that they'd startled him so badly that he'd died of sudden heart palpitations, but without warning his eyes flew open again, and he said, "One of you must fetch Deirdre. She'll know what to do."

Robbie cleared his throat. "Please, sir. We don't know a Deirdre."

"Of course you do," he answered. "Surely if you've eaten anything in Rookskill Castle you've eaten her good food. Her food is right magic, that's what."

"Cook! Miss Brodbeem," Kat said, getting his meaning. Then she faltered. "But she's not here. We couldn't find her. We haven't seen her since before we lost my sister. And please, we have to find Amelie."

Lord Craig waved his hand weakly and shut his eyes again. "Find Deirdre first." And this time he definitely lapsed into a deep sleep.

They all exchanged looks.

"What now?" Peter said.

"I think he's right. One of us should go back to the kitchen and try to find Cook," Kat said.

"I have a better idea," said Rob. "Two of us go to find Cook and one stays here. That way no one is alone."

"Brilliant, Rob," Kat said. "I'll go with you."

"I'll stay here with Lord Craig," said Peter. "I'm armed." He smiled as he lifted the sword.

Kat glanced at the sleeping Lord Craig. "All right. We'll come back straightaway."

She tucked her hand into her pocket and clutched Great-Aunt Margaret's chatelaine.

Rob and Kat stepped into the hallway. Kat gave Peter a little wave. His return smile was so warm, she felt a glow in her cheeks.

Then she and Rob headed down the great stairs.

52

The Tenth Charm: The Eel

SLIPPERY AS AN eel, the Lady thinks. *These three remaining children are tricky. He'll be a challenge, that Robbie.*

But, oh, such fun. Catching an eel with your bare hands is great fun.

Right out of the blue, she remembers doing such a thing as a girl. It was a treat, eel at the table, after days of stale bread and thin broth and that never-ending porridge. She'd been quick that day, her brothers acknowledged it, and as she waded knee-deep in the river her hands had been able to catch an eel and bring it home, and her father hadn't even beaten her that night after they feasted. Such a memory, that.

Which she promptly and firmly puts out of her mind, as her mind and memories are the last human part of her. She hates this part of her, and she hates her memories filled with beatings and worse.

The Lady Eleanor fingers her four remaining charms. The eel, the anchor, the heart, and, of course, the thirteen, the container of souls. Only four charms and this last so heavy, as it is now filled with souls, a great clamoring of souls, and a great weight dragging her down. She walks with a pronounced limp as the chatelaine bangs against her hip. She would have borne a bruise if she had flesh left there.

She makes her way into the dining hall and sits, unable to stand for long, even with her mechanical legs, such is the weight of her chatelaine. She hears the *tap-tap* of a beak against the window glass. It would have been nice if the wolves had made it easy, for this weight is almost crippling. When the charm is full, she will no longer feel the weight. She sits in the dark and ponders her next move.

Which comes to her directly.

53
Witch

THE RAIN LET up about the time they reached the main entry hall. The clock's slow *tock* was the only sound; as it struck three the *gong* echoed throughout the castle, up and down. The gray pall of the day lifted a bit as the clouds broke apart; Kat thought it might be a fine sunset and a clear full-moon night. And a cold night, too, and that thought made her want more than ever to find Amelie.

Rob led the way back through the castle toward the kitchen. As they passed the open doors to the echoing dining hall, they heard a noise from within.

"Cook?" Kat called, and she and Rob ran into the hall.

"I'm afraid not." The Lady Eleanor sat in a thronelike chair at the far end of the hall before the cold fireplace. "Cook is indisposed. But I'm glad you're here. I've been looking for you."

A chill ran up Kat's spine, and both of them stopped dead in their tracks.

"You've been looking for us?" Kat said. "We're looking for our sister."

The Lady nodded. "Looking for little Amelie."

Kat heard the undertone: the Lady knew something. She knew something, and it wasn't nice.

Kat said, "Please don't tell us that she's gone home. Or off with the doctor. Or some other made-up story." Kat clutched at the chatelaine in her pocket, her fingers tight around it. "I don't know what you really are, but you are no lady."

The Lady rose from her chair. Even in the shadows Kat could see a grimace cross her face and her fists clench.

Sunlight broke through the clouds, streaming into the hall in broad bands, and Kat was blinded for a moment as the sun struck her right in the eyes. She squinted and shifted and lifted her hand to her forehead, but before she could get a clear picture again she heard several noises: Robbie let out a shout; the Lady laughed; Robbie's feet slapped the stone floor as he ran toward the Lady; then the sharp squeal as of metal on metal that Kat had heard so often in the night came from where the Lady stood.

The sun slipped away as fast as it had emerged. Now in the shadows at the far end of the room, Robbie faced the Lady. She towered over him as he raised his sword in her direction. Everything about her was menace.

"Robbie!" Kat cried. She let go of her chatelaine and drew her hand out of her pocket, clenching her fists. But she was frozen in place, trapped. Trapped inside her fear.

The Lady reached for the blade and took hold of it in her two hands as Rob struggled to hang on to the hilt, and Kat thought, *There go her fingers, he'll slice right through them,* but no, the Lady bent the blade back and back until it was at a right angle, and she walked, still gripping the blade, toward Robbie, who wore a look of bald astonishment.

How she had the strength to bend an ancient and heavy blade with her bare hands was a terrifying mystery.

"Rob!" Kat yelled, and now her legs woke up and she ran toward him. But too late, too late, for the Lady had reached Robbie and wrenched the sword from his hands and tossed it across the room, where it clattered on the stone, and she took him in one hand by his shoulder. His face contorted in pain as her fingers closed on him.

"Kat!" Rob called, choking. "Hurts . . ."

Kat skidded to a stop only ten feet away as with her free hand the Lady jerked Rob's chin upward and then dropped something over his head and uttered words that forced Kat to throw both her hands over her ears, for the words were harsh and guttural and came rising as if from the stones beneath their feet with a clang and a hammering.

Your soul will sleep within its keep, your life will linger dark and deep; by rock and bone, by blood and stone, not life, nor death, but lost, alone.

Kat thought she was inside some dreadful mechanical device that would grind them all to bits. She shut her eyes tight and fear flooded her, a dreadful weight in her limbs.

All around her went still. Silent.

When Kat opened her eyes, her throat filled with the sorrow and horror of it.

"Rob?" It came out a pathetic squeak.

"Yes, my dear, you have indeed been robbed," said the Lady with a harsh laugh. "Your Rob is now my Rob."

Kat's whole body shook. Rob's blank eyes, his helpless gestures—he was missing, gone, leaving a shell behind. The Lady stumbled and then straightened, and something seemed to lift behind her, black wings at the Lady's back.

Kat tried to plant her feet, but her knees threatened to give way.

One hand of the Lady's was still on Rob's shoulder; he was so limp, she was holding him up.

Kat said in a half whisper, "You're a witch."

The Lady smiled wider, and for a moment Kat thought she saw not teeth in her mouth but metal spikes, sharp and thin and made for grinding, for pulverizing. She shook her head to rid herself of the terrible sight, and the Lady became the Lady again, grimacing but with perfect teeth.

"My dear Katherine, I'm not merely a witch. I have a power you can't imagine. I've already lived many lifetimes. I've made a collection to which I just added. And when I'm finished adding"—she paused and licked her lips—"I'll be perfect. And I will live forever."

"Finished?" Kat took a step away. "Finished adding what? What have you done to Rob? Where's Amelie?"

The Lady's eyes narrowed and she dropped Rob, who crumpled to the floor, helpless. She took a limping step toward Kat; Kat took a step away. "Does it matter? They are mine." Kat saw her hand travel to that magnificent belt, to the chatelaine that hung visible now, the three charms twisting and turning on their chains, as if alive.

Kat rubbed her eyes, wishing she could rub away this madness. And then the full reality struck her. "That's not Lady Leonore's portrait in the hall. That's you. You've been alive for centuries already," Kat said. "You've been casting spells. Spreading confusion, even pitting us against each other. You're a monster as well as a witch."

"I'm a monster?" the Lady said. "I don't think you know what you've already started to become. Your right hand. Have you looked at it in the full moonlight? Have you listened to it in the dark?"

Kat lifted her hand before her. "How . . ."

"Exactly what I would like to know. How?" The Lady smiled again, that cold, bitter smile. She inched her way toward Kat, her right leg dragging, as if she was tied to the floor.

"I don't know," Kat said, her voice small.

"You would call me a monster, when you are becoming one yourself. You call me a witch when you are controlling some kind of magic, are you not?" The Lady's eyes narrowed.

"I . . ." Becoming a monster. A witch. Kat's insides were twisting and turning like the chatelaine at the Lady's waist, writhing like snakes.

"You understand, of course, that monsters and witches can do great things. Why, you, my dear, might even save your father."

"What? Save Father?" Kat pressed her hand against her chest, fearing her heart would break.

The Lady drew closer still. "You think this power I have could not be used for any purpose I choose? All I need is for you to bring me the other boy, and I could save him, your father. I could teach you to use this magic that you possess."

"Peter?" Kat squeaked. "You need Peter? You'll save Father?"

"Yes." The Lady was close now, her voice a low hiss. "Bring me the boy."

"What will you do to him? To Peter?"

"He'll be mine. Like all the rest." She moved her hand, dismissive. Then the Lady coiled her voice around Kat like a rope. "But you won't care, once your father is safe. You'll see how powerful a monster can become, and you'll be glad."

The Lady's voice was liquid velvet. Kat rubbed her forehead. One side of her clamored against this velvet voice; the other cried out for Father. *Bring Peter to the Lady so she could deal with him like the others. Trade all of them for Father.*

Torn into pieces, that's how she felt.

The chatelaine in her pocket made a noise, the charms clattering together, soft, an insistent jingle. Kat shook herself, waking from a living nightmare.

Kat turned and bolted for the door, stumbling blindly. She grabbed the door with her terrible right hand, her monster hand, her powerful, treacherous hand. Kat had to get to Peter before the Lady did.

She couldn't think about her father. She had to put him out of her mind.

54

Pen, Scissors, Thimble

KAT SLAMMED INTO Lord Craig's room. Peter sat slumped in the chair next to the bed, and for a fraction of time she thought he was already under the witch's spell—but then he jumped as the door banged against the wall behind Kat.

Lord Craig did not stir.

Kat turned and shut the door, locked it, and drew a chair up and propped it under the handle so that the door couldn't be opened from outside.

"What are you doing?" She could hear the nervous laughter in Peter's voice.

The words tumbled out in a rush. "She's a witch. She's put a spell on Rob—on all of them. Heaven knows where they are, all the others. That's why they're so strange, so mesmerized. That's what's been happening here. I don't know how she's done it, but now at least I do know why."

"Hang on," said Peter, thoroughly flummoxed. "Who's a witch? Cook?"

"No, no, we never got to Cook. It's the Lady. There's something dreadful about her and she's spelled them all. Everyone. Amelie and now Rob." Kat had to swallow hard not to burst into tears.

Peter's brow furrowed. "Slow down, Kat. Take a breath and explain."

She told Peter what she'd seen, ending with, "She says it will make her supremely powerful. That's why she's done it. To have some freakish power."

She did not tell him that the Lady had offered to save Kat's father. About the bargain Kat could make. And she could not tell him about her hand.

Peter let out a low whistle and scratched the hair at the top of his head. "I have to say, this sounds pretty strange."

Kat clenched her fists. "I'm not making it up. It's all true."

"I didn't say you were making it up."

"I don't make up stories like that," Kat said, heated now. "I'm not a silly girl. I saw Rob! She had him completely under her power, she bent the sword right in her own two hands, she said these terrible words . . . !"

Peter held up his hand. "I didn't mean to suggest—"

"I'm practical." Kat was afraid she might cry, so she paused and bit her cheek. "But there is magic in the world. And it can be evil and dark." Kat took a breath and held it.

Peter watched Kat carefully, then nodded. "I believe you, okay?"

Kat reached in her pocket for her great-aunt's chatelaine.

Peter said, "Now. Tell me again what she did to Rob. Try to remember exactly, moment by moment."

Kat spoke as slowly as she could. "She took Rob's shoulder in one hand. She had this chain in her other hand with something on it. A charm. She draped the chain over his head and said these terrible words—and that's when I shut my eyes, I couldn't help it, the words were like some great black suffocating ooze rising right up from below the floor—and Robbie melted away. He was gone. As if whatever makes Rob the real Rob was gone away, leaving an empty shell."

The voice came from the great bed behind Peter, the voice sounding feeble and distant. "She stole his soul."

Peter and Kat started, then went together to Lord Craig's bedside. He still lay in what seemed a complete stupor, his eyes shut tight. If she'd been alone, Kat would have thought she was imagining that he'd spoken a single word.

"What did he say?" Kat whispered.

"That she . . . stole his soul," Peter answered, his eyes wide.

"My lord?" Kat ventured, reaching for the hand that lay

on the coverlet. "Are you there?" She looked at Peter, who shrugged, helpless. "Lord Craig, please, can you help us? What has she done with him?" And she wanted to ask, but couldn't, *What did she do with his soul?*

And, *Could she really save Father?*

Lord Craig lay utterly still. The sun skated in and out behind the clouds as it lowered in the sky. Just as Kat's body went limp with exhaustion, he spoke again.

"She's stolen their souls. All of them. Deirdre tried to tell me, even when I dinna understand, when I couldna do a thing about it." Lord Craig lifted himself off the bed, staring, as if waking from a long sleep. "I'd no idea what danger you bairns were in, what was happening here, what was happening to me. I'd no idea because Deirdre, bless her heart, dinna have all the pieces and her memory's affected. But now I understand. Eleanor has stolen them, their souls. Locked them in the thirteenth charm."

The thirteenth charm. Kat bent over, her muscles all tense once more, and whispered, "How do you know?"

It was another moment before he spoke again, as he sank back against his pillows, closing his eyes, the strain wearing him down. "I know because I've just put together a string of puzzle pieces that made no sense till now. I know because I once overheard my beloved wife muttering in her sleep about that cursed chatelaine and the thirteenth charm and the souls of children. I know because, as I already told ye, I'm no' dead yet."

Kat feared he would be at any moment, but he rallied yet again and said, "She had that chatelaine from before, but persuaded me that it was a wedding gift. Well, it was, but not for our wedding, no. I thought she was good, a good person. I loved her so, you see. I was wrong." He paused and Kat thought he might pass out again, so she pressed his hand, and he came back. "Her charms, that's what did it."

"Her chatelaine," Kat said. She pulled her great-aunt's chatelaine from her pocket and held it before him.

"Aye, that's it, that's the ticket." Lord Craig lifted his hand and pointed. "Magic," he said, and then his eyes shut tight and he sank, if it was possible, even deeper into his pillows. "She muttered in her sleep about that chatelaine, that thirteenth charm. Attracts magic to it, it does. I thought it was a nightmare she was having. Well, it was. A nightmare of dark magic."

She and Peter both stared at the chatelaine in Kat's hand. "If my aunt was right, this chatelaine is magic, too," Kat said. "Maybe it does more than emit light." Pen, scissors, thimble.

"At the very least they're tools," said Peter, "if we can figure out how to use them."

"That's the question," murmured Kat.

Lord Craig fell deep in slumber again. Peter and Kat spent the next hour searching the room, every nook and cranny and corner. They found the hidden passage next to the fireplace. They dragged a sofa over to block it off. Then they lit a fire to warm the room.

"That's how she's gotten around," Kat said. "All these crazy hidden passages."

"This place was built by a lunatic," Peter muttered.

"Or the whole place is spelled, brick and stone," Kat said.

"I hope we don't have to hold out here for too long, or we'll starve to death."

Kat's stomach rumbled at the thought of food. "I wish we'd been able to find Cook."

"So these things," Peter said, and pointed at her chatelaine, "they're each magical?"

"My aunt told me what they were for, but I didn't believe her. She said the pen is mightier than the sword and can write of its own accord. The scissors can cut through anything. And the thimble . . ." Here Kat paused. "Is for catching souls." Catching souls. Like the Lady Eleanor had done.

"All right," said Peter. "Let's think for a minute. You say you didn't see what she put around Robbie's neck?"

Kat shook her head, misery invading her at the memory of Rob's face.

"Have you seen any of the things on her chatelaine?"

"Yes," Kat said slowly. "That first day, and then again just now. It was a bit like the chatelaine that Storm showed us. On hers I saw a couple of charms. The one that stood out was a heart. And Isabelle spoke of one that she saw." Kat didn't want to describe that one.

He nodded. "So maybe she has a different one of these charms for each person's soul."

"Yes," Kat said, feeling better. "Lord Craig said she's locked them, all the souls, in the thirteenth charm, which I'm betting is hers. Which means she must have had twelve charms to use."

"So let's think. We have"—Peter began counting on his fingers—"that girl you saw on the first day with the fish, the crippled boy we spooked who was in your bathroom . . ."

Kat interrupted. "And the boy I startled in the kitchen with the cats, and those singing voices . . ."

"I'll bet there are two of them from the sound of it, two girls, that's what it sounded like to me."

"Jorry and Colin and Isabelle . . ."

"And Amelie and Robbie," Peter finished.

"Ten," Kat said.

They stared at each other in silence for a minute. Then Peter said, "We're eleven and twelve."

"And then she'll have the thirteenth charm," Kat said. "With all of our souls locked inside. So that she can live forever with a terrible power. While we're trapped in some awful limbo . . ."

The sun slanted through the window in a fat red ray,

penetrating the low clouds and moving toward sunset. The thin line at the horizon flared pink.

"Amelie's soul is trapped," Kat said. Her throat swelled with grief.

"And Rob's," said Peter.

"And all those other children . . ."

Peter walked to the window, where the sunset bathed him in red light. That gave Kat chills, seeing him in the red glow, as did his next thought. "And us next."

The fire snapped, and the sun lowered to the horizon.

"Unless," Kat said as the last of the sun's rays lit the room, "unless we figure out how we can use my chatelaine against her." Kat flexed the fingers of her right hand.

Lord Craig hadn't stirred for a long time.

"I don't know if I have the courage to face her again," Kat said. She pressed her hand against her chest, against the tightness that bound her heart.

"But what else can we do?" said Peter. "Wait it out until we starve? I'd rather just face her now and be done." His voice rang with frustration. He paced back and forth.

The fire warmed the room, and Kat stood before it, rubbing her hands. Her right hand felt especially cold and she fanned it open, catching the heat of the fire. The tall windows that stared out over the lawn were reflective black now. The night was already freezing and the full moon rising. Wispy strings of clouds, the last of the storm, skated across the dark starlit sky. The dark eve of All Hallows', the time when evil walks the earth.

A full moon. Kat would not go near the window, not wanting to see what the Lady meant. Not wanting to see her own hand. Like a creeping sickness, the dark force of worry and fear twisted inside Kat. "We don't know how to stop her," she said.

"Let's think again. You have a pen, mightier than the sword. That can write of its own accord."

"Great. If I have to write the witch a letter, I'll use that." Misery filled her with the taste of metal filings.

Peter pursed his lips. "What are the other charms on your chatelaine again?"

"A pair of scissors that can cut anything . . . Hold on. What if I cut her chatelaine from her belt? Got it away from her and . . . did something with it?" Her voice trailed off, as she had no clue what she'd do with it once she had it.

"By the time you got that close to her, she'd have you charmed."

He was right. Kat slumped into the chair.

"What's the third charm?" he asked.

"A thimble. Supposedly for catching souls."

"Well, maybe you could use the thimble to catch back the souls she already has."

"And how would that work? And do what with them if I even could? Stitch a nice embroidery with them and the thimble?" She couldn't help it; she couldn't keep her voice steady or low any longer.

"Um," said Peter.

Hunger and tension and Peter's hesitation and not knowing what to do got to her. "This is impossible!" She stood up and paced away, her fists clenched. "Ame and Rob and all the other children have been kidnapped, stolen, had their souls ripped out—ripped right out of their bodies—and the same thing's going to happen to us!" Kat's voice was so loud, she could hear it echo. "What are we supposed to do? Guess? My silly old aunt didn't give me any instructions. Just foolishness." Tears filled Kat's eyes and she rubbed them hard. "What exactly are we supposed to do?"

Peter looked helpless, and then said, uncertainly, "Keep calm?"

"Oh, terrific!" That's all Kat needed to hear. She stomped across the room, holding the chatelaine before her. "We're about to die, and you tell me to keep calm! I want to throw this into the fire!"

Peter cleared his throat. "I think that would be a bad idea."

Kat held up the chatelaine, her hand shaking. The silver reflected the firelight, dancing sharp points of light across her skin. Her words came out with a little sob. "I'm frightened.

What if we can't get them back? How can we fight her black magic? What if we can't make it all better?" *Keep calm.* "I don't know what to do."

Peter walked to her side and put one arm over her shoulder. "I don't, either." He pulled away and sighed. He shifted, silent for a moment. "Did I ever tell you about my dog, Dodger?"

"That you left behind in America?"

He nodded. "I knew I had to leave him. So I stopped playing with him, stopped walking him. I could tell he was hurt, and sad, but I couldn't keep pretending. I just . . . I gave up. I let him go, gave him to another family, long before we left for England."

"I'm so sorry."

"There was no use trying to keep him. That's the way I feel right now. Kind of . . . helpless. Like I want to give up." Peter rubbed his eyes, his back to her. "I wish . . . Well, no use, is it? I don't even know why I told you that."

The room filled with the sound of the crackling fire.

"We can't give up," Kat said, her voice quiet. "That's why you told me about Dodger. We do have a choice, and we can't give up, and you're not a bad person for being stuck in a no-win place." Kat was talking as much to herself as she was to Peter. "My great-aunt told me something about faith and hope, and now I think I understand what she was trying to say."

Peter looked at her, his eyes shining.

"There's nothing wrong with wishing, even when you think

it's hopeless," Kat said. "There's something to having faith that it will all turn out." She took a deep breath and clutched the chatelaine tight inside her fist. *Carry on.*

The fire snapped and popped, then Kat said, "I wonder which is worse, having your soul stripped from your body or starving to death?" She looked at Peter, gave him a half smile. "I'm so peckish, I could eat a horse."

"Me too," said Peter. He smiled back, then sighed. "I say we go downstairs. Maybe we can find one of the other grown-ups."

"I'm not sure the grown-ups can do anything against her," Kat said. "Look at them." And she pointed at Lord Craig. "I'm betting he's been spelled. Think about what she's done to Marie, and how odd Storm has become. And the others are gone or confused or both." Kat paused while she took another deep breath. "I think this is entirely up to us."

"All right, then." Peter picked up the sword and examined the blade. "Let's hope this sword is stouter than Rob's. And we might as well go out the door."

"Yes," Kat said. She squared her shoulders. "I'm getting tired of sneaking down hidden passages." She touched the chatelaine in her pocket, her right hand vibrating against it. At the very least it could shed light in the darkness. Kat shivered as her chest grew tight and her stomach hollow. "Right," she lied, "I'm ready."

55

The Witch's Mark

THEY HADN'T EVEN reached the front hall at the foot of the stairs when they heard it: scraping, whining, gears grinding metal on metal. Kat knew those sounds, and they sent sharp, cold chills running up her spine.

She and Peter stood, feet planted, in the middle of the hall, facing the shadows as the sounds ceased.

"Why, Peter," came the Lady's voice. "Whatever are you doing with that sword?"

The fire was cold and no lights had been lit in the hall. The clock was silent, stopped at half past seven. Kat gripped the chatelaine in her pocket. Her mouth was as dry as sandpaper, and her hands were clammy. The moon slid behind a wisp of cloud and the darkness was deep, the only light a yellow glow spilling down from upstairs.

Then, *whirr, slip, whirr,* the Lady Eleanor moved out of the shadows. She wore a black gown, now, that lifted and rose around her like a fluttering of wings, and the belt at her waist glimmered with jewels even in the dim light. The chatelaine dangling from the belt glowed a faint blue; she seemed to bend toward it as if she carried a crippling weight. Her mouth stretched in a grimace, and her white hair cascaded loose about her shoulders. Then, as she reached the center of the hall, a broad band of moonlight struck her, and both Peter and Kat gasped.

The Lady Eleanor was a monster made of metal, of wheels, of snaking ribbons of rubber, of tubes pumping some dreadful blue liquid. Her torso, arms, and legs were all mechanical, with jointed gears and claw hands and birdlike feet and a heart that shone through metal ribs with a coppery glow, ticking with a mechanical tick. Wheels turned on spokes; wound springs pumped; gears clicked together like skeleton teeth. And on top of this metal framework her head perched—and it was her head, human though partly deformed—like the head of a broken doll, hairless, with one gleaming eye and only one ear, and the rest of what remained of her skull was a metal plate.

The Lady Eleanor was hideous.

And then, from some other part of her brain, Kat thought, *No, she's beautiful.* Not beautiful as in the portrait that stared down at Kat now, a mockery of the Lady. No, this monster was really a perfect mechanical device. Gears that meshed with precision, cogs that whirred so fast they were hard to see, belts and pulleys, all working. All shining, all glittering in the moonlight. The Lady was ingenious, a marvel. Like a clock, all the movements perfectly synchronized to create this whole. Kat unconsciously moved toward the Lady, trying to get a better look, especially at that heart, its copper works beating with unvarying rhythm, a clockwork like no other . . .

"Kat!" Peter's voice broke through her reverie as the Lady ground across the stone floor, scraping and clattering toward them. Peter grabbed Kat's arm and pulled so they fell back away from the Lady.

The moonlight drifted behind a cloud and she was again the Lady Eleanor.

But they knew better now, Peter and Kat. They knew she was a witch, and now they knew that she was also a monster. The Lady stopped and a smile spread across her face.

"You can't win."

"Can't win?" Kat asked.

"All of you," the Lady said, "once I have your souls, I will use your innocence and youth to live forever."

"And just how do you manage to hang on to us?" asked Peter. "You can't keep us here forever in some trance."

"Oh, you have no idea." She laughed again, and another passing beam of moonlight exposed her mechanical arm. "You'll live on, but in an altered state. Your souls will feed me." Her claw hand flicked at the air.

"Our parents will come searching for us," Peter said. "They'll know."

The Lady's voice was the grating of metal on metal. "They will forget you. That's an easy enchantment."

Kat's heart pounded in her chest. "Lord Craig—" she began.

"My husband," the Lady interrupted, "will soon be replaced by Mr. Storm." She waved her hand. "I need a husband, but Lord Craig is . . . difficult. Mr. Storm has a far less ethical nature and will be a more malleable consort than my dear Gregor."

"Then, Cook," said Peter, and Kat could hear his voice falter. "Hugo. Marie. MacLarren and Gumble."

"I will deal with all of them. You can't escape. You can't win. I've already won."

"But," Kat said as the blood rushed into her ears and her voice became faint, "but why?"

"Why? Why? Because I was once a helpless child, not nearly so privileged as you. Because I was once a powerless woman in a man's world. Because all I asked for was love and shelter. And instead I got bruises and misery and heartbreak." Her words grated like metal files, broke like shattering glass. "Now I am powerful. I control my fate. I have the life I want to live and I will have it forever."

"You can't do this!" Peter said. His words echoed through the halls.

"Has she told you, boy?" the Lady asked, her voice steady again. "This friend of yours, this Katherine. Has she told you?"

"About what?" Peter said uneasily.

"About her father." The Lady laughed. "Thank you for bringing the boy to me, girl."

Peter moved at Kat's side. "What?"

"No! Don't listen," Kat said, as much to herself as to him. "She's doing it again—trying to set us against each other!"

"No, boy, don't listen," said the Lady. "Because she has betrayed you for her father. Yes. She has."

Peter turned toward Kat now. "What is she talking about?"

"I told her I could save her father, but she had to give you up," came the Lady's wheedling voice. "And she has."

"She's trying to split us apart, because that's all she can do," Kat said. "Don't listen."

Peter lowered his sword, his attention full on Kat. "I'd do anything to save my father." His voice broke. "I bet you would, too."

Kat's heart pounded. "No! My father knows what's right, and he fights for it, and so must I. Don't—"

Kat reached her right hand for Peter and was struck full in the moonlight, and he gasped. Her hand was not a real hand but a clockwork, like the witch, made of gears and springs and cogs. It was, like the witch, perfection. Hideous and perfect.

Peter stepped backward, horror etched on his face. "You! You're like her!"

"I'm not like her! I'm not . . ." Kat's words faltered even as she realized how beautiful it was, how powerful, this mechanical hand.

The Lady was laughing. "Yes! She has already betrayed you, boy, and her brother and sister."

The sword hung from Peter's hand, and he stared at Kat with a combination of sorrow and horror.

And the Lady, with astonishing swiftness, lunged.

Peter yelled and raised the sword. Kat backed away until her heel caught on the step and sent her down on her bottom. From the floor, she watched, helpless, as the Lady caught Peter's sword, just as she had Robbie's, wrenched it from his hands, and sent it flying across the hall. Kat fast crab-walked across the floor after it, to have some kind of weapon, scuttling to the far side of the hall while Peter and the Lady struggled.

Peter was strong and tall, but the Lady was stronger, with her metal arms and spiky claw-hands. He cried out in pain as she twisted his arms back, and Kat grabbed the sword by the hilt and stood to face them.

The Lady had both of Peter's wrists in one clenched claw, and she was forcing him down on his knees before her. With her other hand Kat saw her pull a thin chain from her chatelaine, a chain with a charm that dangled, a charm Kat could see in the full moonlight.

An anchor.

She would anchor Peter's soul.

"No!" Kat shouted, and raced back as the Lady lifted the chain with a grim smile and began to utter terrible words, words that seemed to rise from the very bowels of the earth and envelop them all, dark magic that suffocated and smothered the very light of the moon.

A prison cold, a witch's mark . . .

As the chain slipped over Peter's head, he looked from the witch to Kat and said, his voice coarse and breaking, "Pain. Cut . . ."

And then it was done. Kat watched his eyes grow wide and then dull, blank and staring, and she swallowed a sob.

The Lady dropped him and he crumpled to the floor. She turned to Kat.

It seemed that with Peter's charming she'd grown another foot taller at least. She had taken on a deep blue glow, and now she no longer needed moonlight to reveal her true form, but was exposed as a monster.

"And now for my last charm," she said, her words like oil oozing from between her spiked teeth. "You see, I need your soul."

Kat's left hand gripped Peter's sword, and her terrible right hand gripped the only thing she now believed in: Great-Aunt Margaret's chatelaine.

56

The Eleventh Charm: The Anchor

IT IS SO EASY. Almost too easy.

The boy Peter, tall though he is, and strong—the Lady can feel the strength in him—couldn't fight her. Couldn't resist the spell. Oh, she has grown magnificent. She is mightier than even the magister now, despite the weight of the chatelaine against her hip. Soon she will be stronger than all the human frailties she despises.

She merely has to place the final charm. Pathetic, foolish girl, Katherine. The heart charm is for her.

The heart. Eleanor pauses.

Hearts are about love, are they not? Hearts could be full and could be broken, hearts could be given and could be taken, could be found and could be lost. But the Lady Eleanor now has a heart that can be none of these. Her perfect, rhythmic, metallic heart beats without a waver, without a skip. It will beat forever.

Eleanor once craved love. But her first lord took another wife, a girl so like Katherine in looks that Eleanor shudders.

When she gives the heart charm to Katherine, will it signify anything?

Memories: an eel slips through the child Leonore's fingers, shiny and cold. A man shakes her father's hand and contracts a marriage and rides away on a great stallion. A hope for a child vanishes in the cold Scottish mist. A wedding, not her own, is celebrated as her old heart cracks and shatters.

As the Lady Eleanor makes for the girl, to cast her final spell, to charm Katherine, she hesitates, as if . . . as if the Lady sees something else in the girl, some glow, something that is heartfelt, something about a loving family, some magic perhaps greater than her own, and it has to do with heart and love and memory, and with all that the Lady has lost.

Will the gift of the heart from Eleanor to Katherine be a gift of love? Eleanor hesitates, just for an instant.

Then all thoughts of hesitation vanish. The Lady Eleanor, witch of Rookskill Castle, moves with swift and eager desire toward what she believes is the fulfillment of her dreams.

57

The Twelfth Charm: The Heart

KAT WAS LOST. She had a sword, and she had her chatelaine, but she feared she had already lost her soul. She was already part monster.

Then Father's voice as he left that day, as he picked up his suitcase, came to her, so clear: "Keep calm, Kitty. Carry on. And remember, no matter what happens, keep faith." And Great-Aunt Margaret's voice, like an echo: "In times like these we require other, equally important qualities. Like imagination. And faith. And hope."

Kat raised Peter's sword and braced. She was done for, but she still had to fight back.

She saw nothing in the Lady but her determination to take Kat's soul.

Yet the Lady had raised Kat's charm—and Kat saw that it was the heart—as she came, and only feet away from Kat, she paused. It was an instant, a flicker of a movement, but the monstrous hand that was stretched toward Kat holding the heart charm dropped just a hair, and the Lady hesitated.

In that momentary hesitation, Kat saw the Lady and the Lady's heart now as a perfect clockwork: how the gears meshed, how the wheels joined, how the cogs were placed. All her time spent with her father as he worked on clocks cleared her mind to see the Lady as a mechanical thing.

And something else. The heart. If Kat had nothing else left at all, she still had her own real heart, full of love for her family. The Lady was offering her a heart, as if it was meant out of love. The offering made Kat sad; and then it made her brave.

The Lady came on again with nothing but hatred in her one real eye.

The Lady's own momentum drove her onto the sword blade, and for a fraction of a second Kat hoped that it had stopped her, but no. The sword went right through some moving assemblage of gears and the Lady laughed. Kat let go of the hilt and stepped back, and the Lady took hold of the sword, slid it from her body, and dropped it to the floor.

Kat had nothing left. Nothing except her own chatelaine, which she held in her own monstrous right hand.

The glittering reflection of the chatelaine as Kat lifted it made the Lady pause. Hesitate again. She pointed. "What is that?"

"It's my chatelaine," Kat said. "A gift to me."

Kat withdrew the pen from its holder; she thought of her father making a gift of the pen to Great-Aunt Margaret, and maybe, she thought, just maybe that meant it was from Father to Kat. Her left hand, gripping the pen, shook so badly, she feared she might drop it as she pointed it at the Lady.

"Is that . . . a pen? A *pen*?" The Lady laughed, a long and horrible laugh, throwing her head back as her laughter echoed around and around the castle, reverberating off of bare stone. "I thought you had real magic. And all you have is a pen!"

"Yes, my Lady. This is a pen." Kat shifted the pen into her steady and unnaturally strong right hand and held her arm out straight and pointed the pen directly at the Lady's heart. Yes, the Lady's heart had a weakness, for though it was beautifully made, it was only clockwork after all, and Kat focused on that spot where the gears nicked together, forcing herself to be still and firm and keep her eyes fixed, and her own mechanical right hand tightened around the pen in a grip like steel.

Then Kat said the only thing she could think of, as loudly as she could, her voice ringing around the echoing space of the hall: "And *the pen is mightier than the sword*."

The air seemed to shimmer just a bit, and the pen took on a strong blue glow, and Kat thought, *Oh!* But she held her arm out straight and true, her terrible hand firm, and she pointed the pen directly at the weak place in the Lady's steel and silver and copper heart.

The Lady snarled, and Kat almost shut her eyes against the sight of the wheels and gears, but she held the pen tight, and when the Lady came at her again Kat drove the pen into the Lady's chest.

Where it wedged between two of the gears in that steady beating heart, which ground instantly to a halt.

The Lady froze, the pen shuddering ever so slightly in Kat's hand as the gears meshed, locking the pen between two copper teeth.

58

The Pen

THE LADY IS frozen. Stuck. That dreadful Katherine has driven something straight into her perfect heart. She can feel the gears trying to expel it, small, ridiculously tiny, but powerful, something with a profound magic even greater than her own.

A pen. A pen! And a spell, an incantation. How could the girl have known a spell?

The Lady hates being helpless. When she does manage to get out of this precarious situation, and she knows she will, the Lady will spare nothing, show her no mercy.

Clever Katherine. Far too clever for her own good, and using magic to boot.

The Lady concentrates all her mental effort on ridding her perfect body of this tiny pen throbbing against her perfect heart, this miserable nuisance, this ridiculously tiny pen.

59

The Scissors,
and the First Unmaking: Anchor

KAT STEPPED AWAY, her eyes on the quivering pen.

The Lady was a statue, although her one real eye followed Kat, carrying a raging fury. She was alive, but trapped, unable to speak. The pen, wedged between the teeth of two gears in the Lady's heart, still glowed, though now it was an almost white-hot gold. As long as the pen held the gears, kept them from working, Kat believed the Lady would remain trapped.

I've cast a spell. The pen, mightier than the sword, her knowledge of clocks, and her spell, all had saved her.

All gifts from her father, who might be lost to her forever.

Kat shook herself. Time was not on her side. If the pen was to fall out . . . or the spell to wear off . . .

She ran to Peter. His eyes were blank and staring, although

he could move, and he pushed away from her, as if she was the menace. He'd lost a part of his mind as well as his soul, which would explain the fearful behavior of the other charmed children.

"Peter," Kat said, keeping her voice low and calm. He'd been trying to tell her something, before he'd been charmed. *Cut . . .* That's what she'd heard. "Cut what? Cut the chatelaine?" Kat looked back at the Lady, whose chatelaine still hung from her belt, just as the heart charm still dangled from her outstretched hand. Kat didn't want to get any closer to the Lady; she could see the gears straining at the pen as it quivered.

"I don't know what to do," Kat said, turning back to Peter.

He began to tremble violently. One of his hands clutched at the chain that held the anchor charm.

"Wait. Cut the chain?"

Cut the chain.

She took the scissors from her great-aunt's chatelaine. The chain Peter wore around his neck seemed made of silver, or maybe steel; these scissors were thin and fine. Kat didn't see how they could cut a chain, but she remembered her great-aunt's words: "These scissors will cut . . . *anything.*" Kat reached for the chain.

Peter pulled away, his eyes wide with terror, but she put one hand on his chest and said, "I'm not going to hurt you. I just have to try . . ."

As she took the chain in her right hand, shock zipped all through her, and she jerked away from Peter as fast as he jerked away from her. Her mechanical right hand buzzed and whirred with the shock.

"Well, that was a bad idea," Kat said, shaking her hand. Somehow she now knew that if she took the charm from Peter by force, he would come undone. "So." Although she wasn't sure he understood a thing, Kat said out loud, "This has to be done carefully. I can't touch the chain. But . . ." An idea blossomed. "Hang on. I've got a way to experiment."

She went back to the Lady. Her outstretched frozen arm still held the heart charm—Kat's heart charm. Kat could tell that the Lady, her one eye dilated and unblinking, knew what she was about to do. Kat held the scissors against the dangling chain, took a breath, and cut.

Nothing. The scissors couldn't close around the hard metal.

Kat stepped back, her eyes brimming with tears. She met the Lady's horrible eye. The Lady stared back with venom, an oily spittle trickling from her gaping mouth.

A spell. *Of course!* Kat had to find the right spell, like she had with the pen.

The scissors . . . Her great-aunt had quoted something from Dickens that didn't seem at all right. Great-Aunt Margaret had said Kat had to find the right words on her own.

So she tried, calling out loud and strong, *"Measure twice, cut once."*

But, no. The scissors wouldn't cut.

Then her mind leapt to what her father had said when they'd been working together and she'd swept his watch to the floor. Her father's sad eyes watching her, her misery at having been a silly scatterbrain, and her father's words—she remembered.

She took a deep breath, held out the scissors, and filled the empty, ringing hall with, *"Cut to the chase, or all is waste."*

The chain, as she cut it this time, didn't fall away; it dissolved. It vanished into smoke, leaving the heart charm to drop into Kat's outstretched palm.

The instant after, the Lady's metal right hand broke off and fell clattering to the ground. A smell of burnt flesh filled Kat's nostrils, and a sound like a pained howl rose up from the Lady's chest.

"That's it then," Kat said as she closed her fingers around the charm. "That's how it can be done." The charm was warm in her palm, and the scissors, like the pen, glowed gold. "I think you won't like it when I cut these chains," she said to the Lady's fierce eye. "I think it's not going to do you any good at all. In fact, I rather think you'll be falling to pieces."

Kat returned to Peter now, whose eyes grew wide and fearful again.

"Look," Kat said, showing him her heart charm. "Just look at this for a moment." As his eyes fixed on the heart, Kat slid the scissors under the chain around his neck and, repeating the spell, snipped the chain in half.

The anchor fell away, and he caught it. Kat heard another clattering and howl from behind as the Lady lost yet another broken part.

"Where is she?" Peter said, his voice a hoarse croak.

"It worked!" Kat threw her arms around him, and just as fast, pulled away again. Peter's face turned crimson. "I'm sorry," she said. "I felt so alone . . ."

He backed away from her. "You . . ."

"I'm sorry," she said again. "I didn't tell you about how she wanted me to betray you, or about my hand. I'm sorry." There was nothing more to say. He thought she'd betrayed him, and maybe in one sense, she had. She waited.

"You freed me," he said.

She nodded and swallowed hard against the lump in her throat.

"And the witch?"

"It turns out the pen *is* mightier than the sword," she said, and pointed.

The Lady stood frozen, the pen quivering like an arrow point as the gears worked against it, trying to spit it out.

"I don't know how much time we have before it breaks or she forces it out," Kat said. "And we have to find the others, the other children, before she gets free."

"Then let's go," he said. He tried to rise, but fell back. "I'm a little wobbly around the knees," he said sheepishly.

Kat helped Peter to his feet. She said, "You were right. You were right about cutting the chain."

"There's still the thimble," he said. "I have no ideas about that."

A rough squeal came from the Lady, like an engine trying to start. A gear clicked and whined.

Kat said, "We'd better hurry before she's loose again."

Peter held out his anchor, still in his palm. "What about this? I don't like touching it, truth be told. It feels . . . hot."

Kat had already put her own charm in her pocket. "I can take it if you like."

He smiled and nodded, and Kat put his anchor charm in with her heart.

They ran down the hall toward the kitchen. It was still black as pitch, and there was no sign of Cook.

"What do you think is happening to the witch," asked Peter, catching his breath, "as you cut off the charms?"

"She seemed to lose a part for each of our two charms. Maybe the charms and her mechanical parts are all tied up together."

As if on cue, a grating noise rose from the front hall.

"Where to?" he asked. "We'd better hurry."

"Maybe try to find Hugo?" Kat suggested. "He'll be either in the garage or the barn."

Peter pushed through the back door into the moonlit courtyard, Kat right on his heels. The clouds had dissolved, and it was almost as bright as day; the moonlight reflected off the puddles and wet cobbles, adding to the glow. Kat pulled the sleeve of her jersey over her right hand, not wanting to see it exposed. The castle loomed at their backs, windows dark, like gargantuan eyes. Their feet smacked against the paving as they ran, footfalls echoing off of stone and glass.

In the deeper shadows near the door to the barn, something moved, and both Peter and Kat skidded to a stop.

"Here, now," came the voice of the giant. "Just where do you think you're going, and what are you bairns up to?"

"We have to free them," Kat pleaded.

Hugo wasn't having any of it. He'd marched them straight back to the kitchen and stood barring the door, arms folded over his chest, glowering at them, lighting an old oil lamp that hung inside the door. He had taken Peter's sword and Kat's scissors; they lay on the table at his back.

"Look," said Peter. "We're not the enemy. We want to cut the spell."

"You have weapons," Hugo said. "I'm no' the sharpest tool in the shed, but I don't like weapons."

"But it's so we can save them, not hurt them," Kat said, begging.

"And how do you know about this, hey? How do I know the Lady hasn't spelled you and made you do her bidding?" Hugo's eyes were bright points. Then he softened a little, and said to Kat, "Is your hand all right, then?"

"My hand?" said Kat, startled. "How do you know about my hand?"

"I was the one what took you to the magister so's he could fix it."

"You! Magister?"

"I didna have a choice," Hugo said miserably. "Your real hand was crushed. I did what I had to."

The memory rushed back to Kat, flooding her with images of her crushed hand, of the magister, and of Hugo, as if his words had opened a door.

"Hugo," Kat said softly, "we're on the same side. And I thank you for my hand, even if . . ." She couldn't finish. The thought crossed her mind that she might yet have to pay for this magic.

"We're running out of time," Peter murmured.

A sudden sound like a squeaky hinge, that made the hair on the back of Kat's neck stand right up, rose from beside the great fireplace.

They turned as one. A small door creaked open, and a very small head emerged from the opening, a head with straw-rough hair and a longish nose, followed by a rounded shoulder with a lopsided hump.

Kat sucked in air. The crippled boy.

She was sure he would run back to wherever he'd come from the instant he saw them, but the kitchen was still dimly lit, and he seemed so intent on what he was doing that he didn't know they were there.

Then, from somewhere below and behind him, came a most welcome voice, calling out.

"See if you can find Hugo. Try to concentrate, now, dearie. Oh, I know it's a hard thing, but it's the only thing. You must try to shake off that dreadful stupor and concentrate. Or I shall be doomed to end my days like this, helpless as a snail without a shell. Oh, please, dearie . . ."

"Cook!" Kat called in a coarse whisper.

The boy lurched, hearing Kat's voice; the giant lurched, hearing Cook's voice; Peter lurched out of sheer shock; and Kat lurched, hoping to wedge something to keep that door open before the boy tumbled back inside.

She made it, shoving a long fireplace poker into the gap just as the boy tugged at the door. When he saw it was stuck open, he made a gurgling sound in his throat and disappeared back into the darkness.

"What? What?" came Cook. "Oh, no, it ain't her, is it? Oh, I must be about to meet my maker . . ."

"No, Cook, it's me! Kat Bateson. And Peter Williams. And even Hugo is here." Kat slipped into the opening and stood at the top of a steep stair to a cellar, which she could see by the light of a number of candles all lit in magnificent gleaming silver candelabra.

Lying at the bottom, in a painful-looking heap, was Cook.

Kat rushed down the stairs. The boy vanished into the shadows at the far side of the cellar.

"Oh, thank my lucky stars. I thought I was done for. This poor boy, he can't do a thing. I'd only just got him to go up and try to find Hugo, because all he can do is shine and polish and light the candles and stare into the gloss . . ."

"What happened?" Peter asked, now by Kat's side.

"She pushed me," said Cook sourly. "Caught me unawares and pushed me right down the stairs. She's a nasty piece of work, and a witch; this is sure because of that terrible charming she's done and the way she's spelled this poor lad and the others, too, which I've only just come to realize is what's been going on, and poor Gregor—"

"Hugo, can you get her upstairs?" Kat said.

Hugo lifted Cook from the floor like she was no bigger than a very small sack of potatoes, when she was, in fact, much closer to a very large number of them put together. He had her up the stairs and sitting in the chair by the fire in a heartbeat, where she sagged and gripped her right leg.

"Think it might be broke. Think something is broke, at any rate. Or at least crushed. Or sprained maybe. Or spelled. It don't matter, I couldn't get up, I was helpless as a babe, lying there worrying over you children and Gregor and Hugo . . . Have you seen Lord Craig?" And she gripped Kat's arm.

"We've seen him," she said, "and he asked after you. Wanted you to be found as soon as possible."

A little smile crossed Cook's lips. When she smiled she was pretty. Kat realized she was probably younger than she'd thought before, too.

"But we've got no time now, Cook, for anything but the other children," Kat said. "We've stopped her for now, but I fear she'll make an escape, and then be after us all. Please help us convince Hugo to let us see the others."

"What's this? Stopped her?" Cook looked from Kat to Peter and then to Hugo. "And you didn't believe them?"

"I feared it were a ruse, miss," said Hugo. "I feared they were spellbound by the Lady . . ."

As if the mention of her name caused a change, that terrible sound, that grinding, grating sound, came from the hall where they'd left the Lady and rose to a tortured scream, and they froze, exchanging horrified looks.

60

The Second Unmaking: Dog, Cat, Bell, Devil's Sign, Fish, Hunchback

"SHE'S COMING," KAT said. "We must be quick about it now."

"We have to find that boy," Peter said, pointing to the cellar.

The noise from the hall grew, and with it whining and the movement of gears and a *scrape-hish-scrape*; Kat knew the Lady was free of the pen now, and moving. "No time. She'll trap us down there." She turned to Hugo. "Where are the others?"

"Most in the barn," he said.

"Well?" said Cook, eyeing Hugo. "Get on with it then! Leave me be, here. Just hand me that fry pan. No, the biggest one. Yes, I can handle it, thank you. There. Now I'm armed. The leg is better already, see?" And she flexed it.

Kat snatched up the scissors as she and Peter scampered after Hugo, out the door and across the courtyard, Hugo striding one step to each of their four. He shoved open the barn door and made for the stalls.

Low lamps illuminated the barn. In the second stall a spotted hound lifted her head, her litter curled within her legs, and a ball of a boy that Kat recognized as Colin slept next to her, curled into himself as tight as one of the puppies.

She leaned over him. There was the chain around his neck, with a terrier charm attached. The chain itself glowed a dull blue. She had to be careful not to touch it, now that she knew the consequences. She spoke the incantation and slipped the scissors slowly around the chain.

The scissors melted the chain like butter.

"Ach, lassie," whispered Hugo, as Colin's eyes fluttered open.

At the same time, they heard it coming from the house, through the open kitchen and barn doors: a dreadful scream.

Kat and Peter exchanged a look; they were both thinking about Cook, though the scream didn't sound like hers. But there was no time to lose now. Kat pressed the dog charm into her pocket with the others, as Peter said, "Colin? You all right?"

Colin nodded. "I had the most terrible dream . . ."

"Where are the other children?" Kat asked Hugo, who scratched his head and regarded the golden-glowing scissors with new respect.

"This way," Hugo said.

They climbed a ladder to the loft. Four figures huddled against a wall. One of them Kat knew right off: Isabelle. The other girl she recognized as the poor freezing little thing she'd seen by the pond. And there were two boys, Jorry and the boy Kat had seen fleeing the kitchen with the cats around his feet.

This boy seemed sharper than the others. Maybe the charm hadn't affected him so deeply, or maybe he had an innate desire to protect the other children, but he pushed himself between Kat and the others as if to say, *Keep off.*

"Now, laddie," said Hugo, pleading, "this lass is here to help."

The boy shook his head slowly and spread his arms wide. Kat knelt. "Listen, I have to take that chain off you. And off them, too."

The boy looked terrified at that prospect and clutched at the chain, desperate to keep it on.

"I bet you tried to take one off, right?" Kat said. "I bet you found out that was a bad idea. But see, I have these magic scissors . . ."

Hearing the words come from her mouth made her wonder. She had magic scissors. These children were charmed. The Lady of the castle was a cruel witch. And Kat was able to use magic to free them all.

"Hurry," said Peter, his voice an urgent whisper.

"Please," Kat said.

The boy didn't budge.

Something rubbed at her ankle, and she almost jumped out of her skin, but it was a cat, rubbing its cheek contentedly on her heel. "Oh, kitty," Kat said, relieved, reaching down to rub its ears.

At which everything about the boy changed. He looked from her to the cat and back. The cat purred so loud, Kat could almost feel the vibration. He dropped his arms and bent his head as if to say, *All right.*

Kat didn't hesitate; she cut that chain straightaway, using the spell, and the cat charm clattered to the wood floor.

He leapt to his feet. "Where is she? She can't have them, no. I won't let her have them."

Kat said, "You're very noble, but I must cut these charms from them now or she will have them."

But as she got to work, snipping one chain after another, there came more noise from the house, and then she realized that Peter and Hugo were both gone. She feared the worst but had to press on, and dropped the boy's cat, Isabelle's bell, Jorry's evil hand sign, and then the small girl's fish charm into her pocket.

Seven charms, including her own; she needed to find five more children. And among them, Amelie and Rob. Where were they?

———————————— ❧ ————————————

Kat didn't have to ask John—for that was the cat-boy's name—to help the other children when she left them. He was already comforting Isabelle. Kat slid down the ladder as quick as she could and ran for the barn door.

Dreadful noises came from the house. She bolted to the kitchen to find Cook still wielding her pan and Hugo and Peter looking stunned; the noises came from the hall, not far from the kitchen.

It sounded like a great clanking machine falling to pieces.

"What . . . ?" Kat began.

"We saw her in the moonlight. She's falling apart," said Peter in amazement. "Scattering wheels and gears and I-don't-know-what-all, spread across the floor. With each charm it seems another piece of her falls off."

"It's working!" Kat said, excited. "But where are the others? I'm missing five, by my count, including Amelie and Rob."

"There's the boy in the cellar," Peter said.

"Right."

"I don't know about the other two," Peter went on. "They might be the singing girls."

Kat went for the cellar first.

The poor crippled boy was clearly used to hiding. Used to being chased and used to making himself nearly invisible. He scuttled from one dark corner to the next, and Kat couldn't get near him.

After several minutes—an eternity, as Kat heard the noises from above—she sat down in the middle of a heap of silver spoons and candlesticks, platters and teapots, and picked up a polishing rag.

At once the boy drew closer. She took the rag and made slow circles on her scissors, turning them this way and that, pretending to see her own reflection in the small, sharp blades.

The boy inched his way toward her, as if she held something so irresistible that he couldn't help himself. And then he was next to her, venturing to reach toward the scissors.

She handed him the polishing rag, and then a silver plate, and he bent his head and she slid the scissors around the chain and spoke the charm and, like the others, the chain vanished in a puff of smoke.

The cry came at the same instant and now from almost directly above, and she heard shouts from Cook, Hugo, and Peter. And then a sound that was worse than anything: the sound of silence.

61

Scattered Pieces

IT IS MUCH worse for the Lady than when the magister had taken her true limbs. This is an anguishing pain, a deep ripping and tearing. With each broken charm, a part of the Lady Eleanor rattles to pieces, the very part she had given in exchange for the soul she now loses from her thirteenth charm, and her power diminishes, and she screams for it.

Wheels grate on wheels and she has to crawl like a damaged bug.

Oh, what she will do to those children! What she will do once she has been restored and has secured the magister's help . . . and the Lady screams again at the thought that she will once more be at the mercy of the magister, need his help, be helpless . . . the very thing she vowed she would never be again.

What is left of the Lady Eleanor half crawls, half crab-walks across the floor, heading for the stairs.

There they wait for her—the pearl and the eel. She will see to it that their sister, that wicked Katherine, will suffer over their loss.

The Lady is not done yet.

62

The Third Unmaking: Boot and Chest

THE CRIPPLED BOY put his finger to his lips, then pointed toward the far wall. He moved and Kat followed.

She had to give him credit for being tricky and clever and finding all the hidden passageways in this castle. He led her through a maze of tunnels and secret doorways until they emerged right below the covered parapet outside the keep.

He pointed at the keep itself.

"What?" Kat whispered.

"Angels," he whispered back. "Up in the heavens."

The voices. Angels. Of course. At least two more children were up there, and from what the boy said, they were at the very top of the tower. But in the deepest dark, in that strange tower with its sudden gaps and steep stone steps and hidden doorways, she feared she'd tumble to her death. The moon was about to set, and the night would become black as pitch. And the peculiar keep—would it be possessed of the evil of All Hallows' Eve?

Yet she had no choice but to find her way to the top. She took a step toward it when the boy clutched her sleeve.

"Keep left. Only left. Any doors, any openings, take the left." Then he disappeared, retreating into the shadows as if he was a shadow himself. Kat couldn't blame him; she wished she, too, could disappear.

Keep calm. Keep left.

She found the door at the bottom of the keep from the courtyard and pushed it open with a soft creak. She stepped inside and turned left—and ran straight into a stone wall.

She was flummoxed. How could she turn left into a wall with the opening leading right?

She did the only thing she could think of, the thing she'd done each time she'd run into this obstacle: she pushed.

The wall gave way into utter black. Kat might as well have been blind. Until she remembered.

She pulled the chatelaine from her pocket with her right hand and held it up, and at once it glowed with a blue light so that she could find her way forward, a softer light than when they were on the moors, and she guessed that was because it was missing the pen. She climbed up and up cold stone stairs, pressing her hands on the wall to her left, always left. Once or twice her hand brushed sticky cobwebs and she snatched her fingers away, rubbing them hard on her woolen pants and moving quickly, hoping that spiders weren't crawling into her hair or up her back. Several times as she climbed the wall gave way to another opening and she had to hold out her chatelaine to be sure there wasn't some deep well at her feet, but the boy proved right. *Keep left. Keep calm.*

Moaning and groaning noises rose from deep within the keep.

A blast of cold air from above caused Kat's jaw to tighten, and then she was out in the open. The night was well on, the moon had set, and the stars lay thick and glinting across the sky. It was frigid, but the wind was stopped by the parapet wall, thank heavens, because by the light of her chatelaine she saw them, huddled right up against that wall, in the deepest shadows.

Now she heard them, too, humming softly together, making the most beautiful wordless music, a song so sad and sweet that it made Kat think of home before the war, and Mum and Father together as before, and Rob and Ame snug and safe, and a warm fire and Kat sleepy and her stomach full and her heart full, too.

She began to hum the familiar tune.

They were huddled together, two girls, twins. They smiled

at her, maybe because she sang with them, and they didn't seem the least fearful. When she cut their chains they hesitated only a moment before breaking into song again, this time with a glance at each other and putting words to the old hymn, for that's what it was.

Kat wondered whether they had taken comfort from each other and that was what made them less fearful than the other charmed children, or whether they took comfort from their music, or both.

The girls followed her down the tower. They had to move slowly for fear of the steep stairs, and by the time they reached the bottom and stepped into the court the sky was lighter, a pale gray, and dawn not far off.

The dawn of All Saints' Day. Kat pocketed her chatelaine again. All Hallows' Eve was past and angry ghosts now slept.

They made for the new castle. When they reached the front steps, Kat said, "Go around the back, now, and find Hugo. The giant. He'll take care of you. Or find Cook. They'll see to you now." The girls went off, arm in arm, humming softly.

Kat pushed the door open a few inches, only far enough to see inside. The gray light of dawn grew so that she could make out the stairs and the hallways and the fireplace and the portrait with its shining eyes. And she could see what lay scattered across the Turkish carpet that covered the stone floor.

Bits and pieces of metal. Small wheels and cogs. A hand,

awfully—frighteningly—like Kat's hand. A bit of rubber tubing, and a number of tiny metal parts that she couldn't name. All were scattered in a line starting from the place where she'd left the Lady Eleanor frozen and leading to the stairs. But there was no sign of her—or of what might be left of her. Just pieces, leading up and up the stairs.

Why there? Why go up the stairs and not to the kitchen, where she'd find Peter and Cook and Hugo, and then on to the other children in the barn?

And then it struck Kat: because upstairs was where the Lady had taken Amelie and Rob. That had to be it, the only souls still bound in her thirteenth charm.

Kat made her way in, trying not to step on the broken bits, but she was happy to find in the center of the mess Father's pen. It glowed like a beacon. She bent to pick it up. It was hot to the touch and glimmered the faintest gold, but with her right hand she was able to hold it until it cooled and dulled to silver. She slipped it back onto her great-aunt's chatelaine and into her pocket, heavy now with the weight of the charms Kat had collected.

It was like Kat was following bread crumbs. A watch cog here, a severed chain there. Trailing up the stairs in ever diminishing numbers, the pieces led to the second floor, and then into the hallway.

And then they stopped.

She bit her lip in frustration. Lord Craig's rooms were off to the right, but there were rooms to the left as well, and Kat couldn't be sure which way the Lady went.

Kat started with Lord Craig.

He lay as she and Peter had left him, pale and still. The gray light of dawn had lifted to straw yellow. Kat stood in the room, silent, poised. Lord Craig's slow, deep breathing ... and then the faintest of sounds, a quiet *click-hiss*, came through the open door.

She ran into the hall.

There. From a doorway down the hall and left open a crack came another *click*. Kat bolted and, heedless, shoved the door open, fearing nothing if it meant helping Amelie and Rob, and there she was, the Lady, hideous, deformed—visible in the daylight, now, as the magic must be eroding—a fragmented and broken thing but still powerful enough to be terrifying, and beside her, stretched on a great bed side by side as if they slept—though Kat knew better—were Kat's brother and sister.

Amelie and Rob lay flat and still and lifeless, like stone figures in a crypt. Kat swallowed a sob.

One ragged metal bone protruded from the Lady's shoulder, a bone ending in a vicious claw, and the claw was fixed at Amelie's soft white throat.

63

The Thimble

KEEP CALM.

Kat's heart was pounding and she could scarcely breathe; she was anything but calm. Her eyes went from the Lady's hideous face to the deadly claw at Amelie's throat.

"Come right in," said the Lady. "Please. Come and watch as I begin my renewal. You haven't stopped me, and you won't now. Because I still can make magic and will transform your sister and brother before your eyes. Transform them into something less than human." She paused. "Unless you think you can overcome me? Or perhaps you want to try to become like me?" The Lady laughed. "Go ahead. Use the charms. I challenge you."

Kat felt the weight of the charms she carried. She flexed her mechanical fingers. Maybe she could use her hand and the power within those charms herself. Maybe if she used the magic she would be good, where the Lady was bad.

Why, if Kat had that power, she would end the war, end all wars. She would bring peace to the world, bring Father home— bring them all home, all the fathers. She would be kind and benevolent, not like the Lady. All she had to do . . .

Kat drew back.

All she had to do was find power by imprisoning the souls of children.

"No, my Lady," Kat said, and swallowed hard to keep the tremor from her voice. She had to lure the Lady away from Amelie, for the Lady's dagger claw was still pressing into Amelie's neck. Kat braced and said, as loudly as possible, "I'm afraid I will have to stop you."

The room went still and silent. The pale yellow light of dawn filtered into corners. Kat's very real and imperfect heart beat fast, and she gathered herself together, ready.

"You see," Kat went on, "you're evil, not beautiful. You aren't powerful, and you're not perfect. You're . . . pathetic. Sad, and helpless." She paused, seeing in the Lady's one human eye that she was striking at the Lady's soul. "I feel sorry for you."

With a low rumble, the Lady moved away from Amelie— Kat breathed again—and toward Kat. The Lady dragged one limp leg fragment, a slender piece of steel, and rolled on the other, a hobbled roll on a bent cog. Only one of her arms remained, ending with that single claw. But most appalling was her head: she had only half a skull, and her jaw worked on bent springs. It was hard for Kat, but she kept her gaze fixed.

"Try," the Lady hissed, holding up in that single claw what remained of her chatelaine, the charm with the number thirteen in a circle. The Lady said, "Try to stop me."

Kat pulled out her great-aunt's chatelaine. However well it had served her so far, she had almost no hope for it now. She couldn't think of anything to say, any spell that might work. A thimble to catch a soul?

But out it came, the thimble, and the instant Kat held it up, she remembered.

It was a child's game with a rhyme made up by her father, a game she'd played long ago, and her memory of it echoed with childish laughter; she'd played it before Amelie was born, played it with her father and mother as hide-and-seek. "You're very cold," Father had said. "Ah, warmer now, warmer . . . now you're hot!" And she'd held it up, her mother's old silver thimble, her prize.

Once again it was her father's strong voice that came through her as she repeated the chant that drove the game: *"Hunt the thimble, hot and cold; catch the soul in silver old."*

She hadn't given thought to the chant until now.

The magic took shape, as the air shimmered and the thimble glinted and glowed and grew warm in Kat's hand. Kat trembled, but she hung on, repeating the chant over and over, louder and louder. The Lady shrieked, and all her remaining parts began to quake, and fall, and it was like watching an avalanche as it begins and then gathers speed and rolls inexorably. As she fell to pieces, screaming, something, some vaporous essence from inside her, transformed and reformed and became a smoke that became a wisp that was sucked into the thimble as if into a vacuum tube, and what was left of the Lady Eleanor—the Lady Leonore—was no more than a pile of smoking blue bits of metal and rubber, her parts broken and scattered across the floor.

Her one human eye stared up at Kat, blank. Her perfect heart, at the center of it all, beat slow, slower, and then . . . stopped.

The Lady's dark soul was captured in the thimble that hung from Great-Aunt Margaret's chatelaine and that Katherine Bateson held tight between the strong fingers of her mechanical right hand.

64

The Witch's Bane

A THIMBLE. THAT old nursery game.

The Lady Eleanor—the child Leonore—had played hunt-the-thimble once upon a time, before all the hurt, had played with her brothers, and now from a distant past she hears their laughter, hears her own laughter, hears happiness. She recalls the joy of her first marriage and its promise of love, a promise engraved in silver: *Leonore. You have my heart and soul.* It hurts, that joy, that childish joy, the joy that comes from a very human heart, it hurts her and undoes her, piece by precious piece. Joy and memory and love.

It is your bane.

The Lady Eleanor has not anticipated a thimble.

65

Sturm

KAT DROPPED THE thimble, which had become terribly heavy as it sucked up the Lady's soul.

Then she ran to the bedside, hoping that with the Lady's demise she hadn't spoiled the charms around the necks of Amelie and Rob. She murmured the spell and clipped Amelie's chain and watched. Amelie's eyes fluttered open.

"Kat! Why, there." Ame smiled. "See? Magic, after all."

"Yes, Amelie," Kat said, and went around the bed to cut Robbie's chain, all the while trying not to let the tears fall.

Robbie opened his eyes with a blink. "Where's my sword? Let me at her!"

It took a lot of explaining. And then it took all of Kat's remaining courage to pick up the thimble and what remained of the Lady's chatelaine and put them both in her pocket, where she feared they might burn a hole or make mischief. At least her mechanical right hand was not burned; the thimble was fiery hot until she pocketed it. But Kat had to carry on. Even more so now.

"We're all together again," Kat said as Ame hugged her and Robbie squeezed her hand. "She can't split us apart any longer."

"You did it, Kat," said Rob, his voice ringing with pride.

Kat's cheeks went warm. "We've still got work to do. We have to find the others. And then we've got the next problem to deal with."

"Let me guess," said Rob. "Our so-called Welsh tutor, Mr. Storm. The German spy." He folded his hands across his chest.

"Exactly." Kat helped Amelie and Rob out of the room and down the stairs.

When they reached the kitchen they found Peter, Hugo, and Cook, who had armed themselves with every hard and sharp object they could find to defend the back door leading out to where the other children had been told to remain hidden in the barn, assuming that the Lady would burst in on them at any moment. When Kat told them what happened to the Lady, and took out the thimble and placed it on the kitchen table, everyone went silent for a moment, staring at the now-cold and small silver thimble, this container for a witch's damaged soul.

"'Tis a sad thing," said Hugo, and Cook nodded.

"She didn't start out no good," said Cook. Cook seemed to have fully recovered the use of her leg. "Nobody starts out no good. But she lost her heart along the way."

"Dark magic," said Amelie, her small voice soft. "Dark magic can make someone fall to pieces."

"We'll have to figure out what to do with that," said Peter, pointing at the thimble.

"Yes," Kat said, "we will." She straightened. "But we've got one more problem to solve first, and that's Storm."

Someone spoke from behind her. "Sturm is my name, not Storm. Otto Sturm."

The voice belonged to a very healthy-looking, back-to-normal Mr. Storm. He had a rifle slung over his shoulder. He carried a Luger pistol in his right hand and was aiming it at the group around the table. He wore a too-familiar black greatcoat.

He gestured with the pistol at Hugo, Cook, and Peter, who still held their weapons. "Put down those foolish things. And you"—he gestured at Rob—"drop the sword."

They all hesitated, until he shouted, "Do it!" Kat realized that with the unmaking of the witch, Storm had gone back to himself. He was Sturm, a German spy, and a dangerous one at that.

Everyone emptied their hands. Kat's fingers crept toward the thimble.

"*Nein, Fräulein.* You say it holds the Lady's soul? A powerful weapon in itself that would be, yes? I'll take it," he said, "and all the bits that are left of her Ladyship's chatelaine. If I understand correctly, it is the very artifact I seek."

The hair rose on the back of Kat's neck. *He wants the chatelaine.* What had he said? *This chatelaine is said to have the power of enchantment.* And Jorry had said, *But if this chatelaine thing is found by the Germans . . . Germany might use it the way Vlad did, to overpower their enemies.* And Sturm had said, *Yes . . . something England and her allies would not like.*

If Sturm collected the chatelaine and took it to the Nazis, that terrible dark magic would surely overwhelm the forces of good. And together with the thimble, who knew what dreadful magic could be made?

"Now, *Fräulein.*"

Kat slowly pulled the pieces of Lady Eleanor's chatelaine from her pocket, and all the charms, including the thirteenth. Instead of handing them to Sturm, she laid them out on the table. She couldn't bear to turn this power over to their enemy.

The enemy that held her father captive.

That might even have executed Father by now.

Sturm gestured with the pistol. "Put them in that flour sack. You." He gestured at Cook. "Empty the sack for the *Fräulein.*"

"I knew it all along," mumbled Rob.

"*Ja?* You did, eh?" Sturm laughed. "Too bad you did nothing but play with swords."

Rob bristled, and Kat placed a hand on his arm. *Keep calm,* she telegraphed.

Cook handed Kat the empty flour sack, and Kat placed the chatelaine, the thimble, and the charms inside.

But the rest of her great-aunt's chatelaine remained in her pocket.

"Hand the sack to me," Sturm said. She had no choice. He stuffed the sack inside his large coat pocket. "Now, where are my machine and my short-wave? I know you've stolen them."

No one moved. Then Rob said, "We don't know what you're talking about."

"You lie," he said, and with a gesture that seemed too fast for his size, he grabbed the person closest to him: Amelie. He pulled her roughly to his chest, placing the barrel of the pistol against her head. Amelie's eyes went round and she gave a whimper of fear.

Kat suppressed a scream; Hugo growled and clenched his fists; Cook uttered a sharp "Oh!"

"Where are my things?" Sturm demanded.

"I'll get them," said Peter. "They're right here. I just have to open this cupboard."

"Do it."

Peter opened the cupboard and pulled out a backpack. He sat back on his haunches, looking white-faced. "The short-wave is here, but the code machine is gone."

Kat swallowed hard as Sturm propelled Amelie across the room to see for himself. He grunted. "No matter. For the moment I need only the short-wave." The pistol was still firmly planted on Amelie's skull. "Now you"—and he gestured at Peter—"carry that. And you take this ahead for light." Sturm yanked a large flashlight from his belt and tossed it to Hugo. "We will all go together out to the keep, *ja*?"

Nein, Kat wanted to shout, but they had no choice. Sturm forced them to walk ahead while he held on to Amelie.

The parapet walk was cold. By the time they reached the keep, Kat was shaking all over, though not as much from the chill as from fear. She tried to glance over her shoulder for Amelie, but Sturm yelled at her each time. He marched them into the keep and then, with Hugo leading, they began the long walk up.

They were at the point where the stairs wound in a tight circle. The light from the flashlight was bright, but it bobbled ahead, leaving Sturm and Amelie in the shadows at the tail. With the curve of the stair Kat couldn't see Cook or Hugo ahead or Sturm behind.

"I know what he's going to do," Rob whispered from behind her. "He's going to force us all off the top. Shoot us one by one and drop us over the side."

"Not if I can help it. I've got a plan," came Peter's voice from ahead of Kat. "Use your chatelaine when the time comes." She watched as Peter suddenly leaned left and shoved.

The door gave way and Peter tumbled through and disappeared, the door sliding silently shut behind him.

Kat kept marching upward, her heart thudding. If Sturm found out that Peter was missing, what would he do to Amelie? And, without the thimble, would her great-aunt's chatelaine still have its power? Would its light be dimmed, as it had been when it was missing the pen?

Sturm shouted up, "At the landing, halt. *Halt!*"

They came to the landing, the broad one with the far wall in deep shadow, where Kat remembered a sudden and dangerous opening. They gathered in a cluster, waiting as Sturm pushed Amelie before him. The light from the flashlight wavered as Hugo's hand shook. Kat fingered her great-aunt's chatelaine in her pocket.

"Where is the Williams boy?" Sturm demanded, angry. "Where is Peter?"

"Here!" came a shout as a door behind Sturm slid open. Sturm turned; Peter kicked the flashlight out of Hugo's hand, and shouted, "Now!" Kat withdrew the chatelaine and held it high, hoping against hope.

Ah, that's it!

"Hope!" Kat cried, and then, as loud as possible, *"Hope springs eternal in the human breast!"*

The light that the chatelaine threw off was blinding,

brighter than it had ever been. Even Kat had to shut her eyes. In those few seconds of chaos that followed, with scuffling and shouts, Kat heard Peter call out, "Rob! The opening behind you! Help me push!" And then came a cry as Sturm fell into the blackness beyond the opening of the far wall. He'd tumbled into the pit, and she wondered if he had fallen into deep darkness and maybe broken his neck.

Kat opened her eyes as the chatelaine dimmed. "Ame!" Amelie ran into her arms, and Kat hugged her sister tight.

Peter, Hugo, Rob, and Kat moved to the edge of the opening and, by the diminishing light of the chatelaine, peered over it to see what had become of Sturm.

He was lucky. He'd fallen into a shallow bowl with a bottom softened by bat dung, shallow enough not to kill him but too deep for him to climb out. He sat, shouting in his native tongue, trapped and mucky.

"Nicely done, Rob, Peter," Kat said. "Very nicely done."

Both boys stood up straighter.

"Well. So much for our German spy," said Peter. "Now we just have to alert the authorities and let them take care of Mr. Storm."

"Sturm!" he shouted up. "Otto Sturm!" And he tacked on a string of words that Kat imagined were not very kind, and she was grateful none of the children knew German.

"Look, Kat," Amelie said. She was holding the flour sack.

"Oh, Ame, brilliant!" said Kat. "How did you manage it?"

"It was magic," she said with a shrug.

Kat knew better than to contradict her sister now.

As they made their way back to the new castle, they saw a line of black automobiles trailing into the bailey and policemen in uniform swarming out in all directions.

"How did they know to come?" mused Kat. "Maybe MacLarren and Gumble?"

It emerged that a letter had arrived for Great-Aunt Margaret, written in what looked like Kat's hand. Kat gaped openmouthed, for she'd written no such letter, but there it was, waved about, regaling her great-aunt with tales of German spies set to invade British shores. In fact, a U-boat presumably waiting to connect with Sturm had been located, and new fortifications were planned for construction all along the North Sea right away, all thanks to Kat's warning.

She fiddled with the chatelaine, now back together in her pocket. The pen "will write of its own accord," her great-aunt had said. Perhaps it had.

But the best surprise came shortly after they reached the castle. MacLarren and Gumble emerged from an auto with the encryption machine. MacLarren marched up to Kat and said, "Well, lass, our ruse worked. Thanks to your cracking the code, we were able to make the connection. We tricked them into freeing Jack. Convinced them he was one of their own, a double agent, and needed to assist Mr. Storm in Rookskill Castle. Seems they were sure Storm was onto an important artifact." MacLarren thumbed over his shoulder at the auto and said, "And Jack, here, was key to assisting Storm, since he knows Lord Craig."

From behind him another man stepped from the auto. Jack. A man who smiled in a so-familiar way. And who, as he approached them looking haggard and spent, said, over and over, "I'm so sorry, my loves. I'm so sorry."

"Father!" Kat couldn't help herself; she wept into his collar as he held her and her brother and sister in a tight hug. And she forgave him completely.

Wishes, thought Kat as she hugged and wept and hugged again, *do come true.*

66

The Well

THE AUTHORITIES TOOK the bat-stinking spy Otto Sturm away in a paddy wagon, while everyone else gathered in the kitchen. The twelve children, plus Cook, Marie, Hugo, MacLarren, Gumble, and "Jack," had a magnificent breakfast thanks to Cook, and all were especially pleased when Hugo went upstairs and brought Lord Craig down in a chair to join them.

"I should have known Jack was you," Kat said to Father. "I should have remembered about the bell strike." Her father winked.

Kat plied him with questions. Some he could answer.

"But what was the mission?" she asked.

"Now, Kitty, you know I can't tell you that." His eyes gleamed despite the fact that he looked thin and tired. "But you should know that you've done a great thing." He touched the flour sack with the chatelaine.

"This is a dangerous weapon of great power," said Gumble. "If it had fallen into the wrong hands . . . Well, I hate to think."

"But the Lady wasn't about to give it up except by force," Peter said.

"True," said Gumble. "And she had spelled our Mr. Storm— Sturm—by trying to turn him into her dear husband. That way she could replace the real Lord Craig with the fake, since she deemed Storm to be a less honorable and more malleable sort than her clever husband, and with Lord Craig's replacement she could retain her title and lands. On her way to bigger and better things."

Lord Craig grumbled. He was looking ever so much better now.

"In fact," continued Gumble, "she'd cast a confounding spell about the entire castle and enchantments upon all of the adults here, though each adult was given a different enchantment."

"That's why the castle seemed so confusing. The hallways and such," said Rob, nodding. "But why give us the drugged hot chocolate? Why didn't she just spell us all and take us in our sleep?"

"The kinds of spells that work on adults don't work on children," Gumble said. "You are too young and innocent to be confused by complications, except in the case of the castle itself. I speculate that her charms on you had to be worked in a certain way, and slowly. This is powerful magic."

"What about the wolves?" Rob asked.

"Ah," said Gumble, and placed her finger alongside her nose. "The Lady set them out after Mr. MacLarren and me as we reached the shore where we were to meet Jack. You stumbled upon that same magic, and thank goodness you had your chatelaine. Fortunately for Mr. MacLarren and myself, I know a few magical tricks of my own. But that prevented us from returning to you until we'd secured Jack."

"You are not real teachers, then?" asked Isabelle. She pointed at MacLarren. "You do not know maths?"

"Humph," said MacLarren. "We were recruited and trained especially. I most certainly do know my maths, lassie. And Miss Gumble knows her English."

"We're part of a special division of the war department," said Gumble. "Our mandate is to ferret out unusual things the Nazis might set against us. But I cannot say more than that."

Kat knew more than that, but she kept silent.

Kat's father spoke up. "We've got a bit of cleanup and some decision-making here."

"Right," said Kat, slipping her hand into her father's with a happy sigh.

They swept up the parts of the Lady that were scattered throughout the castle and stuffed them into a second flour sack. Kat fingered the copper heart—still finding it beautiful—before closing the sack's drawstrings.

Then the decision: what to do with the sack of parts, the thimble, and the charms she'd collected from the children, as well as the Lady's chatelaine itself? For, Kat wondered, if the thimble held the Lady's soul, then she might not really be gone.

Magic, as Kat now knew, was powerful stuff. And required payment. She flexed her right hand.

Cook had made a batch of good hot chocolate, and they all gathered around the table in the dining hall to debate the issue.

"I say we burn everything," said Rob. "There's nothing like burning to get rid of black magic."

Kat heard general murmurs of assent.

"But what if burning the charms is bad for us?" asked Isabelle. "What if they still have some little piece of us? They were ours for a time, *oui*? Maybe we should each have our own charms to keep."

"I don't know," said Peter. "I don't think I want to touch mine again. It felt like it was . . . alive, or something."

"Plus, burning them might not destroy the magic. And scattering them around with each of us seems a bad idea," said Colin. "Who knows what they might do to us in our sleep?"

"There's a well out back," said John. "We could dump them all down the well."

"Aye, that's a deep well," said Lord Craig. "And as long as a Duncaster inhabits this castle, we will make it our oath to watch over that well." He coughed a little. "I'm hoping Miss Deirdre Brodbeem will assist me in this task during my remaining years as lord of these lands."

Cook looked fondly at Lord Craig. Yes, she was actually quite pretty, Kat saw, and she seemed genuinely younger, now, and less like a sack of potatoes. It wouldn't have surprised Kat if the jealous Lady had given Cook that lumpy, aged appearance.

"But the thimble," said Colin. "I don't think the thimble should be in the well with the parts and all. What if, what if . . . she . . ." He dropped his voice to a whisper. "What if she escaped?"

They all stared at the thimble as it lay at the center of the table. Kat could have sworn it still glowed.

"I agree," said Rob.

"Me too," said Peter.

"What do you think, Miss Gumble?" Kat asked.

"I think . . . I think we should ask Jack."

"Father?" Kat said.

He stirred. "Things that have great power generally have a way of showing up again, no matter what. I think the thimble needs a bit of safe-keeping, and shouldn't be away out of sight. If Lord Craig can keep watch over the Lady's chatelaine in the well, and no one else knows its whereabouts, then for the time being the Nazis won't be able to get their hands on it. As to the thimble, someone must protect that."

"We're lucky. We've got a free society. So let's vote on it," Kat said. "Who's for dropping the whole lot of the Lady's chatelaine and parts and all, everything except for the thimble, into the well?"

All hands went up.

"And what about the thimble?" Kat asked.

"I think you should keep it, Kat," said Amelie.

Tim nodded. "You."

Everyone chimed in, little by little.

"Because, really," said Amelie, "it belongs on your chatelaine. Which is also magic."

Kat's face grew warm. "Oh." She bit her lip. "I don't know if I can."

"But if it wasn't for you, none of us would be here," said John. "You figured it out and did the trick. You saved us all."

"You used good magic, Kat," said Amelie.

Now Kat's face grew positively hot. John was right. And she almost hadn't. She hadn't believed in what Great-Aunt Margaret had told her. She'd nearly lost the chatelaine. She almost hadn't tried the pen or the scissors or the thimble. And she hadn't believed in herself.

She swallowed and said, "Are you sure?"

"We're sure," said Jorry. "We're positive."

All the children's eyes were on her. Hugo and Marie and Cook and Lord Craig and the teachers and her father watched her, too. She wasn't a grown-up yet, but this was a big responsibility. She picked up the thimble, which had become less heavy over time, and reattached it to the chain on her chatelaine, and stuck it in her pocket. "Right, then. Let's go deal with the rest."

Everyone gathered around the well. Even Lord Craig came out—he was looking better by the hour. They dropped the sack with all the parts and pieces of the Lady into the well first and heard it splash after some seconds. And then in went the chatelaine with its thirteen charms.

Two days later, Mum came with the parents of Peter, Isabelle, Colin, and Jorry to fetch them home. Somehow a letter had reached each of them as well. None of them, of course, knew what had really happened; the letters talked of mistakes made in the hiring of teachers.

Kat was mystified by the letters, which Mum was certain had been written in Kat's hand.

There was a wonderful reunion between Father and Mum that Kat would never forget.

The only thing that still bothered her was her right hand. She hadn't told anyone about it, and didn't think she could, so only Peter and Hugo knew. What would she say about it? It looked normal, and functioned—well, it was astonishing, really. It had saved her, in the end, by being strong, so she could grip the pen and the scissors and hold the thimble. And there was nothing she could do about it. For the moment, she decided to keep it a secret.

She pulled Peter aside.

"I have a favor to ask. Please don't say anything to anyone about my hand."

Peter's dark eyes searched Kat's. "Okay. I won't."

She smiled.

"But it is a little frightening," he said, glancing away. His hair had fallen across his forehead and over his eyes and he hadn't pushed it back.

Her smile faded. So she frightened Peter. Perhaps, she thought, this was the price she paid for using magic. She hoped it was the only price.

Lord Craig invited all the parents to join him in the grand parlor. He was really quite well by this time. Peter and Kat snuck up to the door to hear what he had to say, and Kat could see Father and Mum. Lord Craig made a proposal to all the parents, right there.

"I think this academy might be a brilliant idea, even if it didn't live up to its original purpose. Why don't you let the children stay until the bombing is truly over? We'll get proper teachers for them. We've got plenty of food, what with the farm. And some of these little ones"—Lord Craig dropped his voice, and Kat knew he meant Rose, Tim, Brigit, Alice, and John—"have no other place to go, so they'll be staying on anyway."

Mum caught Kat's eye from across the room. Kat nodded. Her mum said, "I do think that it would be better for them than dodging the bombs."

One by one the other parents agreed, and Kat was secretly pleased, for she'd come to like the other children enormously—even Jorry, to a point, since he'd been humbled by his experience—and Lord Craig and Cook and Hugo and even Marie now that she was herself, and she had a feeling they would all be better off here than in London while the raids continued. For Kat, it was like being part of a very large extended family.

Kat and her father and mother walked out through the chilly grounds. The evening was coming on, and the first star appeared in the night sky.

Kat paused and made a silent wish.

Mum said, "I've a message for you, Kat. Your great-aunt said to tell you not to fall to pieces over things."

Kat smiled. Her great-aunt was another mystery Kat would like to solve. "Please tell her that Scotland is a magical place."

Mum raised her eyebrows and exchanged a glance with Father.

"And tell her . . ." Kat paused. She flexed the fingers of her right hand. She wasn't quite whole, but she wasn't in pieces, either. "I won't fall to pieces now."

Two days later, Kat was working on homework in her room when Marie knocked.

"Your father wants to see you in the small library."

The other parents had gone back to London, but Father had remained at Rookskill Castle to follow up with Gumble and MacLarren. All three were in the library when Kat arrived.

"Please close the door, Kitty," Father said. "And sit." She did.

"You've got a skill, lassie," said MacLarren, "and no mistake."

"Good with puzzles," said Gumble.

"We know that the Lady Eleanor's chatelaine was a powerful artifact, and that the Nazis have been seeking it," said Father. "We've also uncovered information suggesting that other similar artifacts may have made their way to Scotland."

"Aye," said MacLarren, "but we have no idea of the whereabouts of the rest of this treasure, or whether the items have been scattered or lost altogether."

"And," said Gumble, "we've learned that the Nazis are willing to risk a great deal to find any or all of them. As you already know."

"So, dear girl," said Father, "we are hoping that in the

coming months, we can call on your skills from time to time."

A thrill ran through Kat. She could only nod.

"Good. Now keep all this under your hat, will you?"

"Yes, Father," Kat said.

"Oh," he added, "and there's a clock on the second floor that needs attention, if you would care to help me later today. And that watch, too. We need to repair that, don't you think?"

Kat smiled and hugged the watch to her wrist, happier than she'd been in a long time.

67

Time

THE ROOK PERCHES on the edge of the well and casts one beady eye downward. Birds have sharp eyes, especially rooks, and this rook can see it, that charm, that thirteen, the one fallen out of its sack, glowing in the depths with a faint blue light.

The rook wants it, and would even venture down the deep shaft after it, had it not been for the shadow that creeps up from the woods behind and says, in a low mutter, "Be off!"

Off, off, off! cries the rook as it flies away, startling the stoat that has just poked its nose into the air.

War, war, war!

The magister has lost his greatest creation, the Lady. He would weep, but he is not familiar with the concept of weeping and, besides, he has her in another form, and the more important parts of her at that. And he has the mangled hand of the girl as well, a small but powerful thing that may prove useful.

He looks into the well and sees the charm, the thirteen, that glows soft blue, and vows to make the magic, the calling, the bringing of what lies inside the chest within his hut, and he will bend all his skills to this end. He has already paid the price for its use. It will take time, yes, but all things that are important take time. And the war, that turmoil that stirs the air, in which he takes no side but his own, the war will give him time, as it will rage for years to come.

Yes, time, that's all he requires. Magic bides its own time. He glances up at Rookskill Castle, now in shadow, warm yellow light and the laughter of children spilling from the tall windows. Time is what the magister needs; that, and a certain thimble kept on a certain chatelaine worn at the waist of a certain clever girl named Kat.

Acknowledgments

Sometimes scouring the Internet with no real purpose can yield unexpected results. This happened to me one wintery November day when my friend Dotti Enderle posted a picture on Facebook of an eighteenth-century German chatelaine. The decorative charms suspended from the chatelaine were so odd—indeed, unnerving—that I placed the picture on my desktop.

Two weeks later, in a flurry of inspiration, I'd written the first forty pages of what would become this novel. My first thanks go to Dotti for sharing, and for handing me this story. (You can find a picture of the chatelaine in the front of this book.)

At one point in drafting I felt discouraged about everything in my writing life, including the early draft of *Charmed Children*. Kathi Appelt generously offered to read my draft, offering not only critical suggestions but also the kind of encouragement that writers need. This novel—indeed, my career—would not be alive without Kathi's feedback and heart. Thank you, Kathi.

I have the finest critique group in the world, not only because they are smart and thorough and honest, but also because they willingly read draft after draft. Thank you, Kiri Jorgensen, Bailey Jorgensen, Maurene Hinds, Sandra Brug, Kent Davis, and Linda Knox. And thank you also to Michele Corriel, SCBWIers, the YA Binders and WOMG, and my Vermont College of Fine Arts family. A village isn't enough: it takes a whole city.

I've visited Scotland a number of times, but the trip we took in fall 2014 was critical for confirming my memories and deepening my research. Thank you to the many fine hostelries we visited along the way, especially the Golspie Inn, and thanks to our hosts and knowledgeable historians and willing participants in the journey, Nella Opperman and Joe and Helen Cann.

My agent Erin Murphy is the best—the best editor, the best shoulder to lean on, the best agent to rep my work. She's also a wonderful person. I am eternally grateful to Erin for welcoming me into her agency family; it's one of the most important things to have happened in my writing life. Thank you also to Tara Gonzalez and Dennis Stephens and many, many thanks to the EMUs. EMLA rocks!

Everyone told me that my editor, Kendra Levin, was tops and that I'd love her, and they were right. Kendra, you are gentle but firm, and thank you not only for seeing the potential in the raw threads of the story, but for helping me weave those threads into silk. Thank you, Kendra and the entire Viking team: Ken Wright, Joanna Cardenas (who gave excellent feedback), Kate Hurley, Janet Pascal (detail-oriented production editor), Abigail Powers, Jim Hoover (who did the wonderful design), and Greg Ruth (who created one of the most gorgeous covers ever).

And last but never, ever least, thanks to my husband, Jeff, and son Kevin. Kevin, you have the makings of a fine writer (and you give me the best ideas), and Jeff, you forever have my heart.